FLOWER OF POMPEII

A catalogue record of this book is available from the British Library

First Edition: January 2004

ISBN: 1-84375-059-7

To order additional copies of this book please visit:
http://www.upso.co.uk/hildapolhill

Published by: UPSO Ltd
5 Stirling Road, Castleham Business Park,
St Leonards-on-Sea, East Sussex TN38 9NW UK
Tel: 01424 853349 Fax: 0870 191 3991
Email: info@upso.co.uk   Web: http://www.upso.co.uk

FLOWER OF POMPEII

A Historical Romance

by

Hilda Polhill

UPSO

CHAPTER ONE

CLODIUS' PARTY

I lay on a couch in the tablinium, the main sitting room of our house in Pompeii. As I lay there staring at the wall paintings, with their depiction of various fish sporting with water nymphs, I contemplated the party I was to attend that evening. I was excited about it, it promised to be very enjoyable knowing the kind of parties Clodius threw. I stretched out on my couch, I was supposed to be resting in preparation for the coming evening. But I felt restless, I was too elated to keep still for long. I wanted someone to talk to. I rose and went out through the door that led to the peristyle. I spotted my sister-in-law Drusilla seated on a bench. I went over to her. "Ave Drusilla," I sat down beside her.

She looked at me, "You're looking very pleased with yourself," she remarked. Rather sourly I thought.

"It's Clodius' party tonight," I said.

"Oh yes, we aren't invited," she said. "I think he only wants single people."

"Well," I said, "There are going to be several army officers there. Maybe that's the reason."

"Yes, I'd heard about that," Drusilla said.

"I'm looking forward to it, it would be good to meet an interesting handsome young man there."

"They'll be leaving quite soon," Drusilla said. "So there's no sense in getting too attached to any of them."

"Who said anything about getting attached as you put it? I've no intention of getting serious about any man. I was only thinking of an evenings amusement."

"You never do take any man seriously do you Claudia?"

"Of course I don't, why should I?"

"Well you are only sixteen, you've got plenty of time for that. I didn't marry until I was nineteen. But I had a good time while I was single."

"I know you did," I said. "I used to envy you at that time."

"Oh I used to enjoy myself before I settled down with your brother."

"And then you got married," I joked. I supposed Gaius was handsome enough if I thought about it. Which I did not very often. We had our disagreements, but I expected he was different as a husband. I hoped so anyway.

"Oh we have fun together, don't get me wrong, I've no regrets. I'm content enough now."

"You used to have a lot of admirers at one time didn't you?"

"Quite a few, and I had flings with some of them. But not as many as you might think."

As I remembered it, she had had quite a reputation at that time. But perhaps it was exaggerated. I got up from the bench, and stretched, "I'd better go and start getting ready. Meriope will be waiting."

"Have a good time," Drusilla said.

"I will." I wandered indoors and turned in the direction of my bedchamber.

Meriope, my freedwoman was already there, laying out the gown I was going to wear that evening. "Your bath's ready," she told me.

After I had had my bath Meriope began to dress my hair. "Keep still Claudia do!" she admonished me. Meriope had looked after me since the day I was born, so she felt entitled to give me orders. I held my head stiffly in position as she lifted my heavy dark blonde hair, and twisted it into curls on top of my head, in a style I liked, as it suited me well. My flounced dress of flesh pink silk shimmered in the light. It was new and I felt pleased with it. I did not wear much make-up, as at my age I hardly needed it. I had emphasized my green eyes with iridescent green shadow, and black liner that lengthened them. Lifting a flask of blue Syrian glass, I splashed myself with scent.

My friend Flavia arrived at that moment. We had arranged to go to the party together, she looked lovely, as I hoped I did. She wore a gown of palest blue silk, also with a flounce in the skirt. It emphasized her dark prettiness. I turned to Meriope who had followed me into the atrium. "I don't want him to wait for me." I said, indicating the slave who was to escort me through the streets.

"You can't walk home by yourself," Meriope objected.

"I shan't be by myself," I said. "If I don't find a friend to bring me home, Clodius will lend me one of his slaves."

Clodius greeted me with pleasure as I entered his large mansion. It had been difficult to squeeze through the vestibule, (a narrow hallway leading to the atrium in some larger houses), as there had been such a crowd all trying to get through at once. Clodius Publius, patrician about town, had inherited both his home and his wealth from his father, who had died about two years ago. He had no need to follow any calling as he had unlimited cash, and could do as he pleased. Tonight it had pleased him to host a large opulent party, on which no expense had apparently been spared. He was dark and attractive, with black crisply curling hair, and blue eyes.

I took a small cup of spiced wine from a tray held out by a slave, and looked around for something I could admire. It would be impolite not to exclaim over something, perhaps newly acquired since I had last been in the house. The large atrium was painted with erotic scenes of gods and goddesses, disporting themselves with profligate abandon. Suddenly I noticed a blue vase made out of cameo glass. "That's a lovely vase, I haven't seen it before."

"No," he answered. "I only acquired it recently, I'm glad you like it."

"It's beautiful!" Seeing a group of my friends, I started to cross to them. But Clodius detained me. "There are some people I'd like you to meet."

"All right." I allowed myself to be led to where a group of young men were gathered. As Clodius introduced me I noticed one I rather liked the look of. But to my annoyance I saw that a friend of mine, a girl called Julia, had already annexed him. She would! I thought. She always manages to get there first, and steal a march on everyone else. She looked at me, I smiled sweetly at her, "Aren't you going to introduce me to your friend?"

Reluctantly she said, "This is Caelius, Caelius this is my friend Claudia."

He smiled at me, "Ave," he said. Julia grabbed his hand. "There's something I must show you," she said. And with a sweet smile at me she bore him off. I glared after her, I had liked the look of Caelius myself, and now it appeared as it Julia was going to hang on to him all evening. Trust her! And why anyway? Why make such a stir? It was not as if anyone was going to get serious about anyone. These people were only passing through, and would be gone soon. I turned to the other two men and smiled at them. They were army officers, I knew. As was Caelius. Neither of them attracted me at all, but I made polite conversation with them. And asked them where they were stationed. They told me that they were stationed in the Province of Britannia. I had heard of it, it was a fairly new Frontier of the Empire. But it did not interest me particularly.

I looked around for Flavia, I wondered where she had got to. I had not seen her since we first arrived.

We had been separated in the crush at the entrance. Muttering an excuse, I began to push my way through the crowd. Perhaps I would see where Julia and Caelius had got to. And maybe attempt to take him from her. But they had disappeared in the crowd. Finally I spotted Flavia. She was talking to a very good looking young man, who I assumed to be an army officer. I forgot Caelius and Julia. Maybe Flavia would introduce me to her new friend. I joined them. "Ave Flavia, I was wondering where you were."

The officer smiled at me, "I'm sorry if I've kept your friend talking. But introduce us Flavia."

Reluctantly, it seemed to me, Flavia said, "This is my friend Claudia Livillia. This is Marcus Lucullus. He is stationed with the army in Britannia. He was telling me all about it. Have you seen Julia at all?"

"Yes," I replied." I spoke to her a while ago."

"Where is she?" Flavia asked.

"I don't know," I answered I had lost interest in Julia and her officer. I gazed at Marcus. He smiled at me. He was I thought simply gorgeous. He had thick dark hair with auburn high lights. And eyes of such a dark brown they were almost black. He was of medium height, and he wore a blue and gold tunic.

How, I wondered, could I get him away from Flavia. "Have you seen that new vase of Clodius'?" I asked.

"No, where is it?" Flavia asked.

"I'll show you if you like," I said, including Marcus in the invitation. The three of us wove our way through the crowd until we came to where the cameo glass vase stood. "It's beautiful," Marcus said. "Isn't it Flavia?"

"Yes," she replied, "It is."

I looked around for inspiration. It would be time for dinner in a moment. I was hoping that Marcus would escort me to the tables. But with Flavia there as well he could hardly ask me. "Whereabouts did you say you were stationed?" I asked. "In Britannia is it?"

"Yes," he replied.

"It's a long way from here isn't it?"

"Oh yes, it's a long way from Italy."

"What's it like there?" I asked. I was not really interested, but I wanted to keep him talking.

"It's difficult to sum up a place like that in just a few words." He replied. "Maybe later I'll tell you about it in detail."

"Oh yes," I said, "I should like to hear about it."

Did this mean he would prefer to be with me rather than with Flavia? Or did he intend to spend the entire evening with the two of us? I determined to make sure that Flavia was elsewhere for the rest of the evening. How I was going to manage this I was not quite sure. If only she would get interested in one of the other officers. There were plenty of them there, but how could I get her involved with one of them? I could not introduce her to any of them, as I did not know them myself. I looked around for Clodius to see if he could solve this problem for me. But he was involved with a large group of people by now. In any case he would be announcing the meal soon. And I was determined to make sure that Marcus reclined next to me at dinner.

"Oh look!" Flavia exclaimed. "There's Julia. Who's that with her?"

"His names Caelius," I answered. "But why don't you go over and talk to them? She will probably introduce you to him."

She glanced at Marcus. He did not offer to accompany her. If only she would leave us, I thought. Although Julia would not be best pleased. She seemed determined not to chance any rivalry for the young officer she had got hold of. Flavia shrugged, "I don't think I'll bother," she said. "I can see her any time."

It was not going to be easy to get rid of my friend. It looked as though she was planning to hang on to Marcus for the evening. I determined that she should not do so, as I planned that privilege for myself.

Just then Clodius' steward announced dinner was being served. I took hold of Marcus' arm. To my annoyance he held out his other arm to Flavia. The three of us crossed to the dining couches that were spread around the tables, and with one of us on either side of Marcus, we all three reclined together. It was extremely irritating. It looked as though I stood no chance of getting him to myself at all. Well after we had eaten we would see!

Plates of hor-d-ouvres were handed round by the slaves, with cups of sweet wine to accompany it. I helped myself to goose liver pate, and thrush with asparagus. Before we began to eat Clodius sprinkled some wine as a libation to Bacchus. A statuette of whom was placed before him on the table. A shell fish course came next, which we selected from dishes held out to us. By the time we got to the main course the wine was freely flowing. After I had eaten some roast fowl, heavily seasoned with herbs and pepper, I turned my attention to Marcus again. While we had been eating he had got into a conversation with our host, who was reclining close to us. Still at least he was not talking to Flavia, any more than he was talking to me I relaxed, after all there would be plenty of time later. And in any case I could hardly interrupt the discussion between him and Clodius, who was obviously interested in the place where Marcus was stationed.

I poured myself some more wine from the flagon in front of us on the table. I felt suddenly happy and optimistic, I intended to enjoy the party. There was no point in moping anyway. There were other men in any case, only none of them attracted me in the way that Marcus did. I suddenly heard him tell Clodius that he was rejoining his cohort tomorrow. Tomorrow! I thought. That is a different matter, there is no time to be lost then. I would have to get him alone as soon as I could. Just then the dessert arrived, tarts and sweetmeats in elaborate shapes. These were accompanied by a sweet dessert wine.

During the course of the meal music had been played in the

background. But now other musicians entered, and took their places to play for us. There was a flute player, accompanied by a performer on the lyre. Other entertainments followed. It was the usual thing. I wondered when I would be able to attempt to get Marcus to myself. It did not look as though Flavia was going to give up easily. I helped myself to more of the dessert wine, I was becoming more confident with the effects of it.

There was a mime artiste performing now, and everyone was laughing uproariously at his antics. He was impersonating a local dignitary at the moment, and there was much hilarity and mirth at his foolery. I had not met the man myself, and did not altogether understand the jokes at his expense. But most of the men apparently did, although I could see that Marcus did not appreciate the impersonation either. Well he wouldn't would he? He was not living in Pompeii at present, and could hardly have known the person. Although he pretended to find the interpretation amusing.

After this the party would break up into groups, and disperse around the public rooms of the house. I had resolved to get Marcus in the peristyle at the back of the house. With this in mind, I rose from the couch hoping that Marcus would follow me. I attempted to push a way through the throng that was now gathering in the atrium, and overflowing into the tablinium.

Marcus however had been waylaid by what appeared to be an old friend. Whom he had not seen for years apparently. I stopped and pretended to admire an ornament, while I waited for the conversation to end. I hoped it would not take too long, as I was hoping to find a quiet corner of the garden before it became too crowded. Flavia was also hanging around as if waiting for Marcus to follow her. I would have to get rid of her somehow, as it would not be much fun with the three of us together all evening. I beckoned her over and said, "Why don't you see if you can find Julia now?"

"No," Flavia shook her head, "I can't be bothered to look for her in this crush. Besides from what we saw earlier she is already busy."

"They might not still be together," I said. "They might have separated by now."

"I doubt it," Flavia said, "She looked set for the night."

I did not answer, I knew it was true. But how could I get Flavia out of the way?

Eventually Marcus' friend left him, and went to speak to another man he knew among the officers. I turned and looked casually over my shoulder at him. Flavia joined us, to my annoyance. I glared at her, she looked surprised, or pretended to. She must have known why I was irritated with her. Surely it was obvious that we could not both spend the evening with Marcus. But as she had seen him first, I supposed she had assumed she had a prior claim to him. I supposed it was true in a way, but that did not stop me from getting him to myself if I could.

I had decided that I was in love with him. I had never felt this way about any man before, so that had to mean I was in love! As far as I was concerned Flavia did not stand a chance. I only had this evening to get to know him, and induce him into loving me. I knew he would be going away for a long time. But he would return eventually. I had to believe this. And if he loved me he would come back to me. Having made up my mind to this, I turned to Marcus and said, "have you seen the gardens here?"

"No," he answered.

"Well you should see them," I replied. "I will show you if you would like."

"That would be very pleasant, I would be interested to see them." Marcus replied.

I glanced at Flavia, she looked uncertain. She could hardly push herself onto us she knew. I looked around, there must be someone here that she could talk to. Julia and Caelius had long disappeared. I guessed that they too would be in the peristyle.

Putting an arm through Marcus' I led him through the tablinium towards the peristyle. Stopping to talk to another officer for a few minutes on the way, Marcus asked him if he was enjoying the party. He was apparently, and we made our way to where a large bowl of spiced wine was steaming over a tripod at the entrance leading to the garden. Marcus poured a cup and handed it to me. Then he helped himself to a cupful. Holding the cups of hot spiced wine, we left the house and entered the perisytle.

A lot of the guests had gathered here, and were standing around talking in large groups. As we appeared we were greeted by a circle of my friends, who were assembled in the middle of the courtyard around a large fountain, that stood beside a fishpond.

"Ave Claudia," a man called Titus greeted me. "I haven't seen you all evening to talk to. You were a long way from us at dinner."

"Yes," a girl named Antonia agreed. "We wondered when you were going to come and speak to us. Are you going to introduce us to your new friend?" she added.

"Yes, of course," I replied. "This is Marcus."

Marcus shook hands with everyone, and they gathered round us, prepared for a long conversation. I was not prepared for this, I could not be rude, these were my friends and I did not want to antagonise any of them. We would have to stay with them for a while. Although Julia was nowhere to be seen. I wondered how she and Caelius had managed to escape from them politely.

"Have you seen Julia this evening?" I asked them.

"Oh yes, she was here a few moments ago with a man called Caelius. They went in that direction." Said Antonia pointing towards a portico.

I settled in for a long chat with them. I was beginning to enjoy myself now, talking to them with Marcus at my side. We were discussing the social scene, and the various parties and gatherings there would be to attend next. But Marcus had other ideas, and seemed to be bored with standing there listening to us all talking. He put an arm around me and suggested we went for a walk. So taking our leave of my friends, we moved towards a small pathway leading to a colonnade. So far we were the first of the party guests to find our way here, and it was deserted.

Leaning me up against a pillar, Marcus embraced me, and kissed me with passion. I eagerly responded. Just then footsteps sounded behind us. We broke apart. But it was only a slave bent on some errand. I led the way towards a marble bench, and seated myself upon it. "So," I said, "tell me about this place Britannia."

Marcus sat down beside me, and put an arm around my shoulders.

"Britannia is a large island across the sea from Gaul." He explained. "Like Northern Gaul, it's not anything like as warm as Italy. A person needs a warm cloak most of the time."

"What even in the summer?" I asked.

"Yes, sometimes. Although it can get quite hot in the summer. But not all the time, like it usually is here."

"Apart from the weather, what's it like there?" I asked.

"Well I can't answer for the whole country. Our legion is garrisoned at a place called Camulodunum. There is a large army barracks there. And it is, in effect, the principal town or capital. The nearest port is called Londinium. It is a busy place, and we visit it quite often."

"What for?" I asked.

"Well," said Marcus, "it's the place where our supplies are delivered. And some of us have to collect them, and help to transport them to Camulodunum."

"Is that your main food supply?" I asked.

"Yes, it is," he replied. "But everything, weapons, clothing, and everything else we might need is shipped through there."

"And you have to go back there tomorrow?" I asked. "Are you sorry to have to leave Pompeii so soon? Or are you glad to be going back to Britannia?"

"It's all right there, but it is good to be back home here. Yes, I do wish I didn't have to return to duty so soon. Especially now, since I've met you. Still let's not waste time."

He pulled me towards him and began to kiss me again. This time I flung my arms around him, and responded to his lovemaking with enthusiasm. I was by now thoroughly aroused, and rapidly getting carried away. He pushed me down on the bench.

"Not here," I said. "Let's go back into the house. There is bound to be an empty cubicle, but we had better hurry or they will all be taken."

The bowl of wine was still steaming on the tripod. So we each took another cupful as we passed through back to the house. Several of the cubicles were occupied. As we arrived in the corridor two men in brief tunics were just about to enter one of the cubicles. They grinned at us as we passed them, I ginned back. It took all sorts. Eventually we found a vacant cubicle. One small oil lamp was burning within it. I threw myself into Marcus' arms as soon as we entered the little room. He wasted no time, but edged me towards the couch. Unpinning the fibula at my shoulder he drew the dress down to fall around my feet. Then he laid me on the couch, and hastily removed his own clothes. He fell on me like a man starving. I was excited by this and responded avidly. His mouth met mine in a passionate kiss, which grew in intensity as he reached fulfilment. A few minutes later I also climaxed, our cries of attainment mingled. He held me tightly murmuring endearments. Then he sat up, "Jupiter! I needed that."

I laughed throatily, "Has it been such a long time then since you last made love to anyone?"

He sighed, "A very long time in fact."

"Are there no women in Britannia then?" I teased him.

"Not any that I find appealing," he said. "All the Roman woman there are with their husbands. And though some would be willing to have affairs, I don't want to be involved in a situation like that. It would probably end in trouble, as they are mostly the wives of high ranking army or civilian officials."

"So you have to wait until you get back to Italy then?"

"It does seem so, yes. Have you got many lovers?"

"Not so many," I answered. "I had one friend, but he's moved away now. He was my first lover, there have been none since, until you tonight."

Spurious had been the son of a family friend. We had grown up together, he had lived with his father in a small house in the town. His mother had died when he was a baby, and he had never really known her. We had become lovers almost automatically. It had happened one afternoon when we were alone together in our garden. It had been no great romance, I had never imagined myself in love with him. And I assumed it had been the same for him. After that we had met about twice a week, whenever we got the chance. Sometimes at his house, and sometimes at mine. We had never intended anything permanent.

Getting up from the couch, I slipped, still naked down the corridor to the nearby lavatory. No one would see me I knew, or care if they did. They would all be otherwise occupied. All the cubicles set aside for the party guests were now engaged. When I returned to our room Marcus was waiting for me, obviously ready to make love again. I climbed on top of him, and positioning myself astride him, I impaled myself on him. He groaned, and reaching up he grabbed my breasts. I rode him in an ecstasy of pleasure. Afterwards we lay in each other's arms, and gazed at each other. "I wish you weren't going away tomorrow,"

"I'll come back," he said. "I love you."

"And I love you," I replied. "But when did you decide that you preferred me to Flavia?"

"I loved you when I first saw you," he said, "I never preferred Flavia, or any one else here."

"Really?" I asked, "You were in love with me from the start?"

"Of course, why do you think I'm still here with you?"

I was ecstatic! I had dreamed of this happening as soon as I saw him talking to Flavia. But I had not dared to hope he would just admit it like this.

We made love again, and then we dozed off, still in each other's arms. Waking suddenly I knew it must be nearly morning. I nudged Marcus, "I have to go home."

"All right," he said, "I'll escort you. Have you got a slave waiting for you here at all?"

"No, I sent him home when I got here. I didn't want him waiting for me, as I didn't know how long I would be."

"A wise decision," Marcus remarked.

We got dressed, and the door slave let us out, and with arms entwined we walked out into the early morning streets of Pompeii. As we reached my home I turned to Marcus, "When will I see you again?"

"I will call for you later, around noon," he said.

"I'll be waiting," I said.

After kissing him goodbye, I rapped on the door and the door slave let me in. I went to my bedroom, and slipping my clothes off I climbed into bed. I fell asleep immediately.

CHAPTER 2

THE PARTING

I awoke suddenly as Meriope entered my bedchamber. "You were very late coming home last night. Or should I say this morning?" she remarked. "Who escorted you home?"

I smiled, "A new friend. We met at the party, he is calling for me at noon."

"Who is this new friend and what does he do?" Meriope asked.

"He is a soldier," I answered. "He's rejoining his cohort today." I got out of bed, "Bring me a cup of pomegranate juice will you Meriope? I shall have to get ready soon."

She did not ask any more questions, but left to fetch the drink I had asked for. I put on a light wrap, and left my bedroom. Passing Meriope returning with my pomegranate juice, I took it from her, and made my way to the tablinium. I stood at the door leading to the peristyle. I sipped my drink. I yawned. My brother Gaius was coming up through the garden from his apartment. "What's the matter?" he asked. "Too much bed and too little sleep?"

I glared at him, I was annoyed that he had interrupted my dreams about Marcus. He laughed. "Did I disturb your daydreams?"

I refused to give him the pleasure of seeing he had scored a point. "I'm just tired," I said grumpily. "I was late home from the party last night."

"I'll bet," he smirked. "Got yourself fixed up with one of the army fellows I expect."

I turned away from him, I did not want to get embroiled in a discussion with him. He would only spoil everything by making cheap gibes. He always did. He irritated me a lot of the time.

Just then Drusilla emerged from their quarters. "Leave Claudia alone Gaius do." She said. "She probably isn't in the mood for your teasing this morning."

I never was in the mood for his taunting, I thought. Glad that his wife had appeared to put a stop to it. "Good morning Drusilla," I said.

"Did you have a good time last night?" she asked

"Oh yes," I said, "It was a good party, I had a lovely time."

"That's good," she said. "Did you meet anyone new?"

"Yes," I said. "His names Marcus, he's in the army. I'm meeting him at noon. He has to return to duty today. He's stationed in Britannia."

"Britannia!" exclaimed Gaius, who was still hanging around.

I was surprised that he had not got any work to do.

"Isn't that the Province that Claudius annexed when he was Emperor? Quite early in his reign?"

"I suppose so," I answered. "Won't father be expecting you in the vineyard?"

"Trying to get rid of me?" he grinned. "I was just interested in hearing about this place Britannia."

"Well I don't know all that much about it," I said. "Marcus told me something of it last night."

"I expect you had more important things to do didn't you?" he insinuated. "In fact I should think you have probably forgotten what he did tell you about it haven't you?"

"Oh stop your teasing and go to work or something," Drusilla said. She seated herself on a nearby bench, obviously prepared for a long chat with me. Gaius still lingered in the vicinity, hoping to hear more. I wished he would leave. He must have something to do. I wasn't going to tell him everything that had been between me and Marcus. It was none of his business! And even Drusilla need not think I was going to tell her all the details either.

Just then my mother appeared in the doorway behind me. "Not dressed yet Claudia?" she asked. "Gaius hadn't you better be going? Your father is waiting for you!"

"All right," said Gaius reluctantly. "I'm going."

I sighed with relief, then I turned to my mother. "I've got a date, I'm going to get ready." With that I left the tablinium and went to my dressing room. Meriope was there, putting away the clothes I had left lying around. "What are you going to wear today?" she asked.

"Something a bit special," I said. "I may not see him for quite a long time, so I want to look my best."

Looking through the dresses that were hanging there, I picked out a pale green one. After a quick bath, I was soon arrayed in it, and waiting impatiently in the atrium. I hoped he would not be late, or even worse, supposing he did not turn up at all! I began to feel decidedly nervous and edgy. What if last night had not meant anything to him? Or not as much as it had meant to me! What would I do if he let me down? Quite apart from anything else, it would make me look a fool in front of my family and the household. It just did not bear thinking about. I wished he would come, it was already noon.

Suddenly there came a tap on the door. It had to be him! Trying not to appear too eager or concerned I waited for the slave to open the door. A moment later there stood Marcus. The relief and happiness I felt must have shown on my face. Although I tried to hide my feelings as best I could. Marcus came towards me smiling. He kissed me, and embraced me. Then taking my hand he led me towards the door. We walked down the street hand in hand. I was blissfully happy, I did not even think about the parting that was to be so soon. In fact I completely forgot about it for the moment. The sun shone, it was another bright, hot summer day.

"This is a very pleasant town," Marcus remarked, as we strolled along. "Much nicer than Rome, with all it's skyscrapers and tenement buildings."

"Yes," I answered, "I have been to Rome, and Pompeii is much more agreeable. I would far rather live here than there."

We wandered on through the streets until we came to a bar that was not too busy. So far only a few of the tables in the interior were occupied. Although all the tables under the awning outside were taken. We made our way towards a small table at the rear of the bar. We sat down and looked around. Seeing Julia and Caelius in a corner, we both waved to them.

A friend of yours I presume?" Marcus asked.

"Yes," I said, "And I assume you know Caelius,"

"You know his name?"

"Yes, I was introduced to him last night. So he will also I suppose, be returning to duty today?"

"Oh yes," Marcus replied, "It will be the same for both of us. We both appear to have made a new friend."

I smiled, I had no grudge against Julia now. She was welcome to her officer. I was more than content with mine! We would be able to commiserate with each other after Marcus and Caelius had left. The prospect was a pleasant one, or as pleasant as possible under the circumstances.

A waitress approached us and asked for our order. We ordered a fish stew, strongly flavoured with garum, and some wine. The wine came immediately, and we sipped it gratefully. When the fish stew arrived I asked Marcus if he could get garum in Britannia.

"Oh yes," he answered.

"Is it as good as this?" I asked "Here we get the local variety which is very good."

"Yes I know," Marcus answered. "I come from this town too you know."

"Oh yes, of course, I forgot." I said.

After we had eaten we had some more wine. Then we left the bar. Arms entwined we walked along the main street of the town. Past the shops and houses that opened off it, until we came to the River Sarnus, there were not many people here at this hour, and we hoped to have the place more or less to ourselves. The sun was sparkling on the blue Tyrrenian Sea. The cone at the top of mount Vesuvius rose above the climbing vineyards, and olive groves twined around it. It was a beautiful view. Ships were anchored in the harbour, but there was nobody about. Only one or two other couples were scattered here and there, also seeking seclusion.

Finding an isolated spot, hidden behind thick bushes, we fell into each other's arms. We kissed and embraced fiercely. I clung to him, I was on fire with lust. His hold on me tightened.

"Make love to me" I whispered. "Here, now" We would not have another opportunity I knew, it had to be now. We were both inflamed with passion, to stop ourselves at this stage was nearly impossible. And why should we anyway? We sank onto the grass, it was rough here, but I barely noticed it. He pushed my dress up, I wore no underwear, it was too hot anyway. He hastily removed his undergarment. I pulled him down to me, and wrapped my legs around him. As I felt him enter me I moaned in ecstasy. He thrust into me hard and urgently, I cried out loudly, who cared if anyone heard? I returned his ardour passionately, I could not get enough of him, I was completely carried away on a hot tide of lust. The same could be said of him judging by the way he drove himself into me.

It did not take very long, we soon reached a soaring, mutual climax. We lay there intertwined, unable to move for several moments. Finally he seemed to come to, and with a lingering, loving kiss, he arose and adjusted his clothing. I lay gazing up at him.

"Come on," he smiled, "Better pull your dress down."

"Must we go so soon?" I asked

"I'm afraid we must," he said, "I have to go home and collect my things, and say goodbye to my parents."

Reluctantly I rose to my feet, and adjusted my gown.

"Come on," he said, "I'll escort you home, that will take another hour. So we won't be leaving each other just yet."

"All right," I said, "Let's go."

Arms around each other, we started to walk back through the town, away from the Sarnus and the harbour. We strolled through almost deserted streets. The shops were shuttered in the heat of the afternoon. But eventually we did find a tiny bric-a-brac shop still open. We browsed for a few minutes among the little statuettes in bronze and marble. Looking for a momento of this day, finally I picked up a miniature fish made of pink coral. "Oh, isn't this lovely?" I exclaimed.

"Would you like it?" Marcus asked.

"Oh yes I would."

Marcus counted out some coins, and paid the shopkeeper for the ornament, and handed it to me.

"Thank you Marcus, I shall treasure it always."

We then proceeded towards my home. When we reached it we stood outside the door together.

"Let's go inside," I said. "We can't say goodbye properly out here on the street. There won't be anyone about at this time of day. Even the slaves will be resting, except for the few on duty."

"Well just for a few moments then," he said.

Entering the house I led the way to the tablimium, and through to a secluded corner of the garden. "No one should be able to see us here," I said. Then suddenly it was all too much for me. Without warning I burst into tears (Surprising myself as much as I surprised Marcus.) And flung my arms around him. We had been together for such a short time, but I knew I was in love with him.

"It's all right," he said. "Don't cry, I'll come back some day."

"That's just it," I sobbed, "someday! It might be never, you might never come back, and I'll never see you again, ever."

"Of course I'll return, why should I not?"

"I don't know," I wailed. "Suppose something happened to you and prevented you coming back here?

"It won't," he said, "I'm not in a battle zone, it is quite peaceful in Camulodunum."

I would not be consoled, I would not stop crying. Marcus held me in his arms, "Come on now," he soothed. "You must be brave, the time will soon pass, and I'll be back in less time that you imagine."

"I wish I could believe that, I wept. "but it seems an awful long time to me, what will I do without you?"

"The same as you would have done if you had not met me."

"But I have met you," I said. "nothing can be the same again."

"Yes it will," he said. "You'll get over this, as long as you don't forget me!"

"Of course I won't forget you!" I exclaimed. "How could I possibly do that?"

"Very easily, probably," he replied. "You lead a very active social life. There are bound to be any number of distractions."

"Nooooo," I cried.

Just then Drusilla appeared, coming from the main house. "What's the trouble?" she asked. "Stop crying Claudia, and introduce me to your new friend."

I stared at her in annoyance, how dare she interrupt us! Marcus held out his hand to her, "I'm Marcus, I'm trying to persuade Claudia to calm down. But she is convinced I will never return."

"What nonsense you do talk Claudia," she said. "I'm Drusilla,

Claudia's sister-in-law." They shook hands. "Claudia over dramatizes things so much. Of course he'll come back, don't be silly Claudia."

But I was past all consoling, I sank to the ground, still weeping. Marcus looked around, "I really do have to go."

"Of course you do," Drusilla said. "I'll take care of Claudia, you don't want to be late. Do pull yourself together Claudia, you are behaving like a child. Say goodbye to Marcus in a seemly way, he hasn't got all day."

I looked up, "Come on, get up," said Drusilla. "You're making a fool of yourself!"

Tearfully I rose to my feet, Drusilla put an arm around my shoulders, "Come on now, be brave."

"I really do have to go now," said Marcus. "Or they won't wait for me. And I have to collect my gear, and say goodbye to my parents." He held out a hand to me, "Goodbye Claudia my darling." Then he left the house. I turned to Drusilla, "What shall I do? I can't go on without him."

"Of course you can," she said, "Come on, let's sit down here for a while," she indicated a bench. There was nothing else I could do, so I sat down beside her. Still with an arm around my shoulders, she said, "Cheer up, he'll be back, he is in love with you."

"Do you really think so?" I asked.

"It was obvious to me," she answered "From the way he looked at you, and the way he said goodbye to you."

I had calmed down by now, but still felt desolate. "Oh dear, I'm sorry I got hysterical, I just felt so terrible all of a sudden that I lost control of myself."

"Never mind, it was an emotional moment."

I looked around the garden, the chestnut trees were in bloom, and the roses were a riot of colour. But my eyes were blurred with tears, and I could not see them. Much less appreciate the beauty of the scene. I got up from the seat, and still blinded by tears, I wandered through the grounds, down to the water garden. The fish pond, surrounded by statues in niches, was full of exotic fish, in bright and iridescent colours. The whole scene was of course idyllic, if I had been in the mood to appreciate it.

I sat down on a small marble bench, and contemplated the fish through my tears. I was still unable to stop crying, I doubted I ever would.

Drusilla came up behind me, "Come on Claudia, it does no good to give way in this unrestrained manner."

"I can't help it," I sobbed.

"Come on now, it's hardly the end of the world."

"Yes it is, for me it is."

"Nonsense! How silly you are behaving."

Just then Gaius appeared, "What's wrong?" he asked.

"None of your business," I snapped. "I'm going to lie down for a while." With that I fled into the house. I met nobody on the way to my bedroom. Arriving there I discovered the miniature coral fish, which I had placed in a fold of my gown. As I pulled it out and looked at it, tears started to flow again. Falling onto the floor beside the bed, I sobbed uncontrollably again. After a few minutes Meriope appeared in the doorway.

"Whatever are you doing on the floor?" she asked.

I raised my head and glowered at her, I was furious. "Get out!" I screamed, "Why can't everyone leave me alone, it is none of your business. If I choose to lie on the floor it is my own affair, not yours, or anyone else's in this house."

Meriope came towards me, "Stop having hysterics, and get up at once," she ordered. She extended a hand to help me up. Sulkily I took it and rose from the floor, and sat on the bed.

"That's better," said Meriope. "Now are you going to tell me what's wrong?"

"I expect you know," I said. "Everyone in the house probably knows by now."

"Yes, I did hear something," Meriope replied.

"I'll bet Drusilla told you, I expect she couldn't wait to spread the gossip."

"She did say something, but in any case you were making enough noise. I expect the whole household could hear you!"

"I don't care," I gloomed, "What does it matter who has heard?"

"I've never known you get this upset by any man before."

"I've never met anyone like Marcus before."

"Well there's no sense in going on like this is there? It won't do you any good will it?"

"No, but I can't help how I feel can I?"

"No, but I expect he'll be back sometime won't he?" Meriope said. "Now why don't you lie down and rest for a while. I'll get you a cup of wine, and you'll soon feel better."

"All right, thank you Meriope, I'd like some wine."

When she returned with the wine I had calmed down, and was reclining on the bed.

"That's better isn't it?" she said, handing me the wine cup. I nodded and drank deeply, the wine had a soothing effect on me. Suddenly I felt more optimistic, of course Marcus would return eventually, as he had said he would. The time would pass, and we would be together again. How many years though? Two? Three? I felt depressed again, it did not bear thinking about. I would be crying again in a moment if I was not careful. I must try and think more positively. After all there were still parties to attend. Suddenly they had ceased to interest me. Nothing would be any fun without Marcus to attend them with me.

My mother entered the room, "My poor Claudia," she said. "Never mind, the time will pass soon enough, and you'll see him again."

I stared at her, "How will I manage in the meantime?"

"Well it will get easier after a while," she answered. "And think of it like this, it will be something to look forward to in the meantime!" She smiled at me, "Come on, cheer up. It will be just the three of us at supper tonight. Gaius and Drusilla are going out."

That at least was good news. I would not have to face Gaius' snide remarks across the supper table. "All right," I said. "I'll see you then." After that, tired out by grief and weeping, I fell into an exhausted sleep.

CHAPTER THREE

LIFE GOES ON

For some time after the departure of Marcus I was very depressed. Meriope had to force me to get up in the mornings as I did not feel that there was anything to get up for anymore.

"Why bother?" I would say. "There is no reason for me to care what I look like anymore."

"Yes there is," said Meriope severely. "You must keep yourself decent for your family's sake. How do you think they like to see you looking so miserable all the time? Life has to go on and you with it my girl. Besides you owe it to yourself to look presentable, as well as to your family and friends."

I trailed unhappily into the tablinium, and stood by the garden door, the beauty of the well kept gardens almost lost on me as I stood there. Although it was impossible to be completely oblivious to the scene. Slaves were pruning the roses that bloomed everywhere in riotous abandon. The sun shone out of a clear blue sky. I have been told that there is no place on earth so beautiful as this part of the world, and I can believe it.

If only I felt happier! A slave brought me a cup of fruit juice, and I sipped at it, sitting on a garden bench. Everybody else in the house had gone about their tasks, and I was left alone. Alone with my thoughts about Marcus. When, if ever, would I see him again? I wondered. And how was I to cope until I did? I began to feel edgy. I wanted him I realised, and no one else would do, or so it seemed to me then. How could I get excited by anybody else when all I could think of was

Marcus. Being close to him and having his arms around me. I shifted restlessly, how long could I wait I wondered. It might be years before he returned. But then, I thought what will it be like for him? He will be alone too. There was no one for him in Britannia he had told me. I had no reason not to believe him, I had felt how desperate he had been. I was not stupid enough to think it had just been because he desired me so particularly, although I believe that he did that as well. But it was also the long abstinence that had made him the way he was that first night together. In fact that had excited me particularly I remembered. Surely if he could wait so long, go without sex so long, I could at least do the same! I shifted again, and hoped if he could wait so long, then so could I. I resolved that I would not be tempted by anyone, however attractive, until Marcus returned for me. I did not feel like meeting anyone socially at the moment anyway. The social life did not appeal to me at the moment. So I should have no difficulty in hanging on to my resolve.

I continued to sit in the peristyle garden in the sun. I did not feel like moving, there was nowhere to go anyway. Drusilla appeared, coming from her quarters.

"Ave Claudia," she greeted me. "Enjoying the sun are you?"

I nodded despondently.

"Cheer up!" she said. "Surely you're not still moping around are you? It has been nearly a week now, surely you can find something to amuse you."

"A week!" I moaned. "It is hardly any time at all. I might have years to wait before I see Marcus again."

"So what are you going to do in the meantime?" she asked.

"Probably nothing," I said.

"Come on," she said, "Where is Flavia these days? I haven't seen her around here at all lately."

I did not answer her. I remembered how I had almost forcibly taken Marcus away from her at Clodius' party. I doubted she would want to see me again for a while. So what did I care anyway? I was going to keep myself to myself for a long time. I did not care if I saw Flavia or not. She would not be very friendly towards me at present anyway.

But to my surprise a slave appeared in the doorway, and announced that my friend had just arrived. I was astonished.

"Well?" asked Drusilla. "Perhaps she will cheer you up a bit."

Flavia appeared, she looked very pretty. Her dark hair was curled, and framed her face in small tendrils. She did not appear to bear me a grudge about Marcus. But then he had gone away anyway, so she had probably decided to let bygones be bygones. She had nothing to lose in any case, and neither did I. I was pleased to see her. I decided to say nothing about the night of Clodius' party, but showed delight in her presence.

"Ave Flavia" I said. "It has been a while since I saw you."

She laughed. "I thought I would leave you alone for a few days." She said. "I knew Marcus had returned to his cohort. I assumed you would have recovered well enough by now, and be glad of some company."

"I am," I agreed. I realised it was true, I was bored with brooding on my own. And I welcomed the company of my friend. A slave brought us refreshments, and we settled down comfortably to talk.

"Has anything much been going on?" I asked.

"Well not a great deal up to now," said Flavia. "But I think that things will start to liven up a bit soon."

"In what way?" I asked.

"Well I imagine that some of us will get together and arrange some outings in the near future." said Flavia. "You will join us of course?"

"I'm not sure," I said. "I don't feel much like meeting a lot of people at present. It won't be the same without Marcus."

"But you always came with us before you met him," said Flavia "so why not now."

"It was different then, but I've met him now, and I can't feel the same as I did before," I said.

"But he will be away for a year or two probably," said Flavia. "What do you mean to do until he returns? Just sit at home thinking about him all the time?"

I shook my head, "I don't know. I just can't think about anything else at the moment."

Flavia stared at me in surprise, "I've never seen you like this before," she said.

"I've never felt this way about any man before," I said.

We sat in silence for a while. Then after a few moments Flavia asked "Don't you want to see our friends any more then?"

"I don't know," I said. "Sometime perhaps, but not just yet. I'm too unhappy to want to socialise in any way at present."

"But surely—" said Flavia

"Don't ask me to do anything at the moment," I said "It would not take much more to start me crying again at this juncture".

Flavia and I talked for a while longer, then she left me.

Later that day as I sat enjoying the heat of the sun, there was a commotion suddenly. I went into the tablinium to see what was going on in the atrium. I saw my brother Lucius, who had apparently returned home. I ran forward excitedly and threw myself into his arms and hugged him.

"Claudia!" He exclaimed hugging me back. My relationship with him was very different from the one I had with my other brother Gaius. Although he was younger that Gaius, Lucius was several years older than me. We had always got on together, and we were genuinely pleased to see each other.

"This is a surprise," I said. "I wasn't expecting you back so soon."

"I'm only home for a short while," he replied. "I shall have to go back to Rome quite soon."

"How soon?" I asked.

"Within a few weeks," he said

"Have you seen mother?" I asked.

"Not yet," he answered.

Just then she appeared, and ran to embrace him. She also it appeared had not expected him so soon.

"I had a chance of a ride with some friends I met in Rome," he said. "And I decided to pay a visit to my family."

"I'm so glad you did," said our mother.

Slaves were busy carrying his baggage to his room, and preparing a bath for him. I had temporarily forgotten my misery. A special dinner was arranged for that evening in Lucius' honour. Even though it would only be a family occasion I began to look forward to it with pleasure. I called for Meriope to come and help me prepare for the evening. She was only too pleased that I was showing an interest in life again.

We gathered together in the triclinium, sipping wine. My mother and father, Gaius and Drusilla and Lucius and myself. Like my mother Lucius was black haired and dark complexioned. While my father, Gaius and myself were light haired with fair complexions.

Slaves passed the dishes around. The first course was shellfish, followed by roast fowl with herbs and spices. As we ate we listened to Lucius' account of his experiences in Rome. These were mainly of a business nature, and not of great interest to me. My father and Gaius were interested to hear them though, so the talk was mainly of commerce. After dinner we all moved into the tablinium and drank more wine. It was a pleasant enough evening, I felt better than I had for some time. Things would improve now that Lucius was home. We would be able to attend social gatherings together, and perhaps I would enjoy going out again.

The following afternoon Flavia appeared again. She had heard that my brother was home, and had come around to see if she would see him while visiting me. She was pleased to see me looking more cheerful, and asked if I would reconsider joining our friends on some social occasions. And of course bring Lucius along as well. I agreed that that was very likely, and asked when the first event would take place.

"Tomorrow," said Flavia, "Some of us are planning to visit the theatre to see a comedy. Perhaps you would like to come with us."

"I'll ask Lucius," I agreed. "I would like to come. After all life has to go on, and I have to get back into circulation again."

The following afternoon Lucius and I set out to join our friends at the theatre. Flavia was there when we arrived, with about half a dozen of our usual companions. She came up to greet us immediately, and I saw she was hoping to pair off with my brother. I wished them well, it suited me if they became a couple. But Lucius was greeting the others delightedly as he had not seen them for a long time. Antonia took his arm, and led him away from myself and Flavia. Flavia looked disappointed, I took her arm.

"Come on," I said. "Let's go and find our seats. The play will be starting soon."

We filed into the theatre. The play began, it was the usual sort of comedy, about a slave who takes charge of his master's affairs. Not at all true to life, no slave would really behave like that, but it made hilarious comedy, and was very amusing to watch. It certainly cheered me up.

"I don't think that that will last very long," I said. Glancing towards my brother. "He is not serious about her. She just came up to him and took charge. He is pleased to be home, and he has not seen any of them for a long time. He will likely play the field a bit at first. You will just have to wait for the right moment, and find the right opportunity."

"I hope you're right," replied Flavia. "I really do like him you know."

"Yes," I said. "I know you do."

Just then Lucius came over to us. "Lets go home Claudia," he said.

I looked at Flavia, "you see?" I whispered.

Antonia looked disappointed. She had expected that Lucius would have remained with her, but he preferred to come home with me than to go anywhere with anybody else. We said our farewells, and I took his arm as we turned our footsteps in the direction of our house.

CHAPTER FOUR

BACCHIC REVELS

After the theatre party Lucius and I attended several social events together. Flavia was always included in these, and she continued to hope that Lucius would be persuaded to return her feelings for him. But Lucius did not seem to be aware of her devotion, or if he did, he chose not to notice it. I think he preferred to be unattached for the present. He was not staying in Pompeii for very long anyway, as he had to return to Rome and his studies quite soon. To get involved with a girl now, would only lead to heartbreak later on for both of them. But Flavia would not see this, and spent her time worrying when she could have been enjoying herself. I tried to tell her this, and urged her to take more pleasure in the proceedings. And that Lucius would probably think more of her if she were not so obviously in love with him.

"Just ease off a little," I advised her. "Pretend that you don't care when he shows interest in another girl."

"I'll try," she said, "But it will be hard to pretend."

"He's not really interested in any of them," I said.

"I know," said Flavia. "But I can't help being jealous."

At a party one night, a man I had never met before came up and began a conversation with me. As we talked he asked me if I had heard of the Bacchic Revels. I said that I had heard vaguely about them. He told me that it was celebrated at a large house some way outside the town gates.

"You could apply for initiation," he said.

I asked him what exactly this would involve.

"It would take the form of a ceremony," he answered. "You and your friends would enter the room naked for the initiation ritual. I can't tell you at this stage the precise order of the rite of initiation. That would be explained to you just before the ceremony began."

It might be fun, I thought. I would suggest the idea to Flavia I decided. It might cheer her up a bit, and stop her moping after Lucius so much. I told the man, Faustinius was his name, that I would think about it, and consult my friend. I did not intend to include any of my other friends at the moment, just Flavia.

I looked around, and caught sight of her leaning dejectedly against a pillar, I went over to her.

"Cheer up!" I said. "I've got something to tell you."

"Lucius has disappeared somewhere," she said. "I don't know who he has gone with."

I sighed. "Perhaps he hasn't gone with anyone in particular, maybe he has gone for a breath of air. It is hot in here."

"Do you really think that that is all," she asked hopefully. "What did you want to tell me?"

"I have just been talking to a man named Faustinius," I said. "He has been telling me about the cult of Dionysius. It sounds quite interesting. He suggested that I, and some of my friends should join it. I thought that you and I could go together. It could be fun, and worth a try anyway."

"All right," said Flavia, "why not? As you say it's worth a try. Find out when the next one takes place."

"I will," I said, and went to find Faustinius again. He was not very far away, in fact he was watching me as I came towards him. He was tall and thin, with a narrow, rather fawnlike face, with dark hair.

"Well?" he asked, "will you come?"

"Yes," I answered. "My friend Flavia will come with me. When is the next meeting?"

He told me it would be in two days time, he would meet us, and escort us to the villa. We made arrangements about where and when we would meet him. It would be late he told me, we would go under cover of darkness. I felt excited, it was something new after all, and I liked new experiences. I told Flavia the time and place where we would be meeting with Faustinius.

Two nights later, just when it was starting to get dark, Flavia and I met

Faustinius as arranged. I introduced him to Flavia. He was riding in a chariot, and we got up beside him. He drove through the narrow streets of the town, towards the Herculaneum Gate. Driving through the gate, we continued on to the mysterious villa. This was some way beyond the gateway, we passed one or two other large houses on the way. It was further away from the town that I had realised. I began to feel rather nervous. The weather was still very hot, so there was no fear of being chilly in the scanty garments I was told we would have to wear for the ceremony, and the celebration that would follow. Some of which would take place in the open air. But I could not halp a shiver of trepidation which I tried to repress, as we approached the large house.

Arriving at the mansion, we dismounted from the chariot, and stood outside waiting for Faustinius to hitch up his horses. We then followed him to the entrance of the Villa, which was immediately opened for us by the door slave. We then followed Faustinius into a large room rather sparsely furnished. The reason being that this was where the main ritual was performed, I discovered later. There were both men and women, rather scantily clad, reclining on couches placed around the room. There were even a few children I saw to my surprise, as I had thought it an adult cult.

After we were also seated with wine and cakes, a lady who was introduced to us as the high priestess, rose from her seat at what appeared to be an altar. She had been sitting with her back to the room when we came in. The wall paintings depicted what was obviously the ceremony of Dionysius that we were going to see performed. I was still feeling nervous, and the pictures were indeed awe inspiring. I shivered slightly again, and the priestess noticed. She smiled at me.

"It's not as frightening as it may look," she said, indicating the paintings. I smiled back at her.

"It looks quite scary," I said.

But the wine was beginning to take effect, and I was starting to feel relaxed and euphoric suddenly. There were herbs in the drink I saw, and this may have been the reason for my changed mood. I began to look forward to the ritual, and the revels that would follow. I had been promised amusement by Faustinius, which was the main reason I agreed to join the festivities.

The actual ceremony would not take place tonight, but three nights later. This was just a gathering so that Flavia and I could meet the other members of the group. And be told something of what would be involved.

The high priestess, a plump, dark lady called Clodia, explained to us that we would all meet at the villa, the same as we had tonight. Garments would be provided for us to wear. We were introduced to the other members of the cult, both male and female, who seemed to be about equal in number. They appeared a solemn lot, and appeared to take the whole business very seriously. They were pleasant enough to us, but I had the feeling that they were slightly suspicious of us, wondering why we had come, and what our interest was in the Cult of Dionysius. A few practically ignored us.

More wine was poured, and we chatted for a while. Some of the Mystery was described to us, but by no means all! For that we had to wait until the rite itself took place.

Three nights later we again met Faustinius, and drove to the Mystery Villa outside the Herculaneum Gate. This time we were again greeted with cups of wine mixed with herbs. If anything this was more strongly flavoured with herbs than before. The effect of them was even more pronounced. After we had finished our wine we were taken to the bathing area and told to take a purifying bath. Even though we had both had a bath before we left our homes. We were told we had to have a ritual bath with special herbs to prepare us for the initiation rite.

The initiation was to be held in the large room with the Dionysiac wall paintings. Flavia and I were led blindfolded into the room. Then we were led around the room, stopping at each corner. Someone, Faustinius I think, was chanting something at each corner. After the blindfolds were removed from our eyes we were at last able to see the scene that was taking place. A naked young boy read out the ritual, two women flanking him on either side, as he read from the scroll. A man was playing a lyre throughout the ceremony.

We were then both ritually scourged. Although this appeared frightening in the painting, it was really only the lightest of touches with the scourge wielded by Faustinius. After the ceremony we were led to the temple of Bacchus. One of the priestesses knelt and drew a veil from a phallic symbol. This was meant to represent the phallus of Dionysius. Everybody then prostrated themselves before the sacred symbol, rather solemnly I thought, and Flavia and I followed suit. The whole procedure was taken very seriously from beginning to end.

Afterwards we donned the flimsy garments that had been given to us, and took our places with the other celebrants. And we all filed out of the temple towards a huge fire that had obviously been lit while we were inside the temple. Food and wine was passed around as we sat around the fire. Incense was thrown onto the fire. And between that, and the wine, that again had herbs mixed in it, a feeling of ecstasy and euphoria soon overtook us all. After the meal, music was played. Drums and cymbals crashed around us, and more herb infused wine was handed round from a large cauldron. I soon began to feel intoxicated, it was a very pleasant feeling, and I felt encouraged to help myself to even more to the strong wine. The serious part of the proceedings was now apparently over, and the revels had started in earnest. The smoke from the fire to which more incense was being thrown from time to time, by a priest or priestess who happened to be close to it, increased the heady feeling that we all now had. Faustinius, I had already noted, had a quite high position in the hierarchy. He was obviously one of the higher priests, and was close to the woman who was in charge, and, I learned, owned the house.

Someone took hold of my hand, and we seemed to run up the side of the mountain in our flimsy, transparent robes, with our hands joined. The men followed behind us, and when we reached the slope of Vesuvius, some the them paired off as if by prior arrangement. I had by now become separated from Flavia, and was wandering in a kind of daze among the vines and bushes of the wooded area we were now in.

I looked around for Flavia, but could not see her. I began to worry about where she had got to. I did not think it a good idea for us to be separated. We were among a crowd of strangers whom we knew nothing about. It was a bad idea for us to become split up. Just then Faustinius appeared, from somewhere behind me it seemed. Taking my hand he pulled me after him among some bushes. I followed him reluctantly, lots of people were by now entwined in passionate embraces. But I had no intention of getting involved in that kind of thing, as I had sworn to be faithful to Marcus. But Faustinius seated me and himself in a small glade. He looked more faunlike than ever, as he produced from somewhere two large goblets of a different kind of wine to that which we had been drinking earlier. He handed one to me, and proceeded to sip at the other one himself. I thought that there could be no harm in it as he was drinking it himself, and so I took a mouthful. It had a pleasantly sweet taste, so I drank some more. Faustinius smiled, and also drank some more wine. After a while I became confused, and was not sure exactly what was happening. Suddenly I found Faustinius' arms around me. It was not unpleasant, indeed I began to enjoy the feeling of his hands on me. Before I realised what was happening, I felt a searing sensation of ecstasy suddenly, and it was as if I had swooned for a moment with pleasure. Then everything seemed to be in a haze, and I was lying on the ground. There was no one else in the immediate vicinity. I lay there for a while in a stupor, I was not quite sure exactly what had happened. Whether Faustinius had had sex with me, but it seemed the most likely explanation for the sensation I had felt. Well there was nothing that I could do about it whether he had or not, and I was sure he had. I had barely been conscious at the time. I was enjoying myself I realised, and I was too euphoric to mind much about anything that had happened, or might happen.

Still intoxicated with wine, and what were obviously drugs, (although I was not thinking quite so specifically then) I rose to my feet. Rather unsteadily I made my way back to the fire which was still burning. Several of the other participants had already returned, and were reclining around it, looking somewhat stupefied, as I must have done. I had by now almost completely forgotten about Flavia. I was past caring about anything. I was not even worrying about how I was to get home, it did not seem to matter at all!

I think I must have fallen asleep, I do not know for how long, but suddenly someone was shaking me awake. It was one of the priestesses. I had to be home before daylight I was told. There was a married couple whose names I did not catch, (or if I did I cannot now remember) whom I was told would take me back to town with them, and drop me off at my own door.

Suddenly I remembered Flavia, I looked around for her, but I was told she had already left. Sleepily I climbed up beside the people who were offering me a lift, and was driven back to the town. I could not recall even reaching my home, and getting into my bed.

The next thing I knew, Meriope was bending over me, waking me up. I shut my eyes again, I felt terrible! What had I been drinking, or even eating the previous night?

"Where were you last night?" Meriope asked. "You left the house without telling anyone where you were going. Or even that you were going out at all! Where have you been, and what have you been doing?"

"That's my business," I snapped. "I don't have to tell you or anyone else what I do."

"Yes you do," she answered. "Why should you object to telling us where you went, unless you were up to no good, which I presume you were."

I had had enough, I had a searing headache, and I felt distinctly queasy. I was certainly not up to being questioned by anyone. I burst into tears suddenly.

"I'm ill," I wept. "I'm not up to being cross examined."

"It's your own fault if you're not well," said Meriope. "If you won't say where you've been then leave it for the moment. Here quick!" she handed me a bowl just as I was violently sick. I lay back on the bed exhausted, I told Meriope I wanted to be left in peace to sleep.

"All right," she said, "I'll leave you alone for now, but later I shall want to know more. I'll tell your mother you do not wish to be disturbed."

I was asleep before she left the room. I awoke much later, and called for Meriope. She came immediately.

"Well, how are you feeling now?" she asked.

"Not well at all," I replied.

Meriope busied herself tidying my bed, and making me more comfortable. When she had completed this task, she again started to question me about the previous night. And what I had been doing to get myself in such a state. I did not reply for a while, but she persisted in knowing what had gone on. Eventually I told her something of what had occurred.

"Bacchanalia!" she exclaimed. "That used to be a banned cult. Goodness knows what goes on at those rites. You want to be careful my girl, getting yourself involved in that."

"It was all right," I said defensively.

Although I could not clearly remember all that much about what had gone on. I had been in a stupor for much of the time I had been there. And come to think of it, what had happened to Flavia! I could only vaguely recall being brought home by a married couple. I could only dimly recall them.

Just then my mother came into the room, followed by Drusilla.

"Are you all right Claudia?" my mother asked. "You don't look at all well"

"Well I don't feel very well!" I snapped. "I'm sorry mother, I should not have spoken to you like that," I apologised.

"Never mind that," said my mother. "Where did you go last night. I presume you had a lot to drink, wherever it was."

"Quite a lot," I confessed. "Probably more than I usually have."

"Where was it exactly that you went?" my mother repeated.

I again explained about the Mystery Villa, and the rites, (Or some of them) which had taken place there.

"I have heard about these people," she said. "And I don't think that they are suitable to get involved with."

"They were all right," I said. "It was fun, really it was. There were some serious parts, but mainly it was a party."

Meriope returned with some broth. "Here," she said, "drink this, it will make you feel better. And help you get your strength back."

"I'm not hungry," I said.

"Try to drink some," my mother said. She took the cup from Meriope, and lifting my head from the pillow, she put the cup to my lips. I drank some of it obediently. It did make me feel better. I lay down again. "I would like to sleep now," I said. "I'll see you later."

"Very well," my mother left the room. But Drusilla who had been listening quietly, without saying a word, waited until the other two had left. Then she came forward, and sat on the end of my bed.

"What was it really like?" she asked eagerly. "I've tried to persuade Gaius to let us go to one of them, but he refused. I don't know why, they can't be that bad. Are they?"

"To be honest I can't recall all that much of what happened." I said. Even the initiation ceremony was confused in my mind now. "I'm sorry, it was quite fun, although some rather peculiar things did go on I think."

I remembered Faustinius, and what had occurred between us. I was sure he had raped me. And also, what had happened to Flavia? I was worried about her, but surely she would have been escorted home by someone as I had been. But there was nothing I could do about it until I was well enough to leave my bed.

CHAPTER FIVE

MARCELLUS

It was a few days later, more than a week after the night of the Bacchic revels. I had recovered, and was up and about again. A dinner party had been arranged by my parents. Flavia I had heard was home, and had arrived there quite safely. Although I was still curious to know what had happened to her on the night of the mysteries. She also had been unwell I had heard, so we had not had a chance to meet and compare notes as to what had happened at the revels.

The people who had been invited to dinner at our home that evening were a family of cloth merchants. I had not met any of them. It appeared that my family had only recently become involved with them. Although we were in the wine trade, and they were in the clothiers trade, it seemed that the two families had interests in common. Probably to do with investments I surmised. I was not all that interested in the details in any case, but I was quite happy to help to arrange the dinner party.

I entered the kitchen where the cook was starting to prepare the meal for that evening. A large earthenware cooking pot was already heating on the stove. There was not a great deal of room in the kitchen for all of us. My mother and Drusilla and myself, as well as the slaves. Mother was supervising the preparation of the meat we were to eat that evening. It was to be a large fowl, boiled with herbs first, in the pot that was on the stove. Afterwards, when it was half cooked, it would be removed from the pot and put in a stew pan with oil and garum, other herbs would be added, with a little wine for colour. Finally, when it was almost completely cooked, wine and honey would be added, and the bird would be basted in it's own gravy, with a dash of vinegar added.

I was delegated to oversee the desserts. These were mainly pastries to be fashioned into shapes in dishes specially designed for the purpose. I sorted out which shapes should be used for this occasion. It was of course extremely hot in the kitchen, which was by it's nature small, as kitchens always are, unfortunately. By midday we were glad to rest, and have a light snack in the small garden. After which we all rested for a while.

After we had rested, we prepared ourselves for the evenings festivities. Although I was not expecting it to be a very exciting evening, I still dressed with care, in a bright yellow dress which suited me rather well. Apart from myself and Lucius there would not be any younger people there. Marcellus, the son of the people who were coming to dinner, was over thirty I had been told. So I was not counting on having a particularly good time. In fact I was assuming I would have a rather boring evening. So I was quite content to oversee the final preparations for the dinner. Which meant I was not there when they arrived. This did not worry me at all. I would meet them eventually.

As it happened I did not join them until the meal was just about to be served. I slipped into the triclunium just as the first course was being presented. I took my place on a couch next to my brother Lucius. I was introduced to the guests, they were around the same age as my parents, perhaps a bit older. Except of course for the son Marcellus. As soon as I saw him I could not stop looking at him. He was absolutely stunning, with thick curly dark brown hair, and superb good looks. He was the handsomest man I had ever seen, I could scarcely believe my eyes. I thought I knew some attractive men, but this man! I was lost, devastated, I could not stop myself from staring at him.

"Claudia," said Lucius, "the man is waiting for you to choose an hor d oeuvre, hurry up, other people are waiting to be served."

"Sorry," I mumbled.

I chose the first thing that came to hand. I was barely aware of what I was eating anyway. Trying not to stare at Marcellus, I kept my eyes on my dish of shellfish. The main course was then handed round. The fowl was accompanied by fennel, stewed leeks and onions, and peas.

As we ate I glanced surreptitiously at Marcellus again. He caught me looking at him and smiled at me. Embarrassed I looked away quickly and drank some wine. When Marcellus was involved in the conversation again I risked another glance at him. He really was devastatingly handsome, I forgot to eat. Lucius looked at me.

"What's the matter?" he asked. "Why aren't you eating, are you not hungry?"

"I'm all right," I said, and forced myself to eat some of the meat and vegetables. When I looked up again Marcellus was gazing at me. I stared back for a moment, then turned away and made an effort to start a conversation with Lucius. No one else seemed aware of anything unusual, they were all absorbed in their discussion about money, from what I could gather from the conversation.

After the dessert which was shaped pastries, with fruit to follow, a flask of best Falernian wine was passed around, together with a bowl of spices for those who liked their wine with seasoning. I liked a dash of flavouring myself, though not too much in this instance as it could detract from the taste of the wine, which was I knew a particularly good one. While the wine was being passed around I was again drawn to gaze at Marcellus. The conversation was livelier now. They had stopped discussing investments, and joking and laughter had replaced it. I grew bolder with the effect of the wine, and now I stared more openly at Marcellus. He met my gaze head on, he stared back. I flushed and looked away again. Stealing another glance I saw he was regarding me steadily, he smiled at me, I smiled back, it would have been rude not to. Just then Gaius engaged him in a conversation, and he had to turn his attention away from me. Even in profile, perhaps particularly in profile, he was wonderful to look at. I wondered if I would see him again after tonight. I sincerely hoped so. I would, I decided find a way somehow to ensure that we met again. I did wonder why I had never met him at any of the social functions I attended. Maybe he had been away from Pompeii for a while. But in that case he might go away again, and our paths might not cross again, or at least not for a long time.

Eventually it was time for the guests to leave. As we shook hands in the atrium Marcellus again looked hard at me. I stood in a dreamy daze until my mother said "Come on Claudia, don't stare at people so."

Flushing again, I pulled myself together and said goodnight to Marcellus and his parents as they left to go home.

"Are you tired Claudia?" asked Drusilla. "You did not seem able to concentrate tonight, or to join in the conversation at all."

"I did not understand all the talk about investments," I said. "And yes, I am tired, I'm going to bed."

With that I left them all, and made my way to my bedroom.

It was the following afternoon, I lay on a couch in the tablinium. I could not stop myself from thinking about Marcellus. I was daydreaming, imagining what it would be like to be with him. What kind of a lover would he be! The thought made me tingle all over, I hardly dared to think about it. As I reclined there on the couch there was a knock at the door, which I had drawn shut so I could have more privacy. A slave was there, he said there was a man to see me. I pulled myself together, who could it be I thought.

"Show him in," I said. "And bring us some wine." To my astonishment Marcellus walked in. I rose to my feet. "Sit down," I bade him, indicating another couch. "There's nobody else here, my father and Gaius are out."

"I know," Marcellus replied. "It's you I've come to see."

"Me!" I exclaimed surprised.

"Yes, you," he replied seating himself beside me on the couch.

The slave returned with the wine, and set it down near me. Then he left the room, we were alone together. I poured the wine for us, and handed a cup to Marcellus. We sipped at it, looking at each other. I did not know what to say.

Putting his cup down, Marcellus took mine from me, and set it down also. Without saying a word, he pulled me into his arms and kissed me passionately. I was only too happy to return his ardour, I was wildly excited, he could do anything he wished with me. This he then proceeded to do, laying me down on the couch. I wore only a thin silk robe, this he easily parted. I clung to him breathlessly, our desire was mutual, there was no way I could have prevented the total fulfilment of our joint desires. Afterwards I pulled my robe around me slightly, and settled down beside him, cuddled as close together as we could get.

"Why?" I wondered.

He laughed, "Surely that's obvious isn't it? You didn't take your eyes off me all last evening. What did you expect? It was clearly what you wanted."

I could hardly deny it, it must have been obvious how I had gazed at him all through dinner. It had not affected his appetite though, although I had had difficulty in eating much at all. I snuggled closer to him, "Will I see you again?" I asked, hoping fervently it was not just an afternoons amusement to him.

"Of course you will, why wouldn't you?" he asked.

"I wondered if you were going away somewhere," I said

"No, I'm not going anywhere," he answered, to my relief.

"I think we will be seeing a lot of each other."

I sighed happily, "I'm so glad."

We remained in each other's arms for a while, then I suddenly realised we were not very private. We were lucky that nobody had come in while we had been together. I arose from the couch, my hair must be disarranged I thought. I adjusted my gown, pulling it more securely around me, and tried to straighten my hair. It was only loosely gathered in a topknot, and most of it was hanging down by now.

Marcellus had also risen from the couch, and was preparing to leave. Perhaps it was better that he left before one of my family found us together. It would only require explanations that I did not feel up to just now. Later would be time enough for that I decided. If Marcellus and I were to be seeing each other regularly. I wondered when we would meet again, soon I hoped. I turned to him, still trying to adjust my hair, strands of which were hanging around my face by now.

"When will I see you again?" I asked.

"Tomorrow if possible," he answered. "I will come at about the same time I came today. Will you be alone again?"

"I'm not sure about that," I said. "But you can come here anyway. I will be in this room again. But we took a chance today, the peristyle door is open, anybody could have been passing."

He shrugged as if this was unimportant. "We'll be more careful. Is there a place we can be more private?"

I nodded, I was a bit annoyed by his casual dismissal of what could have been an embarrassing situation. If a slave had seen, for instance, the whole household would know. I did not wish my personal arrangements to be openly discussed in the slave quarters.

After he had left I went to tidy myself before the other members of the family appeared. I would tell them in my own time I thought, there was no hurry. Meriope appeared in my room suddenly, and began to help me with my hair.

"It's all right I can manage," I said. "Where did you come from anyway? How did not you know I was here?"

"I heard your guest leaving," she answered. "How involved did you get?"

"That's my business," I snapped. I did not care to be cross examined. She shrugged, "All right."

My hair rearranged, I changed into a less informal gown. I had not been expecting company when I put the other one on. Which was why I was so scantily clad. I went to join my mother and Lucius in the tablimium. All the signs of my earlier activities had been removed, so no one knew I had received a visitor.

The following morning Flavia arrived unexpectedly. I took her to the garden, I was pleased to see her, and eager to know what had happened to her on the night of the revels.

"Who brought you home?" I asked.

"I'm not sure," she answered. "I woke the next morning in my own bed. I don't know how I got there."

"What happened?" I asked curiously. "Who did you get involved with? Was it Faustinius?"

"He was there," she said. "There were a crowd of a dozen people together in a grove. We were chewing some leaves."

I stared at her, "What sort of leaves?"

"Laurel most likely," said Flavia.

"They cause hallucinations," I gasped. "Anything could have happened to you. It probably did, and you know nothing about it!"

"That's likely what happened," she said. "It was fun though, didn't you enjoy yourself?"

"So so," I said. "Some peculiar things seemed to go on." I told her about Faustinius, and what had occurred between us.

"I'm not really sure what did happen," I said. "He gave me a different sort of wine, at least I think it was wine."

"What do you mean you think it was wine?" Flavia asked

"Well the odd effect it had on me it might have been some kind of distilled drug for all I know. I was in a sort of trance state, I did not really know what was going on. But I'm almost sure that Faustinius raped me."

Flavia stared at me, "Aren't you positive?"

"Almost," I answered.

"Are you sure it was rape?" she asked. "The state you say you were in you could have agreed to it, and then forgotten."

I shook my head, "I don't think so."

"Would you go again?" Flavia asked.

"I don't think so," I repeated. "Not at present anyway."

"Why, because of what happened?"

"Not only that, there are other reasons," I said.

"Such as what?" she asked.

"I had a lot of trouble from the family, not to mention Meriope. They don't think it advisable for me to continue to go there."

"And that's the only reason?"

"Not entirely," I said. "There are other things, For one thing I've met the most marvellous man."

"When," she asked, "and where?"

"Here, about two night ago. He came to dinner with his parents."

"Who is he?" she asked.

"His names Marcellus, his family are cloth merchants, they are involved in some business investments with my father and Gaius."

"What's he like?" she asked.

"Well first he's wonderful looking," I answered. "I could not take my eyes off him all through dinner that evening. And yesterday afternoon he came to see me."

"What happened, what did he say?" Flavia asked.

"He is coming again this afternoon he said. And as to what happened, we made love." I said.

I told her exactly what had occurred the previous afternoon.

She gasped, "In the tablinium? With the garden door open? You took a chance didn't you? A slave might have seen. Not to mention one of your brothers walking in."

"I know," I said, "we will be more careful next time. I just wasn't thinking at the time. Not until afterwards anyway. He agreed we should be more discreet next time. I can't wait to see him again."

Flavia looked envious. "You seem to be having all the luck at present. There's me trying to get Lucius to notice me, and you don't even seem to have to try to get the most attractive men! First Marcus, and now this one."

I nodded, "I don't think you should have any great hopes of my brother. He will be leaving soon anyway."

"How soon?" she asked.

I shook my head, "I'm not sure, but I think it will be within a few weeks. Maybe two or three. Not any longer. Why don't you look around, there are plenty of good looking men about, even in our own circle of friends. Why waste your time worrying about a man who in any case isn't intending to settle down, or get involved in any way at the moment. You could have much more fun if you found someone else."

"Well you haven't wasted much time have you?" she said annoyed. "A few weeks ago you were going to wait until Marcus returned, weren't you?"

"Yes I know," I said. "And I did mean it. It wasn't until I met Marcellus that I even thought about anyone else. But he is unbelievable to look at."

"What's he like though, apart from his looks?" she asked.

I was uncertain how to answer her, the truth was that as a person I really did not know much about him. I had heard that he had been married, and was now divorced. But I knew nothing of the circumstances. I shrugged.

"I'll soon find out when I get to know him better won't I?"

"Maybe," said Flavia, she rose to depart. "I'll see you soon."

After she had gone I went to join Lucius in the tablinium. I could hardly wait until the afternoon to see Marcellus again. I would take him to a small room that we had beside the triclinium. We should be completely private there, as I hoped that nobody would know we were there.

Towards the time I was expecting Marcellus to arrive, I wandered towards the tablinium, intending to wait in there until he came. To my annoyance my brother Gaius was reclining on a couch in there, reading a scroll. This was a blow to my plans for the afternoon. What to do now I wondered. Just then Marcellus arrived in the atrium, Gaius rose from his couch to greet him.

"Marcellus!" he exclaimed, "how nice of you to call, it is good to see you."

They shook hands, and Gaius led Marcellus into the tablinium. The tow men settled themselves down for a business discussion. I trailed in behind them and threw myself onto a couch against the wall. Gaius looked at me in surprise. "Claudia I did not realise you were there, You remember my sister Claudia, Marcellus, she was at the dinner party the other night."

Marcellus smiled at me, "Yes, Ave Claudia, it's nice to see you."

I smiled and nodded. Marcellus turned back to Gaius.

"Claudia can you se about some wine for us?" asked Gaius.

I arose, and went to find a slave, I ordered refreshments and returned to the tablinium with the man carrying the tray of wine following behind me. Gaius poured the wine, we all sipped at it. I had decided to wait to speak to Marcellus somehow before he left. After about two hours he rose to leave, I jumped up. "I will see Marcellus out," I said to Gaius. He shrugged, "All right." He shook hands with Marcellus again. "I'm glad you came, it has been interesting to talk."

I led the way out of the tablinium, and drew Marcellus to the side of the atrium, where we could not be seen by Gaius. "When will I see you again?" I asked.

"I will call for you the evening after next," he said. "We will go to my dining club, there is a function being held there, will you come?"

"Yes," I answered, "I'll be happy to come. I've never been to a dining club before."

He smiled, "You will enjoy it, it will be something different for you. I can take you to a lot of places you haven't been to before."

"Oh yes please," I whispered.

So I would be seeing Marcellus often then. I was so happy, I looked at him, my knees felt weak. He looked so handsome standing there beside me. The tunic he wore seemed to accentuate his broad shoulders, in fact he was perfection I thought. If only we dared to go into the room I had intended. But the door slave had appeared to usher him out. Trembling with excitement and desire, I retired to my bedroom to rest, and dream in peace about the immediate future.

CHAPTER SIX

A LOVE AFFAIR

Two nights later I awaited Marcellus in the atrium. I was both excited and nervous as I had not heard from him since that afternoon two days ago with Gaius. I had got myself ready, I was wearing a white gown edged with silver, which fastened across one shoulder leaving the other one bare. Around my neck I wore a silver necklace with matching bracelets and earrings and armband. I was a bit early, I hoped that Marcellus would not be late. It would be embarrassing to have to wait too long in the atrium with the slaves passing to and fro, and I thought staring at me. As it happened, fortunately, I did not have very long to wait before the door opened and he appeared. I caught my breath, he also was wearing white. A pure white linen tunic which looked superb against his bronzed skin. In fact he looked magnificent, his astonishing good looks shown to advantage in the most electrifying way. I gazed at him in, I must admit, complete adoration. He looked me over too, and I imagined liked what he saw. With his arm possessively around me we left the house.

Outside four attendants were waiting with a litter, when we had stepped into it they lifted it up and carried us to the dining club which was some way away. Rather too far to walk, in fact it took about half an hour to get there. But reclining inside with Marcellus' arms round me was enough for me. I was almost sorry when we arrived.

We were greeted by the host for that evening just inside the door. Who, after he had shaken Marcellus' hand, and been introduced to me, ushered us into the dining area. We stood around for a while with small glasses of spiced wine in our hands. Marcellus was obviously well known there, for he seemed to know everybody. There were I noticed, quite a lot of unattached men there, only a few had brought women with them. Some of them seemed surprised that Marcellus had brought me. They were obviously used to him being there alone, and did not seem sure what to say to me. Although there was quite a crowd there, it was not overcrowded. These clubs were select, and had a fairly limited membership. Women were allowed only as guests, and were not permitted to become members in their own right. This seemed perfectly satisfactory to me, it was not the sort of place I would come to unescorted. But with Marcellus beside me I was completely happy.

The company was a mixture of all age groups, but I was by far the youngest person there. I glanced round at the other women as we took our places on the dining couches. There was a couple there I thought I had met somewhere before, but I could not recall where, or in what circumstances. Or even if I had met them before, and was not mixing them up with someone else. But they appeared to recognise me by the way they were gazing at me across the table. I turned away from them, I was rather embarrassed by the way they kept staring at me. And as I did not remember who they were, I wished to avoid being addressed by them. The first course was being passed around, I selected an hor-d-ouvre and turned to look at Marcellus. He was deep in conversation with the man seated on the other side of him. I ate my hor-d-ouvre in silence. I did not know anyone else anyway. The man on my other side showed no interest in starting a conversation with me. In fact he seemed more interested in his food than anything else. He was a large man who seemed the type who would join this sort of club solely for the dinners. His girth made it obvious he enjoyed his food and plenty of it. In fact he barely answered when someone did address him.

The main course was a large fish brought all the way from Rome I was told. I wondered how they managed to keep it fresh for so long a journey. Because it was fresh, nobody would eat it if it was not. It would be packed in ice or course, I knew, until just before it was cooked. I wondered idly how long it would take to get here. Marcellus turned to me, "Are you all right Claudia? I am sorry if I am neglecting you, but

Titus and I have some business in common. He is in the clothiers trade as well."

I smiled and nodded, "I'm managing all right."

He picked up a flagon of wine and poured me a cup. He then poured one for himself and lifted it to me. I responded and we both drank.

"This fish should be good," he went on. "The main reason for the meal tonight is because we acquired this trout. It is unique to the River Tiber."

"Oh," I said "I have heard of this fish. It's known to be very good."

The fish was served, it was flavoured with herbs, including parsley thyme and fennel. We helped ourselves to garum and vegetables from bowls held out by the slaves who were waiting on us. I wondered where they came from, if they belonged to the club. And if so what they did when there was no dinner party. Later I learned that they belonged to various club members including Marcellus. Everyone was quiet for a while enjoying the fish. Any fish is popular, and this was something special.

As we were relaxing before the dessert was served, the woman I thought earlier I had recognised spoke to me across the table.

"Did you enjoy yourself at the Rites?" she asked

I was startled, that was where I had met them before! What to answer? I could hardly deny being there that night. I must be careful how I answered, presumably everyone here knew that they were members of the Cult.

"I'm sorry," I said, "I cannot quite recall who you are. I met so many people that night."

"We drove you home," the woman replied. "I hope you were all right. You didn't seem too well when we left you."

"No," I mumbled, "I was quite unwell for several days afterwards."

"Oh I'm sorry to hear that," said the man. "But you recovered obviously."

"Yes," I answered, "I'm all right now."

"That's good," he replied.

Marcellus was looking at me in surprise. Some of the other guests were also looking at me. I did not know what to say, I knew a lot of people did not approve of the Dionysaic Cult. By the way Marcellus was looking at me I thought he might be one of them. "You attend the Bacchic Rites?" he asked.

"Only once," I said, "last month."

"You must tell me all about it some time." He said.

Just then the dessert arrived, thankfully I attended to the business of selecting a dish from the trays that were being passed around.

As we were leaving I again encountered the two people who had driven me home from the villa on the night of the Revels.

"I hope we shall see you again," the man said.

"Who brought you to the Villa?" his wife asked. "Was It Faustinius?"

I nodded, then ran to join Marcellus at the door. "We can walk from here," he said. "I sent the carriage home. We'll go to my house."

"Yes," I agreed.

Arms entwined we set off down the cobbled street. It was a comparatively short walk from the club to Marcellus' house. We stopped to kiss passionately once or twice, so that by the time we reached the house we were impatient to make love. We entered a large room and fell onto the nearest day couch. I clung to him avidly my desire for him mounting. He entered me almost immediately, thrusting hard his passion matching mine. I responded equally enthusiastically. We could not get enough of each other, our need for each other intense and wild. Finally we reached a tempestuous consummation, I felt drained and satisfied.

Afterwards we both drifted off to sleep. I awoke to find myself on the couch with my dress in disarray around my waist. Marcellus lay beside me still fast asleep. I sat up, I would have to find my way home soon I knew. I was not at all sure of the direction we had taken the previous night. I would have to wake Marcellus I thought, and ask him to either escort me home himself, or get on of his slaves to take me there. I nudged him, he awoke and stared at me as if he was surprised that I was still there. Although how he expected me to find my own way, I do not know.

"I ought to go home," I said

He sat up, "I'll take you."

We arose from the couch and straightened our clothes. It was around sunrise, I would be able to get in unnoticed I thought. Outside my door we embraced, I wondered when I would se him again. I did not like to ask, I hoped he would suggest something. Unfortunately he said nothing about another meeting, I went forlornly to my bed.

Two days went by without me hearing from Marcellus, and I was getting worried, when suddenly one afternoon he arrived. He was with my father and Gaius, and his father. I rushed to get them refreshments, then I tactfully left them to their business discussion. How to ensure that I saw him before he left? I could not interrupt them before they had finished, I would not be so rude. I hung about in the atrium, there was no one else about, Lucius had returned to Rome a few days earlier. The other women would be resting in their rooms I imagined, so I was surprised and disconcerted when Drusilla appeared suddenly.

"What are you doing Claudia?" she asked.

"I might ask the same," I answered.

"Have you seen Gaius?" she asked.

"Yes, he's in there with my father and Marcellus, they are talking business I assume. They have been there a while."

She looked at me, "I suppose you are waiting for Marcellus, he has not been here for several days has he?"

"No," I agreed.

"I thought he was your new suitor," she said

I did not answer her, there was nothing to say anyway. We sat down on a bench together, there was no point in denying that I was hoping to speak to Marcellus when he came out of the tablinium.

After about two hours the men emerged, they were in excellent spirits, laughing and joking together. My father saw me and Drusilla. "Ave girls," he said. "I'm so glad you're both here, I've got some good news for you" He indicated Marcellus and his father, "Marius and Marcellus have agreed to join us for the Games."

I perked up at that, this meant that Marcellus and I would be together at the Festival of Augustus, I smiled at my father.

"That is good news I'm so glad." I smiled at Marius and Marcellus, I certainly meant it. It was only a few days to the Festival which was at the end of August. So it would not be long before I saw Marcellus again. I glanced at him, he smiled at me and winked. I wondered if he had suggested the idea. It was certainly a good way of being together with both families. It would perhaps be a suitable time to announce that we cared for each other. Assuming Marcellus cared for me as I did about him. I tried not to stare too obviously at him, which was hard because I could barely take my eyes off him as usual. He wore a short summer tunic of a deep shade of blue, he looked magnificent!

The next day I went round to visit Flavia at her home. I wondered if she was still annoyed with me about the day I told her to stop dreaming about my brother Lucius. I was shown into a small room at the side of the atrium, she rose to greet me.

"This is a surprise," she remarked.

"I'm sorry I haven't been to see you sooner," I answered. "But a lot has been happening!"

"Yes I suppose it has, there's never a dull moment for you these days is there?"

She sounded bitter I thought.

"Has Lucius left yet?"

I nodded, "Yes he has, I don't know when he will be back again."

I seated myself beside her, "are you coming to the Games?"

"Yes I suppose so," she replied.

"Who will you go with?" I asked, "your family."

"I expect so," she said.

"Marcellus and his parents are going to join us," I said. "It will be fun."

Flavia looked morose, "Have you seen him lately?"

"Yes, yesterday afternoon he came to our house with his father. That was when the party for the games was arranged. But last week he took me to his Dining Club."

"What was it like?" she asked.

"The Club was fun and the dinner was good," I said, "but there were two people there, a husband and wife, I thought I knew from somewhere. But I couldn't think where I'd met them before. Then they spoke to me, they happened to be the couple who brought me home on the night of the Bacchic Rites. They announced it right across the table with everyone listening. Including of course Marcellus."

"Did it matter?" Flavia asked.

"I'm not sure whether it mattered or not." I said.

"Did Marcellus say anything about it?" she asked

"No, but that doesn't mean that he won't later" I said. "We had other things on our minds after we left the club. But that doesn't mean that the subject won't come up another time."

"Would he object do you think?" asked Flavia.

"He might," I answered. "Some people think it's not a reputable cult. Including my family."

"Well I'm going to go there again," Flavia said. "If you won't come with me I'll go anyway."

"Why," I asked, "are you so anxious to return there? Some of the things that went on there were questionable to say the least."

"I enjoyed myself," she retorted. "It was the best fun for a long time. But then I'm not having such a good time as you are at the moment."

"The Festival is always enjoyable," I said. "You will surely find an interesting man soon."

"I don't know," she sighed. "I'm not having much luck in that direction at present. Besides I love Lucius and am not really interested in meeting anyone special."

I sighed, "I've told you you're wasting your time. He's not said anything about you to me at all. There's no reason to assume he'll become interested in you even when he returns home for good. Which is in any case a long time ahead."

Flavia looked sulky, "all right, but in the meantime I intend to continue attending the Dionysaic Revels."

I got up to leave, this conversation was going nowhere at all. Why was she being so stupid? She was a very pretty girl, she could easily find herself a lover if she really tried. It was not because I was any more attractive than her that I was having such luck at present and she was not. There was no difference between us. No I reflected, it was her attitude to life at present that was preventing her from enjoying herself.

"Come to the Baths with me tomorrow," I suggested. "We can watch the men exercising in the paleastra. You might even see one you like, there are usually some good looking ones training there."

With any luck I thought, Marcellus might be there. It would be nice to see him working out nearly naked. "Will you come?" I asked.

Reluctantly Flavia agreed to accompany me the next afternoon. Why was she being so boring? I wondered. It was almost as if she did not want to be amused, but preferred to mope about and complain about my good fortune in contrast to her's. It was as if she got a kind of perverse pleasure in being miserable. To make me feel guilty perhaps, it was annoying. But I was determined to try and help her enjoy herself.

The following day Flavia and I met, and walked together to the largest of the Bath Installations in the town. I had one of the younger slave girls with me, to attend me and carry my towels and oils. I intended to go through both the tepid and hot baths, finishing with a dip in the pool to cool off. Afterwards we relaxed and sauntered round the porticoes to watch the men training in the paleastra. Swathed in towels Flavia and I stood with some of the other women spectators. I suddenly saw Marcellus, he was on the opposite side to where we were standing, so I could not attempt to speak to him. I would see him at the Games in a few days anyway. In spite of the blistering heat, (it was the hottest time of the year) he was exercising vigorously. His oiled body made darker by the sun. He obviously made a habit of this to be so sunburnt. I watched in delight, he wore only a loincloth as did the other men there. In spite of our intimacy I had never seen him so nearly naked before. On the two occasions we had been lovers we had not bothered to remove all our clothes. I had temporarily forgotten my companion as I was so absorbed in gazing at Marcellus. Now I turned to her, "that's Marcellus over there in the far corner. Isn't he handsome?"

Flavia nodded, "yes, he is, you have struck lucky again! There is no one else here who would appeal to me."

I looked at her, she was so pretty I thought again. I could not believe she was not able to find herself a beau. There was not another man in the palaestra as good looking as Marcellus, that was true. Quite a lot of them were middle aged, some even elderly. They did not of course exercise themselves anything like as strenuously as Marcellus, or some of the other younger men there.

"Lets go home," Flavia said

I was trying to see if I could catch Marcellus' eye across the palaestra. But he was not looking in our direction. I had hoped for a word with him before we met at the Games, when both our families would be with us.

"Why don't we stay here a bit longer?" I answered. "It is pleasant in the shade of the colonnades."

But Flavia was bored, there was no one here to hold her interest she said.

"All right," I said. "we'll go home."

With a last lingering glance in Marcellus' direction I followed my friend back into the bathhouse. We collected our clothes, and feeling refreshed, with the help of our slaves we dressed and tidied ourselves. We stepped out into the furnace that was the streets at this time of day, and made our way home.

On the day of the Games we set out early for the Amphitheatre as the spectacle began quite early in the morning. We met Marcellus and his parents outside, and made our way to our reserved seats. As we were people of some importance in Pompeii, we had our own private enclosure. Other people had to wait for the main gates to be opened, and had to queue for seats. They would all get in of course, there was plenty of room in the covered galleries, as well as in the tiered wooded seats below. The sun was already hot, and the temperature would be well into the nineties later. For this was August, the hottest month of the year, dedicated to the Emperor Augustus. This Festival was an annual event, looked forward to by everybody in Rome and Pompeii and everywhere else in the world where Roman citizens lived.

As we took our places in a semi-circle, myself and Marcellus with Gaius and Drusilla sat together on one side, and our parents sat on the other. I noticed that Marcellus resembled his father in looks, I had not thought about this before. His father Marius was an older version of Marcellus. His mother Lucia was lighter of hair and skin. She had light brown hair and hazel eyes. She was also very attractive, so it was no wonder Marcellus was so good looking. My father glanced at me, his blonde hair and almost patrician good looks enhanced by the purple bordered tunic he wore.

"Enjoying yourself are you Claudia?" he asked.

I nodded happily, it was set to be a perfect day I thought. The men would not talk business today I knew, as this was a public holiday. Just then a fanfare blast was blown by military trumpeters, the Games were about to start.

I gazed forward eagerly as the first pair of gladiators entered the arena. They would fight evenly with swords I saw. They saluted the city officials, the decurions who sat in their own special enclosure.

The fight got started, the two men were well matched. This was only a warm up event to set the mood for the day. Most of the audience were still chattering among themselves, I looked at Marcellus, he turned and looked at me. Drusilla and I were both wearing diaphanous dresses of a very fine cotton. Mine was in a shade of azure, Drusilla's a coral colour. He grinned at me.

"I like your dress," he remarked. "I can almost see right through it."

"It's cool and comfortable," I answered. "And the latest fashion, you should know, you're in the cloth business."

"Yes," he said, "but I've never seen it shown to such advantage before."

I looked around the stadium, "a lot of women are wearing it. Surely it's good for business isn't it?"

"Did I say I was complaining?" he asked.

He put his hand on my thigh for a moment, I caught my breath. His touch sent a thrill through me that was almost electrifying. I felt good in my thin gown, Drusilla and Gaius were intent on the fight. She looked good in her flimsy dress, I hoped Gaius liked it, I was sure he did. Marcellus was now watching the ring where now other gladiators were entering in pairs for one to one combat. This was better I thought.

While everybody was intent on the performance I glanced around the amphitheatre and saw to my horror Flavia, with some people I recognised from the Bacchanalia! In fact Faustinius was sitting behind her. Next to her sat one of the young men who had been there on the night we were introduced. This was something I had not expected to see, I had not realised she was so involved with them. Suddenly Drusilla said to me

"Isn't that Flavia over there, who are those people with her?"

"I don't know," I lied.

"Some of them look vaguely sinister," she remarked.

"Perhaps" I said sounding bored. "I want to watch this contest. Flavia's affairs are not my business."

I would have to speak to her as soon as it was possible. She either had not seen me, or she pretended that she had not. I wondered why she was behaving so furtively if she thought these people were all right. But there was nothing I could do at the moment, or on this day at all. I refused to let my fears for Flavia spoil the day for me. Come to think of it, in her present frame of mind she would probably enjoy my worry. I turned my attention back to the Games, by now several of the gladiators were down, with the victorious ones standing over them. It only remained for the chief decurion to give the official signal by raising his thumb. It was mainly a formality, nobody expected him to give the death sentence by lowering his thumb. These were light hearted games, this was a Festival, who would want unpleasantness on such a day? Some of the men were wounded of course, as the fighting was real. It would not be so exciting if it was not. Some might even die of their wounds, an occupational hazard in their profession. I studied the fallen gladiators, one of them looked as though he might already be dead. The attendants were now entering the arena carrying stretchers. I watched as they lifted the wounded onto the stretchers, and carried them off.

"Are they seriously hurt?" I asked, "can we find out?"

"I don't know," said Gaius. "I suppose we could, it is the interval now, Marcellus and I will go and fetch refreshments for us. Maybe we will be able to learn something at the stalls."

The vendors of food and drink had concessions outside the amphitheatre. Some of them even managed to get their stalls inside, which meant that they had the advantage of not only getting more custom, but of seeing the show as well.

I turned to Drusilla, "shall we go for a walk?" I suggested. She agreed and together we made our way to the latrines, I hoped I might see Flavia there. The queue was enormous of course, especially at the women's latrines, there was not alternative for us. I tried to look for Flavia, then I saw her, she was ahead of us in the line, in fact I think she was deliberately avoiding me. When she emerged while we were still waiting, she almost ran to join her friends. Her dress was, if anything, more daring than mine I noticed.

"Flavia didn't stop to speak to us," remarked Drusilla.

"Perhaps she didn't see us," I said.

Afterwards we joined the men who were carrying laden trays, with which we all returned to our seats. We ate hot pies and drank cool wine. I saw that Flavia had returned to her seat, they were also eating and drinking. The young man next to her did not I saw pay a lot of attention to her, apart from what was polite. So no relationship there I thought. The second half of the entertainment was now beginning, I leant forward. This time there was to be a contest between a gladiator armed with a sword against one with a retirius, a net and trident. This was more entertaining than straight dual sword fighting. The man with the retirius held out his net against the man with the sword, and defended himself with the trident. He would try to enmesh his opponent in the net, then stand over him with the trident raised until the signal was given if he was the victor. This time the retirius did win, after a long struggle. There only remained the finale which was to be a pitched battle between all the surviving gladiators (by which I mean those not wounded in previous events).

Marcellus turned to me, "enjoying it?"

I nodded.

"You seem very interested in that enclosure over there" he said.

"My friend Flavia is with them" I answered. "But I don't think she has seen me."

"She seems very engrossed with her friends" he said

"Yes," I answered, "I'll see her another day, it's not important."

"I just mentioned it because I happen to know that some of those people with her have a rather bad reputation," he said.

"Do they?" I muttered.

"Yes," he replied staring at me. "Do you know any of them?"

"I might have met some of them," I admitted.

"I would be interested to know where," he said

Just then the gladiators entered for the finale, and he turned his attention to the arena to my relief. I wished I had not let my gaze wander to them so often during the show. The last thing I wanted was Marcellus asking me questions I could not answer satisfactorily. I did not think that any of my family would tell him of my adventure with the Dionysaic Cult.

The pitched battle had begun, so I temporarily forgot my problems in the excitement. The two lines of contestants faced one another across the arena. The crowd was rapt, no sound in the amphitheatre. Gladiators in chariots rode in to fight against each other as a final attraction. This was thrilling stuff, as some of them were fought off the chariots, and leapt onto the back of the galloping horses at top speed. Some not so lucky or so adept were trampled, some managed to crawl to safety. But some lay there unable to move as the horses and chariots rode over them. Casualties were likely in this, I knew. The loud organ music accompanying this event made it impossible to hear any cries for help.

People were standing up in the audience shouting for one or other driver. Carried away I stood with everyone else.

It was almost impossible to be sure which was which of the charioteers in the arena. They fought against each other with swords and knives. This was taken from actual battles. It was the nearest most of us would ever see of real combat. There were real soldiers borrowed from their legions for this display.

Although it was only a mock up, the fighting was genuine with no quarter given. The excitement was intense and tangible in the amphitheatre as spectators got carried away. Some women fainted, but most seemed as tense as the men. I was, I admit transported by the thrill of it. Forgetting to be worried about whether there were casualties among the participants. This was approved entertainment, it did not do to get too upset about hurt or even dead fighters. If anything happened they knew the hazards, but most of them were in control, even when it appeared as if they were not. They were professional soldiers, and doubtless faced worse in war. This was spectacle put on for the games.

When it was over we all made our way out of the amphitheatre. There was still the chariot racing to come later in the Festival, which we all looked forward to. We all agreed we would attend this together again. We joined the crowds in the streets streaming out of the amphitheatre, and flocking home in twos and threes, or in parties as we were.

CHAPTER SEVEN

THE CHARIOT RACE

When we reached our home a meal had been prepared which we ate informally in the tablinium off small tables, instead of more formally in the triclinium. After his parents had taken their leave Marcellus remained with us for the rest of the evening. When my parents had also left us, and gone to bed, the four of us stayed talking in the lamplight that cast greenish shadows, reflecting from the painted frescos that decorated the walls. Finally I got to my feet.

"I'm going to bed," I announced. I glanced briefly at Marcellus, he smiled at me.

Reaching my bedroom I undressed and lay naked on the bed. I lay on top of the coverings, it was too hot to get underneath them. I lay there dreamily, I expected Marcellus to join me, he would I knew, easily find my room. In spite of the long day I was not really sleepy. I ran my hands down my body, I was pleased I was slim, I would hate to be fat I thought idly. A short while later Marcellus appeared, he came straight in. "I assume you were expecting me," he said.

"I hoped you'd come," I replied. I shifted on the bed and gazed at him by the light of the one lamp I always kept burning all night. He wasted no time but was soon undressed, he came over to the bed, his bronzed skin gleaming in the lamplight. I held out my arms to him, he came to me quickly. We made love fiercely, almost violently, the day's events accentuating our desire for each other. Afterwards we lay talking softly to each other.

"You're beautiful," he said.

"So are you," I replied. I started to stroke him, I could not help my craving for him, or resist touching him when he was near me. He was stroking me too, our joint caresses grew more heated, before we could control ourselves we were making love again. It was slower this time, at first anyway. But I could never control myself with this man. I clung to him eagerly, fervently, as he drover further into me, I could not get enough of him, I just wanted more and more all the time. Our loving finally reached it's peak, and we collapsed in each other's arms. We lay entwined for a while, not wanting to let each other go. When we ultimately broke apart I fell asleep immediately. In the morning when I awoke I reached out for him, but found I was alone. I wondered when he had left, I was disappointed but not downhearted. We would soon meet again, perhaps today even.

Suddenly I felt hungry and went in search of some breakfast, I joined Drusilla and Gaius in the small garden. They looked at me, Gaius grinned, "Marcellus give you a good time last night?"

"Yes as a matter of fact he did," I answered defiantly.

"What time did he leave?" Drusilla asked.

"Some time ago," I replied. "Is he coming round here today?"

"Possibly," Gaius shrugged, "I'm not quite sure."

I took a fig from a bowl on the table and began to peel it. "Are mother and father up yet?"

"Yes they had their breakfast some time ago" Drusilla said. "I wonder why Flavia ignored us yesterday. You must have noticed it Claudia."

I nodded, I did not know what the reason was why she had behaved so oddly at the games, I intended to find out as soon as I could. I would have to visit her at her house as she was unlikely to come here if she was trying to avoid me. I was afraid to leave the house in case Marcellus turned up, Flavia would have to wait for a while I decided. Gaius and Drusilla got up from the table.

"We're going out for a walk to see what's going on!" Gaius said.

"All right," I said. I was not even dressed yet, otherwise they might have asked me to join them.

After I had had a bath and got dressed, I hung around the tablinium and garden on the chance that Marcellus might come. There was nothing planned for today, the Festival would continue tomorrow with various theatrical entertainments. We would attend some of them, I hoped

Marcellus would accompany us. Towards noon he appeared, much to my delight, I was alone in the garden, he came straight through to me. Gaius and Drusilla followed behind him, they had met in the street they explained. We all seated ourselves around the fountain, the sight of the cool water refreshing in the mid-day heat.

"What's it like outside?" I asked.

"Busy, there are a lot of people about. The baths will be opening soon, it will be impossible to get into any of the bathhouses today," Marcellus said.

Gaius nodded, "We're going to the mime at the Odeion tomorrow," he said. "Are your parents coming as well Marcellus?"

"I should expect so," Marcellus replied. We'll all sit together again of course."

It was a statement not a question, I smiled. It was time for the midday meal, we ate sitting round the fountain, it was an idyllic day I thought.

The following afternoon we all met at the Odeion theatre. The mime was one of the more high minded type, (of which there are very few), in honour of the occasion. It was still very amusing, and somewhat scurrilous in it's depiction of both gods and men. The small theatre was packed, I could not see Flavia there, so I assumed that she had gone elsewhere, to one of the other events in the town that day.

The next day was the day of the chariot race, perhaps the most popular event of the whole Festival. Again we had our own private enclosure which we occupied with the Vinicius family, as at the Games. I looked around the amphitheatre, to my dismay I saw Flavia again, with the same crowd she had been with at the games. I said nothing but gazed furtively at them, I would not put it past them to have put some sort of spell on the race to make sure that one charioteer was victorious. I had heard of such practices. They would bury some charm in a tomb outside the town in the Street of the Tombs, to ensure some unfortunate driver would overturn his chariot and get trampled on. There was one member of the group who looked important enough to be at the centre of some such crime. I gazed at my friend, she looked animated, even excited about something, but she was not looking in our direction. She would deliberately avoid doing so I was sure, after the way she had dodged me at the Games. I would have to get to the bottom of this as soon as I could.

"There's Flavia with those same people again," Drusilla pointed out.

Both Marcellus and Gaius looked at me, Marcellus said, "There's Caius Sabinus with them, how did she get involved with him? He has a very dodgy reputation. He might even own one of the charioteers. If so he will stop at nothing to make sure he wins the race!"

I nodded but did not reply, I was sure there was something crooked going on. And Flavia had to be implicated somehow, if only by association.

"Are you going to try to speak to her?" Drusilla asked.

"I don't know," I muttered, "not today I don't think. It won't really be possible."

"You'd better visit her tomorrow then," said Drusilla. "I'd like to know what she's mixed up in."

"How did your friend get herself associated with these people?" Marcellus asked. "Those two people at the club who you knew are with them."

"Yes I can see them," I answered.

"You've never told me how you met them," he said.

I was saved from explaining just then by the entrance of the competitors in their chariots. Each one wore a short sleeveless tunic and a leather hat. The reins were fastened to their belts.

Each chariot was draw by two horses. The charioteers were now each in his separate enclosure with the barrier down in front of him. The crowd waited, holding it's collective breath, for the chief decurion to give the signal for the race to start. As he lowered the white cloth the barrier rose and the contestants all shot out together. The first lap of the race had begun. One of the 'eggs', as they were called would be removed before each lap of the race commenced. I leant forward as the race gathered momentum, all four chariots were neck and neck at present. There was nothing between any of them.

The first lap ended and the second one started, one of the chariots was out in front by now and one of the others was catching up. I hoped there would not be a collision, as this could be dangerous, resulting in injury or death for at least one of the drivers. This to me would have spoiled the event, I had not yet found out if any of the gladiators had been killed during the games. Gaius and Marcellus would know, I must remember to ask one of them. I tried to study the contestants more closely, which was difficult at that distance. As with the gladiators it was mainly the profiles that the spectators saw as they went past. By now three of the 'eggs' had been removed, and things were getting exciting. It was less likely that there would be an accident with only one pair of horses, with two pairs it was more likely. In fact this, the first race of the day went without a hitch, and one of the charioteers was duly crowned.

After the interval there was one more race to be run. There would be four horses per chariot this time, but only two competitors. Money was being betted on the outcome of this one, much more than on the previous one. We mingled with the crowds outside the amphitheatre. We bought cold sausage meat, and a flagon of ready watered wine. I tried to see Flavia but the crowds were too dense at first. Then I thought I caught sight of her with Faustinius, and some of the others from their group. By the look of some of them they had been up to no good.

"Those people your friend is with," said Marcellus. "Are laying large bets on one of the competitors in the next race."

"Oh are they?" I asked, "what's wrong with that, lots of people are betting on this race, including I should think my father and Gaius."

"Oh yes," Marcellus answered, "my father too, but I only bet on a dead cert, and I should think so do your friends."

"Why aren't you betting on this race then if you think it's a dead cert?" I asked.

"I don't," he replied. "But that lot know something no one else does. I wouldn't be surprised if it was fixed somehow."

Just then Gaius and Drusilla appeared. "We've just put a bet on the next race," said Drusilla.

"Have you?" I asked, "have you any idea which one is going to win then?"

"Not really," Gaius said, "but it's a bit of fun to have something on it. Are you betting Marcellus?"

Marcellus shook his head, "No, I was just telling Claudia, I only bet when I'm sure of the outcome."

"But half the fun of betting is the uncertainty," said Drusilla.

"Not for me," said Marcellus. "I don't like taking risks with money."

"Well Flavia and her friends were laying high stakes," said Gaius.

"Did you bet on the same one?" I asked

"Well no, should I have?" he asked.

I shook my head, "I don't know."

"Something's going on," Marcellus remarked. "I don't trust those people. They're into all sorts of things. Bacchanalia is only a part of it."

"You mean they belong to the Dionysaic cult? Asked Drusilla.

"I should think Claudia could answer that," said Marcellus.

"Did you meet them there Claudia?" she asked.

"Not all of them." I mumbled. "In fact I met hardly any of those people."

They all stared at me in silence for a moment, I felt uncomfortable. It was not as if I knew anything. Whatever Flavia was doing, it had nothing at all to do with me.

"Let's go back to our box," Gaius said eventually. "So we can eat our lunch before the race begins."

Relieved I agreed, and we made our way back to our seats.

Both my parents and Marcellus' *Marius* were already there when we returned.

"There you are at last," my father said. "We're waiting for our food."

"Yes," said Marius, "you've been a long time Marcellus. We've been getting hungry."

"Sorry," said Gaius, and handed round the sausage meat. The wine was poured into the beakers we had brought with us, it had kept cool in the jug.

When we had finished our meal I looked across to where Flavia was sitting. They had just returned to their seats, I assumed they had eaten outside, maybe at a cookshop or wine bar. Everyone had now returned to their seats as the chariots entered. Both of them were drawn by a team of four horses, they were both confined behind the barrier, one at each end leaving the centre empty. The decurion dropped the white cloth, and the barrier lifted, both charioteers shot out together. The first lap went without incident, the second 'egg' dropped, and they started the second lap. Just as everything seemed to be going well, one of the charioteers who was slightly behind at this point in the race appeared to veer sideways. It seemed to be accidental, and he soon righted himself, and all appeared well for the moment. The next two laps went smoothly, in fact if my suspicions had not been aroused by the things I had heard during the interval, I would not have thought anything was likely to go wrong.

It was during the sixth lap, the next to last, that the charioteer who had previously seemed to swerve by mistake, now drove his chariot almost into the other one. The other tried to control his team but his opponent now pitched his horses ever closer forcing him towards the spina. There was nowhere for him to go, there was going to be an almighty crash any minute now. My fists clenched as I watched what was beginning to look like cold-blooded murder. The other spectators were getting restive, wondering what was going on. This appeared to be deliberate not accidental, and the crowd was displeased with this change in their entertainment on this day. By now the two charioteers were engaged in what appeared to be a life and death struggle for survival. The next moment there was a loud crash, as the charioteer who was being attacked smashed into the spina, or outer barrier. The audience was standing shouting, some fought to get out. This was a terrible thing to have happened, no one was sure of what to do. The chief decurion was unable to do anything, stretcher-bearers ran out into the arena to rescue the fallen charioteer.

Pandemonium broke out amongst the crowd, people were fighting to get out of the amphitheatre. I turned to Marcellus, who put his arms around me protectively, as did all the men in our party. My father with my mother, Marcellus' parents, Gaius with Drusilla.

"Come on," he said "We'll try to fight our way out of here."

This we did by clearing a pathway in front of us, mainly by pushing out of the way anyone who tried to impede us. It was everyone for themselves, social niceties were ignored. Finally we were out in the street, the sun hot after the shade of the covered amphitheatre. Still holding tight to each other we cut a swathe through the crowds milling about in the street.

"We'll make for our house," my father said. This we did, arriving hot and sweating, the coolness indoors a welcome relief. I had not had a chance to see what happened to Flavia and her friends, I would have to go and see her as soon as I could.

This I managed the next day, things had clamed down by then. The Festival was over, the chariot race being the finale to it. I was shown through to the garden, where Flavia was sitting by the fountain.

"Ave Flavia," I greeted her.

She turned her head to look at me, she did not look especially pleased to see me I thought.

"I saw you yesterday, and at the gladiatorial games," I waded straight in. There was no point in beating about the bush I decided.

"So you saw me," she said, "what of it?"

"I wondered why you were avoiding me at both events. Because you were avoiding us, me and Drusilla anyway."

"What do you mean I was avoiding you? It was not possible to chat, we were too far apart."

This was true of course, but there was the occasion outside the lavatories, I mentioned this. "It would have been possible to have spoken to each other then."

"I don't remember that," she answered.

I did not believe her, but chose not to argue the point, it would serve no purpose. "Who were those people you were with on both days?" I asked.

"Friends or mine," she answered.

"I recognised Faustinius," I said. "And some of the others. They were members of the Dionysaic Cult weren't they?"

"So what if they were?" she asked defiantly. "They're my friends, I've been there again to another ceremony."

"What was it like?" I asked, "was it the same as the one we went to together?"

"More or less," she said, "there were some different people there. The first one was mainly an initiation ritual as you must know."

I nodded, that was true of course, I wondered when she had been back there, I asked her.

"Two nights ago," she said.

I was shocked, that put it just before the chariot racing. Did she know anything about what happened in the amphitheatre the day before.

"It was terrible about what happened yesterday wasn't it?" I said.

"Yes," she answered.

"I heard your party were laying large bets on that race." I said

"There's no law against betting is there?" she asked sarcastically.

"No of course not," I answered. "It's just that sometimes a race is fixed, and considering what happened, it might be possible that that one was."

"Who are you implying fixed it then?" Flavia asked. "you think, that just because you disapprove of them, that my friends are responsible don't you?"

"I don't know," I said. "But Marcellus said that one of the men in your group was Caius Sabinus. He has a very bad reputation he said, I'm not happy about you mixing with his kind."

"He was perfectly pleasant to me, I only met him the night before, at the ritual."

"What sort of ritual was it?" I asked.

"It was a secret one, only people with a high enough degree in the Cult can take part."

"What about you, surely you are not high up enough yet?"

"No not yet," she replied. "But I shall be soon, if I attend enough ceremonies."

"Why are you getting yourself so deeply involved in this? I just thought it would be a bit of fun when I suggested we attended a rite together."

"It's far more serious than that," she said. "Once you become initiate you are, or should be, committed to it."

"I never intended to get implicated to such a degree, and I don't think you should either. Drop it now before things go any further." I beseeched.

Flavia shook her head, "It's not just a matter of getting involved, they can help me get things I want."

"What sort of things?" I asked apprehensively.

Flavia looked away from me evasively, "That's my business."

I sat down on the bench beside her. "It's a man isn't it? Who is he, anyone I know?"

It couldn't possibly be my brother Lucius could it? Surely he was too far away, even she could see that. She did not answer me, but looked away obliquely.

"Who is it?" I asked again

"It's none of your business," she finally answered. "Why don't you just carry on with your own pleasure. You've got enough of it at present from what I can see. Yes I did see you at the Games, and at the chariot race yesterday, and you had plenty of attention. Especially from your new lover."

I was shocked at her outburst, but tried again to make her see reason. "All right don't tell me who it is, if it is a man you like. But for your own good don't get too involved with these people and their affairs, whatever they are."

"I'll do what I please," she replied. "Just because your precious Marcellus doesn't approve of someone, we all have to disapprove I suppose!"

"It's not just that," I said. "It's that I'm worried about what you're getting into with the Dionysaic Cult. What do your parents think about it? Don't they mind? They must surely have some idea of where you are going."

"They don't know," she admitted. "I tell them I'm visiting friends, they don't think to check up."

This was sounding worse by the minute. "You won't get away with it indefinitely," I said.

"Maybe not," she agreed, "But I am at the moment and that's what's important." She glared at me, "You'd better go, since all you can do is find fault with me and my friends."

I was shattered, we had never fallen out in a serious way before.

"I'm sorry I ever suggested that we attend the Dionysaic Rites." I said, "In fact I feel responsible for taking you there."

"You didn't take me there, we went together that's all." She said.

"It was my idea," I said. "I saw Faustinius was with you, I shouldn't think he's a very good influence."

"Just because you imagine he raped you when you were in a drunken stupor."

"I didn't imagine it," I snapped. "he did rape me."

I could guess the reason for that. He was using sex magic to involve me more deeply in the Cult. I did not say this to Flavia now, there would be no point. She was far too angry with me at present to even listen to anything I might say. I got up.

"All right I'm going. I just hope you come to your senses before anything terrible happens."

With that I left her, there was nothing more I could do.

CHAPTER EIGHT

FLAVIA AND PHILOCRATES

For several days after my encounter with Flavia I was distressed. What should I do I wondered, I still blamed myself for all that had occurred. It was I who had first suggested the Dionysaic Rites outing, I who had discussed the idea with Faustinius, and persuaded Flavia to join me. But then I thought, it was not all my fault, she had chosen to accompany me, she had known as well as I had that there was an element of risk involved. But apparently the risk did not bother her in any case, she had returned to the villa again of her own free will, with no encouragement from me. But in a way that was even more worrying, whatever was she getting herself into? These people were, from all I had heard during the festival, a dangerous crowd. People who would stop at nothing to gain their ends, whatever they might be. If only she would meet a decent man and forget about these people. In retrospect I was not upset by her criticisms of me and my relationship with Marcellus. She was I realised jealous, and that did not help our friendship. I did not want to break with her over this, but I knew she would not listen to anything I might say, or any advice I might offer at present.

This also caused problems with Drusilla, who was curious to know what was happening with Flavia. I had tried to keep out of her way after I returned from Flavia's house. But living under the same roof this was an impossibility. In fact I had not been back long from visiting Flavia when she waylaid me in the garden.

"Did you see Flavia?" she asked, without giving me a chance to think up an explanation of her behaviour. And of who she had been with at the Games and the chariot race.

"Yes," I answered, I picked a fig off a tree and bit into it. The juice ran down my chin, once having begun to eat it I had no choice but to finish it. I did not really want it anyway, I was not hungry. I just had to do something while I thought of what to say.

Finally I decided on the truth, more or less anyway. After all Flavia was quite openly consorting with these people. In fact apart from her parents, it appeared, everyone knew. In which case any lie I told now would probably be discovered later, so why put myself in the wrong? I faced Drusilla and took a deep breath. "She has been to the Revels again it seems. She has met most of those people we saw her with there. But I don't think she's involved in anything illegal, whatever they may be implicated in. In fact I think she's probably innocent of what they are really up to."

"What about what happened yesterday at the chariot race?" Drusilla asked.

"She agreed with me that it was quite dreadful. I honestly don't think she knew anything like that was going to happen," I said. I was not going to say anything about what Flavia had said to me, about being able to get the things she wanted for herself. At present I would keep that information to myself. It may not have been so sinister in any case, I might have overreacted. She probably only meant trivial harmless things. Drusilla sat down on a bench, "what did she say?"

"Only what I have just told you. She did object to my interfering, said it was none of my business what she did."

"What did you say to that?"

"I told her to be careful, not to get too committed to the Rites, or the group. But she wouldn't agree there was anything to be concerned about. She said they were her friends."

"This sounds ominous." Drusilla remarked. "What do her parents think about it?"

"They don't know, she didn't tell them where she was going. And if they saw her with that crowd at the games, they probably wouldn't know who they are, or what they are involved in."

"No I suppose not, she's taking a risk though."

"Yes," I said, "I can do nothing about it, she refuses to see reason."

We sat there musing over Flavia and her situation, then Drusilla said, "It's time for the noon meal, let's go."

After this Marcellus and I were so involved with each other and our mutual social life, that I did not see or hear anything about my friend for a while. Eventually however, it was inevitable that our paths collided. At a party I was attending with Marcellus, I saw her with an attractive young man. I was intrigued at once, I wondered who he was, and where she had met him. I determined to try and speak to her as soon as I could, perhaps she would introduce me to her new friend. There was something familiar about him, I was sure I had seen him somewhere before. I was puzzled, but not particularly worried.

I remarked to Marcellus, "there's Flavia over there, I haven't seen her for weeks. I must speak to her."

Marcellus put his arm around me, "I'll come with you."

There was no way I could prevent him accompanying me. Although I would have liked a word in private with Flavia. Together we made our way towards her and her escort, he looked foreign somehow, I noticed. "Ave Flavia," I said. "I'm glad to see you, it's been a long time. This is Marcellus, I don't think you've met."

She stared at me for a moment, somewhat disconcerted I thought, then turned towards her companion. "Ave Marcellus, this is my friend Philocrates."

I shook his hand, "Ave," We stood there together uncertain of what to talk about. I still could not place Philocrates, but by his name he was definitely foreign. Of Greek origin, surely I thought. He appeared to be some sort of athlete, I studied him covertly. Marcellus was frowning I saw suddenly, what could have upset him? He inspected Philocrates, then turned away and scrutinised an elaborate vase on a plinth, in a corner of the room near where we were standing. I turned back to Flavia. "How have you been?" I enquired. "Have you been to any other parties recently?" It was something to say, I was not really interested in where she had been, I wanted to know more about her new friend. But I could hardly ask that kind of question in front of him.

"A few," she replied

I wondered where, as she had not been at any of the functions I had recently attended. I still could not guess what was wrong with Marcellus, he appeared disapproving of my friend and her companion. Philocrates also did not speak, and with Marcellus in a mood, it was left to me to make conversation with Flavia. She gave me no help in this at all, then her new man said something to her in a low voice, and with a muttered excuse to me she followed him out to the peristyle. I was alone with Marcellus, I tuned to him, "Is something the matter?" I asked.

"I should say there is," he answered. "Did you not recognise that man you friend was with?"

"Not altogether," I said, "But I seem to know him from somewhere. Is there anything wrong with him?"

"I'm surprised you didn't remember him. He's the charioteer who caused the death of his opponent at the races last month. He is the freedman of Caius Sabinus, does anything he requires of him. I certainly don't think him a suitable companion for your friend, and I'd rather you did not get involved with him, even if it means not seeing her at present."

I was stunned, "I knew nothing about this. I have not seen Flavia for some time, not since we quarrelled just after the race."

"I realise that," said Marcellus. "I cannot imagine why her parents let her consort with him."

"I don't suppose they know," I said. "She told me they don't know where she goes when she attends the Rites of Bacchus. I'm surprised they haven't yet discovered that something unusual is going on."

"Well someone's got to put a stop to it," Marcellus said. "She is playing with fire, Caius Sabinus is a dangerous person to get mixed up with. Even if that young man is genuine in his interest in her, he is tied to Sabinus, even if he has been manumitted, and is no longer a slave. There's probably a reason for that, as a freedman he can move around more easily."

"Oh dear," I said, "What has she got herself into?"

"A great deal of trouble," Marcellus answered. "Her family must be told before anything monstrous occurs."

"I can't tell them," I objected.

"I think you must," he said. "I will come with you to see them if you wish."

"I won't know what to say," I tried to squirm out of it. "It would mean admitting I took her there the first time."

"I don't think you can blame yourself for that. After all if it had stopped at the once as it did with you, there would be no harm done. But you could not know it would go so far with Flavia, or who she would choose to get involved with."

"But what will I say?" I agonised, "They'll probably blame me anyway."

"Surely they won't if you explain what happened. Someone has to prevent this going any further."

"Flavia will never speak to me again if I go to her parents and split on her behind her back."

"That's a chance you'll have to take," he answered. "As I said I'll come with you, I'll even explain to your friend that I'm responsible."

"She'll never speak to me again," I repeated. "I can't be the one to break up her relationship."

"Someone has to," said Marcellus. "She's already under the influence of Sabinus in some way. He can manipulate her through his freedman, as I've made clear. Surely you don't want that?"

"No," I said, "But I still don't relish telling her family."

"We have to and there's and end to it," Marcellus snapped. "Come on we may as well enjoy the rest of the evening."

We arranged to meet the following afternoon to go together to see Flavia's parents. Marcellus did not come in with me that night, I was not in the mood, I was too upset, and he did not insist, or make any attempt to persuade me. I regretted this immediately, making love would have helped me feel better I realised. How stupid of me not to have asked him in.

The following afternoon we set out for Flavia's home. When we reached the entrance we asked for the master and mistress. We were informed that they had gone away on business to Hispania, and would be away for a few months. The daughter was there we were told, if we wished to see her instead. We declined, but I said, "please don't tell her that I was here. This is a matter between us and her parents."

The door slave agreed not to tell her, but I knew he would recognise me, and that this was bound to get out. Although I was relieved not to have to confront her family in this way. After all several months was quite a long time, when they returned all this might be over, and there would be no need to tell them anything. This I remarked to Marcellus, but he did not agree, repeating that someone ought to be told so this could be stopped.

We had removed to a wine bar in the town, and were sitting over cups of their special.

"Really we ought to have confronted Flavia," said Marcellus.

"Yes," I answered, "I did not think. Not finding her parents at home distracted me, or we could have spoken to her."

"I think you still could," said Marcellus. "Not today, it's too late, we cannot go back there now, but another day."

"Yes," I said, "Of course! I can invite her to my birthday party. That will be an excuse to pay a visit."

"Do you want me to come with you?" he asked.

"Perhaps it would be better if I went alone," I said. "Then it would appear my main reason for calling is to ask her to the party."

I thought about it for a moment or two. "That would be the best way, then there need not be any unpleasantness."

"No," said Marcellus, "There need not be any unpleasantness, as you say. But find out how deeply she is involved with Caius Sabinus and his cronies."

"I will," I answered, relieved at being able to at least delay for a while Marcellus' zeal in making Flavia see the error of her ways.

The next morning I again presented myself at Flavia's door. I was shown in immediately, and found her in the tablinium. I prayed she had not heard of our aborted attempt to visit her parents the previous afternoon. Apparently she had not. She looked up from a scroll she was reading. I wondered what it was.

"It's a new novel," she said. "It is called 'The Satyricon'. It is by Petronius."

I nodded, I had heard of him, he was a novelist and poet, and a close friend of the Emperor.

"Is it interesting?" I asked.

"Yes, it was given to me by a friend," she said. "It is set in a town very like Pompeii."

I seated myself on a nearby couch. "I am having a party for my seventeenth birthday, I hope you will come."

"Yes," she agreed, "I'd like to come."

"Good, I'm so glad," I said. "Most of our friends are coming, I'm looking forward to it. It will be fun."

We talked for a while about life in general, I did not mention Philocrates, and neither did she. But I did enquire if she had been to the mysteries again. She shook her head, "Not recently, not for quite a while."

I was relived that there was no need for an argument about that. The time passed pleasantly enough, it was like old times between us. When I finally took my leave, I said, "I'll see you at my party then?"

"Yes," she replied, "I'll look forward to it."

I put my arms around her, "I'm so glad that we're friends again."

She nodded, "Me too."

"And so you said nothing at all about her involvement with Caius Sabinus and his henchman?" Marcellus asked in disbelief. "I thought that that was the main reason you went to visit her."

I was shaken, I had forgotten this was my motive for calling on Flavia. In the relief of making up our quarrel it had slipped my mind completely.

"But it's a start isn't it?" I asked. "She'll come to my party and we can take it from there, can't we?"

Marcellus looked grim, "your birthday party is hardly a suitable place for a confrontation is it now? We cannot risk a scene here, it would be most inappropriate, surely you can see that."

"I did not mean to confront her," I retorted. "Why should I anyway?"

"What then?" asked Macellus.

"I don't really know, but I am not going to start another quarrel with her." I said, "why can't we just let her alone to enjoy herself? Why must we spoil her fun?"

"It's for her own good, she is going to be in some bad trouble, if she isn't already."

I did not answer, there was no point in arguing, but I was unhappy that it should be necessary for Flavia to lose her lover. After all maybe the relationship was perfectly innocent, and they might, (I hoped) have simply been attracted to each other, whatever loyalties Philocrates had to Sabinus. In which case would it not be permissible for the friendship to continue? I tried to suggest this to Marcellus, but he was adamant.

"We cannot afford to take that chance," he said. "I've explained to you the risks involved to your friend. But you don't seem to care so long as she is happy."

"That is important," I replied. "And she would never forgive me if I caused trouble."

Marcellus sighed, "All right, we'll leave it for the moment and see what happens. With luck it might wear itself out between them in a short time."

I agreed, relieved to have succeeded in forestalling him. As he said it might not last, then there would be no problem to solve. I busied myself in preparations for my birthday party, and no more was said on the subject of Flavia.

On the evening of the party our home was well lit with oil lamps, and chandeliers were suspended from the ceilings in the tablinium and the atrium. I had invited all my friends. Marcellus arrived early, as had been arranged between us, so he could be by my side as I received the guests. Lamps on tripods stood at regular intervals. As we produced our own olive oil on our farm, we did not stint on the illumination.

As Marcellus and I waited together we smiled contentedly at each other. Nothing I thought could spoil this evening. I was wrong. The party guests began to arrive, some of them in pairs, some separately. Titus and Antonia I saw were together. Julia arrived with a young man I had not seen before. Good looking I noticed, trust her! She kissed me and introduced her friend.

"This is Drusus," she said. "He is recently come to Pompeii. This is my friend Claudia."

I introduced Marcellus to everyone, it looked like being a good gathering I thought happily. Suddenly I saw Flavia arrive, to my dismay she had Philocrates with her. This I had never considered happening, although I realised I should have done. I stole a glance at Marcellus, he looked furious, I knew he would blame me for not foreseeing this, and forbidding her to bring him. Desperately I fixed a smile on my face as they approached, a scene now would not be wise. I hoped Marcellus would not say anything at this juncture, it would have to be sorted out later, not here, now. I need not have worried, he was tact itself as he shook hands with them both. I did not know what to say to Flavia, although she did not know how we felt about her friendship.

"It's lovely to see you," I said, I did not include Philocrates in this, but she did not seem to notice.

By now everyone had arrived, and small glasses of spiced wine were being passed round by the household slaves. The meal was laid out mainly in the atrium, but some tables had been set up in the tablinium.

The triclinium was not in use tonight, as it was too small for such a large party. Couches were set out around the tables. Hot food was kept warm on charcoal heaters on the large serving table at the side of the atrium. There were also cold salads, with cured ham, and spicy peppered sausage meats. Dishes of olives and nuts were spread around, for people to help themselves to as they stood around in groups talking, with their wine cups in their hands. I made my way round the rooms. Talking and being greeted. I was wearing a new gown in pale yellow silk, sleeveless, with a gauzy stola draped over one shoulder. A lot of my girl friends admired it, including Julia. She was in pale lilac in a similar style, we were very fashionable. I studied Drusus, he was I noticed a rather flashy looking young man, with rather unruly dark blonde hair, I wondered where they had met.

"I've not seen you for a while," Julia said.

"No," I replied. I had been mixing with Marcellus' associates lately, not seeing my former friends.

"Your new man looks nice," said Julia. "How long have you known him?"

"About three months," I said. With Drusus standing there, I could not ask her the same question. She, however, supplied the information freely. "That's about the same amount of time I've know Drusus. He is a professional gladiator, but he comes from a good family."

I nodded, it was not unusual for a young man of good family to enter the gladiatorial profession. It was a good way of making a lot of money fairly quickly. She told me he had come to Pompeii from his hometown of Capua, to join the gladiator school here. Marcellus appeared beside me, he nodded to Julia and Drusus.

"Phito wants to know when he should serve the food," he said.

"All right," I said, "tell him we will seat ourselves now, then he can serve the hor-d-oevres straight away."

Marcellus nodded and moved off.

"Come on," I said to Julia, "you can join us at dinner."

I led them to a couch in the atrium near where the serving tables were situated, so I could keep an eye on the servers. Marcellus rejoined us. Flavia I saw was seated on a couch on the opposite side of the atrium with Philocrates beside her. I decided not to worry about them, and enjoy my birthday party.

Most of the guests had brought me presents, I wore a gold necklace which my family had given me. It was a lovely thing, made like a chain of small flowers. I also wore matching drop earrings, given me by Marcellus. They had obviously combined in this, I was delighted with the set.

The hor-d-ouvre was served, and wine poured into glasses. I turned to Julia whom I had placed beside me so we could converse as we ate. "What have you been doing lately?" I asked. "Did you enjoy the festival?"

"Oh yes," she replied. "Drusus was of course involved in the combat at the games."

"Where exactly did you meet him?"

"I went to a party at the Gladiators barracks and he was there."

"Who did you go with?"

"Some people I knew slightly were invited, and I tagged along with them. It sounded like fun, and I had been on my own since Cealius left. I was hoping to meet someone there, and I did."

I told her how I had met Marcellus, and that our two families were now very closely linked, both by business and socially.

"He's very handsome," Julia said. "you're lucky to have met him in such a way. I've never had that opportunity."

"Neither have I before," I said. "But you've managed all right anyway haven't you?"

"Yes, but I had to try a lot harder. That wasn't the first function I had gone to hoping to meet an attractive man."

Just then Marcellus turned to me and engaged me in conversation. Julia turned to Drusus as the main course was served. We preferred the cold food, ham and sausage meats with salad, rather than the hot food tonight. It was lighter, as the weather was oppressively hot at the moment. There would be a storm soon I thought. It would come suddenly, as they always did this time of year. Especially when it was as warm as it was now.

The wine flowed freely after the meal was finished. We had drunk in moderation while we were eating. We reclined around the tables and nibbled fruit with the wine. Julia and Drusus were cuddled close together, and I lay in Marcellus' arms. I did not care now what anyone else was doing, this was my evening, and I was enjoying it. I kissed him on the lips, I felt marvellous, nothing mattered now, I was so happy.

Everything was wonderful. Several couples had wandered into the garden, but most stayed around the tables sociably. We would presumably all spend the night with our lovers, so why seek privacy now? Flavia and Philocrates were still seated where they had been at dinner. Although nestling close they were not engaging in any overt loving behaviour. Not as much as I was, I guessed she was being careful of how she conducted herself in my home. I was not sure why, unless she realised her lover might not be socially acceptable to the rest of us.

I was not sure how she knew this, but Marcellus' attitude at the party where he had been introduced to us might have been noticed, by her at least.

It was getting late, one or two slaves were standing about in case we needed anything, but most of them had retired to bed. I arose from my couch, several people were coming to take their leave, thanking me for a lovely evening. When the last of the guests had departed I dismissed the remaining slaves, and went to my room. Tired I sat on the edge of the bed, Marcellus had followed me and was standing across the room from me. He looked annoyed, his polite manner vanished.

"I suppose you did not know your friend was going to bring that man to your house?"

I stared at him, shaking my head "Of course I had no idea she would bring him. I didn't invite him, it just never occurred to me he would accompany her here tonight."

"It should have, I assumed you had told her not to bring him."

"How could I have? I told you we never even mentioned him when I called on her." I said.

"So you did," he answered. "I should have remembered that. I had forgotten how stupid you were about that."

"Don't let's quarrel now," I pleaded, "its late and I'm tired."

I removed the gold necklace, it was beautiful, I put it on a side table. Marcellus still stood, I removed my gown and slipped under the cover. If he was going to stand there all night there was nothing I could do about it. Finally he stripped and joined me in the bed. "All right," he said, "Let's forget about Flavia." He drew me gently into his arms. "What a fool you are sometimes." I froze, this was not what I wanted to hear at the moment.

"Relax," he soothed. He was caressing me, desire mounted, suddenly he was making love to me. I responded with equal passion.

The next morning I awoke to find him beside me, he was already awake.

"Are you staying for breakfast?" I asked.

"I should think so," he said. "I want a word with Gaius before I leave."

We lay there together for a while. Then I turned and pressed myself against him. He stirred, and put his arms around me, we began to slowly make love, at first anyway. Ecstasy was already building within me when he turned me over to reach his own climax. I came again as I felt him reach his orgasm. I was shaking and sobbing, he held me for a long time. I was so happy I wanted to stay like this forever. But slowly he withdrew, and leaving the bed, he dressed in the same elegant tunic he had worn for the party. I also arose, and throwing on a loose robe, I followed him from the bedroom.

We joined my mother and Gaius in the small family dining room. My mother looked at us as we entered. "The party was a success last night I hear," she said. She was not at all surprised to see Marcellus with me. She would have expected him to stay the night after the party. He often did anyway, we were an established couple. Although he did not always stay for breakfast, sometimes leaving before I awoke.

"I'm glad you were able to stay for breakfast today Marcellus." She said.

"Yes," he answered, "I'm happy to do so."

Neither Marcellus or Gaius discussed business at the table, but as soon as they finished eating Marcellus said, "I'd like a word Gaius."

He agreed, and the two men left the room together.

CHAPTER NINE

FLAVIA'S REFUSAL

After Marcellus had left the room I was alone with my mother. I decided to ask her advice about Flavia. I turned around to face her, "Flavia turned up with a rather shady young man."

She stared at me, "What do you mean by shady?"

"Well," I said, "it was the charioteer who caused the death of his opponent at the Festival."

She looked shocked. "What can she be thinking of to get involved with a character like that? Surely her parents don't approve of the association. What do they say I wonder?"

"They're in Hispania," I said. "No one knows when they'll be back. In the meantime, who knows what she'll do."

"What does Marcellus think about it?" my mother asked.

"He disapproves very strongly, we've had arguments about it," I answered.

"Arguments! What sort of arguments, surely you're both in agreement about this? There's no question of allowing this to go on, someone must put a stop to it."

"Yes I suppose so," I said, "But what can we do?"

"Can't you speak to her?" asked my mother.

I hung my head, "I can't bring myself to upset her. That's why Marcellus and I are in disagreement over this."

My mother thought for a moment. "I could come with you to visit her. I could say things that you could not."

I nodded, I did not relish the confrontation, but I supposed it had to be faced. It would maybe be better than taking Marcellus with me. She might be more inclined to listen to my mother. On the other hand she might not. She could still be angry with me for interfering. I wanted a little time to pass after my party before the next encounter. I mentioned this to my mother, she agreed. "All right we'll give it a couple of days, but no longer. How did she meet this man anyway?"

What to answer? I could deny all knowledge, after all I did not know the precise circumstances in which they had met, although I could guess where it had happened. I shook my head, "I'm not sure, she introduced him to us at a party about two weeks ago. I had no idea she knew him until then. Then to my horror she brought him here last night."

My mother frowned, "I'm concerned to hear that. I would rather she did not bring him to this house."

"It was all right, nothing untoward occurred. They behaved perfectly well," I said.

"Even so, I cannot condone the association, and I don't want him here."

Three days later my mother and I set out to visit Flavia. We went in the morning, soon after breakfast. As soon as it was proper for calling. I did not want the embarrassment of meeting Philocrates leaving, if he had spent the night with her. Nor would I want to go so late as to arrive at the time of the noon meal so she would feel obliged to invite us to eat with her. As it happened we got there about mid-morning. Flavia was supervising the household slaves in her mother's absence. She left her work to speak to us, she looked a bit suspicious, wondering perhaps why my mother had accompanied me, considering her own mother was absent. She looked dishevelled, her hair hastily pulled up and pinned on top of her head. We sat in a small sitting room to the side of the atrium. My mother said, "I hear your parents are in Hispania."

"Yes," Flavia agreed.

"How long are they away for?" asked my mother.

"I'm not quite sure, several months at least I think."

I let my mother do the talking for the moment, I was unhappy in the situation. She ploughed on.

"I hear you have been seeing that charioteer who caused trouble during the festival of Augustus. I cannot think this at all a suitable friendship for you. I presume you family know nothing about this, as they must have seen what happened during the chariot racing."

"Yes they did," Flavia admitted. "And not they don't know I've been seeing him. It didn't begin until after they had left. I expect they would disapprove as much as you and Claudia do. But it's my life and I can do what I like with it."

"No you can't," my mother was angry now. "I don't know in what circumstances you can possibly have met him, or what made you get yourself involved with him. But you are causing your family great harm. I don't know why your parents left you alone here, but it seems they made a mistake, as you obviously can't be trusted to behave decently. This relationship must cease, surely you can see that."

Flavia got to her feet. "No I don't see, I'm happy with Philocrates, and other people accept him."

"They don't," I said, "you bring him to peoples homes, and they receive him for the same reason I did, you give them no choice. But what will happen is that eventually they will stop inviting you, knowing that he will accompany you. Do you want to be ostracized by all our friends?"

Flavia looked sulky, she sat down again. "Why can't everyone let me live my life the way I want to?"

"Because," said my mother, "the way you say you want to live your life is unacceptable, if it includes a close friendship with a man like that. Quite apart from what he did during the race, the man is little more than a slave. At least he used to be a slave until quite recently. Now as a freedman he still serves the same master. And not a very reputable one at that!"

"Caius Sabinus is all right," Flavia said. "I don't know what everyone has against him."

"You should know," I said. "You know the crowd he runs with. You've met most of them."

Flavia got up again. "I don't have to listen to this, this is my house Clauida."

"It's your parents house," said my mother. "you don't own it, but Claudia and I are leaving."

I had no choice but to follow her out of the room and out of the house.

The threatening storm was about to break, the atmosphere was oppressive, and lightening was flickering around Vesuvius. I shuddered, I did not relish being caught in it. The rain when it came would be drenching, quite apart from the rest of it. My mother took my arm,

"Come on let's hurry, there is obviously nothing to be gained by reasoning with Flavia."

We quickened our pace, it was only a short walk to our own home from Flavia's but just before we reached our door the storm finally broke. A huge crash of thunder followed an immense flash of lightening, we were soaked through within seconds as the rain poured down in a torrent. Rivers ran down the streets as more thunder and lightening loomed behind us. Used as we were to these storms, they were still alarming sometimes, although this one had been menacingly close for days.

As Meriope helped me change my wet clothes I told her about what had occurred with Flavia. "She refuses to see sense in this," I said.

"It's a pity you ever got involved with the Bacchic cult," Meriope said. "I could have told you something unpleasant would happen."
I sighed, "I* know, but it's too late now, the trouble has started."

"What does your friend Marcellus think about it?"

"He's furious about Flavia getting herself involved with that man." I answered. "It's causing arguments between us, I think he blames me in a way, as it was my idea in the first place. Although we were both keen to attend, and Flavia says it was just as much her plan as mine. She went of her own free will and does not regret it. But I never imagined anything like this would happen. It never entered my mind that we would meet someone like him socially, as a result of it."

"You must have realised that disreputable people would be there," Meriope answered.

I shook my head, "I didn't think."

"And that's where you made your biggest mistake," she said.

Marcellus would be arriving after lunch, he knew we were intending to go to see Flavia today. I was terrified of what he would say when he heard how we had fared. I insisted on seeing him alone, I didn't want my mother dragged into any unpleasantness that might occur between us. It was not her fault that any of this had come about. I was waiting in the tablinium when he arrived. He walked straight in.

"Well?" he asked, "did you see her?"

"Yes," I admitted.

"And your mother accompanied you, did she succeed in making your friend see sense?"

I took a deep breath, "Flavia absolutely refused to see reason. She said it was her life, and none of us had any right to interfere in her affairs."

"It sounds as if she was very rude to both of you," he said

I nodded, "I think it was particularly hard for my mother. She was shocked at Flavia's manner, saying no one could tell her what to do."

"What?" he asked, "tell me exactly what went on between you this morning."

I told him precisely what had taken place that morning. He looked worried, there was really nothing to be done about it. Until Flavia's family returned, we were powerless to prevent her doing just as she pleased. So long as it did not precipitate a catastrophe of some sort, why not leave her to her fun for a while I asked. "After all" I continued, "Quite a few of our associates are freedmen, it is not so terrible is it?"

"You don't understand a thing about it if you think that." He snapped. "Of course some of our associates, and even some of our friends are freedmen. But there's a world of difference between them, and Philocrates. Apart from anything else, he is still in the employ of his master, he's not a free agent, he has to do as he is told. It's probably illegal for him to consort with a girl like Flavia."

"But things like that do go on," I said.

"Yes, but in secret usually, they don't attend functions and parties together."

I was subdued, I knew of this of course, there had been elopements, and this would be a disaster for Flavia and her family. I dreaded to think what would happen if it came to that. I was nearly in tears, I had had a dreadful day all round. I felt as if everything was against me. I rose from the couch where we were sitting, and went and threw myself down on another couch that stood against the wall. I did not know what to say to him anymore. He came over to me, and leaning down he lifted me up and put his arms around me. "Don't worry about it anymore, just leave her alone for a while. There's really nothing you can do about it. Let's leave it to run it's course, she'll likely soon get tired when she finds herself isolated from her friends. Come on," he urged as he lowered me down onto the couch. "Let's forget Flavia and her problems."

We heard no more about Flavia and Philocrates for six months or so. They held themselves aloof from society, we assumed that they were still together. Then one day the following April, we heard her parents were home. At last things will be sorted out now, I thought.

But the following day her mother appeared at our door. She looked distraught, my heart sank, I had imagined everything would be all right now they were home. She was closeted with my mother in the tablinium. I was summoned to join them. Flavia's mother looked at me, "do you know where Flavia is Claudia?" she asked.

I shook my head, I was stunned.

When did you last see her?" she asked.

"Not for six months at least," I answered.

"Why was that?" her mother asked. "You used to be so close, why have you not met for so long? Did you quarrel?"

I met my mother's gaze, she said, "It's not Claudia's fault that they haven't been close lately Priscilla. In fact Claudia and I went together to visit your daughter a few months ago. I'm sorry to have to tell you this, but Flavia was extremely rude to us that day. We both tried our best to talk sense to her, but she refused to listen to anything we said."

"But why?" asked Priscilla. "What was the reason you needed to make Flavia see sense? What was she up to?"

Neither I nor my mother spoke for a moment, then she said, "Have none of your slaves told you anything of what has occurred? Did they not know if she had eloped or anything?"

"Eloped!" exclaimed Priscilla. "Eloped with whom? No one has said anything about any kind of clandestine affair. Are you implying that Flavia was involved with an unsuitable man?"

I nodded, "I'm afraid so. My mother and I have tried, as she had explained, to make Flavia see reason, and stop seeing this man."

"Who is he?" Priscilla asked.

My mother and I exchanged glances again, then I said, "He's a freedman in the employ of Caius Sabinus. Or he was before he ran away with Flavia."

"How can this have happened?" Priscilla asked.

We finally told her everything, omitting nothing. We told her he was the charioteer who had killed his opponent during the chariot race last August. She of course knew about this, she was horrified. "That was deliberate murder." She said. "How could she have met him? He is a rank outsider, I know the man he works for. An undesirable character, presumably he was the instigator of the dreadful occurrence at the Race. I had no idea at the time, but I see now it was very probable. Did you meet this unsavoury young man Claudia?"

"Yes," I said, "I was introduced to him at a party somewhat

reluctantly by Flavia. Then she brought him to my birthday party here a few weeks later."

"What did you do then?" asked Priscilla.

I shook my head. "There was nothing I could do but allow him to stay. I couldn't make a scene. But I warned Flavia later that people would soon stop inviting her if she persisted in bringing him to social affairs. As I have not seen her since, I presume that is what happened."

We sat in silence for a while, Priscilla looked distressed still. What to do? I wondered, I did not know what to suggest, I had no idea where they might have gone. To one of the other local towns perhaps, although they would probably not have stayed so close to Pompeii I guessed. I wondered if Sabinus knew, could he even be behind it? Although it would hardly have helped him in any way to lose his trusted freedman. I failed to see any advantage to him in this.

We discussed the best course of action to take. To search for them would be almost impossible as my mother and I pointed out to Priscilla. She began to cry, she had had a terrible shock. I went to find Meriope, she would be able to sooth Priscilla if anyone could. She followed me into the room carrying a tray of herbal tea, which we all three drank while we debated what would be the best thing to do. Somewhat calmed by the brew, but still very upset, Priscilla asked our freedwoman if she had any ideas about what could be done about finding Flavia.

"Have you got any idea how long they have been gone?" Meriope asked. "Surely your household slaves must know?"

"They said they had not seen her for about two weeks." Priscilla answered. "They assumed she was with friends. They did think it odd that she did not tell anyone, not even her personal maid. She must have packed her own belongings, most of her clothes are gone."

This startled me, this sounded serous, as if she did not intend to return. If she had only been going for a short trip she would not take so many of her clothes I reasoned. I glanced at Meriope, she too looked shaken. I felt guilty again, I realised if I had not suggested the Bacchic Rites, this would not have occurred. She would never have met such a person at Philocrates. Tears filled my eyes, Meriope shook her head, "It's not your fault," she whispered under cover of refilling my cup. I drank some herbal tea, it helped, I felt a little better.

Priscilla said, "My husband is getting a search party together, but we've really no idea where to begin looking for them."

It all depended on how far they had got, two weeks was not that long, but it would give them a head start.

"I'll ask Marcellus if he has any idea of where they could have made for," I said.

I decided that I was unable to go to the function Marcellus and I had planned to attend that evening. When he arrived I was huddled on a couch in the atrium. He stared at me, "Why aren't you ready? We're due shortly."

I remained where I was, "Flavia's disappeared," I burst out.

"We think she has probably eloped with Philocrates. Her mother was here this morning, she was in a dreadful state."

"When did this happen?" he asked.

"About two weeks ago, so the household slaves say."

He looked appalled.

"What can we do?" I asked.

He sat down on the end of my couch.

"I thought you might have some ideas," I said.

He said, "Two weeks is quite a long time, they could be anywhere by now. We've no idea which way they've gone, or what form of transport they took. Whether they boarded a ship, or of which of the town gates they may have left by. No one could begin to look for them."

"What are we going to do?" I wailed.

Marcellus shook his head. "Nothing can be done now I'm afraid. We should have been informed within hours, or at least a day of her disappearance. Any kind of trail they may have left will be cold by now."

I explained that it had been thought she was visiting friends at first, and none of the slaves had thought anything was wrong. Finally we agreed Marcellus would go round to Flavia's home to question the staff next day. To check if anyone had any information that might help us locate her. But he warned me not to get my hopes up too high, as finding them now was unlikely.

As indeed it proved to be. Although Marcellus questioned all the household slaves, none of them had had the slightest inkling of anything like that being planned by Flavia. They said that they were all aware that the man she was implicated with was a freedman, an ex-slave, as they denigrated him. There was, said Marcellus, obvious disgust at the goings on in the house, and outside, it the last few months. But what could they have done about it, it was not their place as they pointed out to criticise the daughter of the house.

There was nothing to be done about it, all we could hope for was that she would understand what a mistake she had made before it was too late. I hoped we would see her back at home before too many months had passed. If I had known then, what a long time it would be until I saw Flavia again, I would have been far more worried than I was then.

CHAPTER TEN

THE RETURN OF MARCUS

It was nearly a year since Flavia's disappearance. It was April once more, the problem with Flavia had been pushed to the back of my mind, other considerations had made the shock recede. My own affairs were flourishing, Marcellus and I were very happy in each other's company, too happy maybe. But I had no premonition then of any personal unhappiness to come.

I was in Marcellus' bedroom lying on the bed, waiting for him to join me. He had held a reception in his house that evening for his business friends and acquaintances. My brother Gaius had been there with Drusilla. My parents had also put in an appearance. Marcellus' parents were there too. I had acted as hostess as I often did when he gave a party or reception. I was spending the night at his home as I occasionally did, although he usually came to mine. I had supervised the tidying up after the function ended, and had then retired. I lay there anticipating Marcellus' arrival, and hoping he would not be too late. The curtains drawn across the sliding window that opened directly onto the garden were heavy felt in a dark red colour. The nights were chilly, it was not yet summer.

Marcellus entered, pushing aside the curtain that was drawn across the entrance. I sat up and smiled a welcome. He removed his toga carefully, I held out my arms, he came to me, his superb body kept trim by weekly exercise. I had myself seen him practising at the baths. His dark skin was already bronzed, we had had some hot days already this year. His skin felt smooth as I ran my hands over him, I was so much in love, and so I assumed was he. This assumption seemed correct as he returned my caresses. Our passion mounted as we kissed, he laughed softly. "In a hurry my golden girl?" he teased.

"Is that what I am?" I asked, diverted for a moment.

He twisted a lock of my dark blonde hair around his finger. "I would say so."

My desire grew fiercer, I wrapped myself around him, he entered me, triumphantly it appeared to me. I came suddenly, he paused, then slowly started to move again. My own passion grew once more as his thrusts became more urgent. "I've been longing for this all evening," he said.

"Yes," I replied, "me too."

"I couldn't wait to be alone with you." He cried out suddenly, and as we peaked together my cries mingled with his. We held each other tightly for a while, I felt blissful, life was perfect it seemed to me that night. I told him so, he agreed, we were happy in each other's arms, nothing could go wrong.

The following afternoon I was lounging in the garden enjoying the spring sunshine. Drusilla had joined me and we talked desultorily about our affairs in general, and lovers in particular. She and Gaius had had a disagreement and she felt disgruntled. My liaison with Marcellus continued to flourish as she pointed out. It appeared to annoy her that I was so content. But this trouble she was having with Gaius would blow over I said, their marriage was very stable basically, I had no feeling of it going seriously wrong. In this I was proved right, unlike my own life as it happened. But everything appeared sublime at that moment with no shadow on my horizon. As we lay there on our couches Julia was suddenly escorted through to us. She came over to where we reclined and threw herself onto a spare couch beside me. I ordered some herb tea to be brought to us, and then I turned to her. She looked upset I noticed, it appeared everyone was bringing their troubles to me today, I examined her closely. "Is there something wrong?" I asked.

"It's Drusus," she said, "I can't find him!"

"What do you mean?" I asked.

She burst into tears, "He's disappeared!"

Just then the slave arrived with the tea, I poured for the three of us. Julia continued to sob, she had been with Drusus for about eighteen months now, maybe a bit longer. There had even been talk of their getting married. It would be quite acceptable, even if he continued to fight in the arena.

Drusilla aroused from her own problems was alert. "How can he have vanished completely?"

"I'm not sure," Julia wept. "Everything was perfectly all right between us, I thought we were happy together. We were discussing getting married. He was very enthusiastic about it."

"Have you looked for him?" I asked.

"Of course I have," she answered. "I've looked everywhere he might be, but I can't find him, I'm sure he's trying to escape from me."

"You can't be sure of that," Drusilla said. "Perhaps he's had to leave town in a hurry for some reason, and did not have the time to get word to you."

Julia stopped crying, "do you think that that could be the reason?" she asked hopefully.

"It could be," Drusilla replied. "Come on drink some tea."

Julia drank obediently, I also sipped some tea, then I said, "Can't you find out from the barracks where he is?"

"I know he isn't there," she answered. "It's the first place I'd look."

"I meant," I said, "why don't you ask the Lanista. Surely he'd know where one of his gladiators has gone."

"I can't just ask him where Drusus is, I'd be too embarrassed."

"Drusilla and I could come with you," I suggested.

Julia looked uncertain, "I don't know, I hate to have to ask him."

Finally it was arranged for us all three to go together the following morning. We met Julia in the Forum as agreed the previous afternoon, and made our way to the gladiator's barracks. The men were training in the gymnasium attached to the school when we arrived. We hesitated, not sure what we should do next. Julia hung back. "We can't just go up to the instructor and ask him if he knows where Drusus is."

I peered though the railings cordoning off the exercise area from the street outside. I tried to see if I could see Drusus, but it would be impossible anyway, they all looked alike from here, we could not see their faces. "He might be there," I said. "But we can't attract their attention at the moment."

Julia turned away, "I'm going home, there's nothing to be gained by hanging around here."

"We've come this far," said Drusilla. "We can't just give up now."

I wavered between following Julia, and remaining here to try and find out where the man had gone, or indeed if he had gone anywhere. I looked at Drusilla, she was older than us, and I hoped bolder. "We'd better find the lanista," she said.

"How can we?" I objected. "We can't just go in and knock on the door."

"His apartment is over the top of the barracks," Julia said. "I don't think this is a good idea."

"You want to find out where Drusus is don't you?" asked Drusilla.

"Maybe, but I'm still scared of going in there."

"You've been there before haven't you?" I asked.

"Only to a party the first night I met him, and I was with other people then. They knew where they were going," said Julia.

We stood outside the gates uncertainly for a moment, footsteps sounded in the narrow street behind us, a man appeared. He looked at us standing there. "Looking for someone?" he asked.

We stared at him, then Drusilla said "Yes, we are looking for Drusus Lenius."

"He's not here," the man said. "He's on leave, had urgent business to attend to at home in Capua. He left here rather hurriedly." He eyed us with interest, probably wondering which one of us was involved with Drusus.

"Will he be gone very long?" I asked.

He shook his head, "You'd have to ask the lanista, he'd know as he gave him leave."

Julia came to life, "Thank you for the information. That's all we really need to know." She turned to us, "Let's go."

We followed her, past the larger theatre and into a wine bar where we sat down and ordered some wine. When this had been bought to us Julia drank deeply. I looked at her as I sipped my own wine, "Don't you want to find out when Drusus will be coming back?"

She shook her head, "Why didn't he tell me he was going away?"

"Perhaps he didn't have time," I said.

"He could have left a message," she said.

"Who with?" I asked. "He wouldn't have expected you to go to the barracks, so where could he have left a message?"

"Julia's right," said Drusilla. "The man could have sent a note by a friend, someone could easily have left it at Julia's home."

I nodded, there was nothing secret about their relationship, word could have been got to her. Well we would have to wait and see what occurred when Drusus returned to Pompeii. Julia was upset, but things would probably work out between them.

Marcellus was at our house when Drusilla and I got back. Gaius was with him, Marcellus smiled at us. "I'm glad that you are both here," he said. "We've just had a consignment of materials arrive, I thought you'd both like to join us to have a look at them."

"Ooh yes please!" I answered. "Come on Drusilla, let's get ourselves ready. We'll be with you in a few minutes."

"We'll wait here in the atrium," Marcellus said.

A few minutes later Drusilla and I joined them. I thought this might be a ploy on Marcellus' part to heal the rift between Gaius and Drusilla. I walked ahead with him leaving the other two to follow. They had no option but to walk together. I glanced at Marcellus, he winked at me, so I was right I thought. We made our way through the crowded streets. People were on their way to the baths at this time of day. Some of them would likely have appointments to keep. As we jostled our way down the street the sun beat down on the cobbles, we were glad to get into the shade afforded by the overhanging houses in the narrower streets.

At last we reached the home of Marcellus' family and entered the atrium. Grateful for the coolness inside I sank down onto a bench, Drusilla joined me. I studied her to see if the walk through the streets with Gaius had improved relations between them. I did not want to ask her, and she gave nothing away by her demeanour. Gaius was talking to Marcellus, he turned to us, "Come and have some refreshments." He led the way toward the peristyle garden where slaves served us with cool wine and bread and cheese. I was famished suddenly, I hadn't eaten since an early breakfast, and then not very much.

After we had finished our lunch Marcellus rose and led the way to a room used for business dealings and trade, where the goods were laid out for our inspection. I gasped at the variety of colour and fabric, I walked around examining them. There were shimmering silks and brightly coloured cottons. Thin wools, all the new cloths for the summer season.

"Well," said Marcellus, "what do you think?"

I reached out and touched a bale of silk. "I love it," I breathed. "When will it be on sale?"

"It goes on display in the Hall of Eumachia tomorrow," he answered. "But you may both choose some material for a gown which I will have made up for you."

I was thrilled, so was Drusilla. "Thank you Marcellus," she said. "That's very generous of you, we are so grateful."

"Not at all," said Marcellus. "It's the least I can do for my friends."

Examining the materials closely, I finally, after much deliberation chose a dress length of scarlet silk. I would have it made into a sophisticated evening gown, which I anticipated wearing to various occasions with Marcellus. He smiled, "Yes I look forward to seeing you in that."

I was excited, I watched Drusilla, she chose a length of bright green silk. Also for an evening dress I assumed. She turned to Gaius, "do you like this?" she asked him.

"Yes I do," he answered, "it will suit you very well."

I was pleased to see this, it seemed everything was fine between them once more. We were all four of us happy together. If I had known what was to come! But I did not, and so I was elated with the way things were going.

Two or three weeks went by. One day Julia appeared again. We had not seen her since the day we all three went to the barracks to look for Drusus. This time though she was excited and happy. "Drusus is back!" she wasted no time in small talk. "He returned last week, it was family trouble. His brother came to fetch him, he had no time to leave any messages. And he was too busy when he got home to have time to get word to me."

Well if she was content with this explanation so much the better I thought. "I'm pleased for you," I said. "What was the urgent news then?"

"Oh, he said it was his mother, she was taken ill. But she has recovered now, and he has returned to the gladiator's school here. Oh Claudia, I'm so fortunate to have him back. I really do love him, this has made me realise how much."

"Good," I said, "do you know what was wrong with his mother?"

She shook her head. "Not really, but at least everything will be all right now he's come back to me. He came to see me as soon as he could after he got back."

We talked for a while, I was still delighted with my own love affair, and was not concerned with criticising other people's. With Gaius and Drusilla reconciled, nothing it seemed could mar our pleasure.

Nor did it for several more weeks, there were plenty of activities to attend, and sometimes we all four went together to functions. One evening we all attended a concert at the Odeion, the smaller of the town's two theatres. As we sat there listening to the music, Marcellus whispered to me, "I've got something to tell you later."

I nodded, I hoped it was good news, but afterwards as the concert concluded and we left our seats, I asked him what his news was.

"You may not like it," he said.

My heart sank, "what is it?" I asked.

"I'm afraid I have to go away for a while," he answered.

"What!?" I exclaimed in horror. "What do you mean? How long for and where to?"

"It won't be too long I hope," he said. "I have to go to Syria to visit some silk merchants."

"But that's a very long way from here!" I almost shouted. "I'll never see you again."

"Of course you will," he said. "I'm not going to live there. It's only a business trip. I'll be back as soon as I can."

"How long?" I asked.

"About six months to get there and back, and attend to business while I'm there."

I was furiously angry, I walked away from him, pushing past the crowds leaving the theatre. I caught sight of Gaius and Drusilla. His blonde head was bent over her dark one as they kissed passionately, as several other couples were doing. It had been very sensuous music. I was nearly in tears, this should have been a romantic evening for us too I thought. And now Marcellus had spoiled it, had spoiled everything. My life was in ruins it seemed to me. Blindly I tried to run, my red silk skirts hampering me. Marcellus caught up with me, he took my arm, I pulled away from him.

"Come on Claudia," he said. "You are making an exhibition of yourself. You can't run in that dress, it's too tightly fitted. Let me at least escort you home."

"I never want to see you again," I said. "Gaius and Drusilla will see me home."

He laughed, "I doubt it, did you not see them just now? They have no time for anyone but each other tonight. That music had that effect, although not it appears on you."

"How dare you," I retorted, "How dare you expect me to be amorously inclined towards you after what you have just told me?" I was outraged suddenly, I glared at him.

"Let's not waste the time we have left. I'll soon be back, I promise." He put his arms around me, no one gave us a second glance, there was much more passionate lovemaking than this going on at the moment. Anyone who did not have a companion was hoping to find one. The prostitutes would do a roaring trade tonight I knew. One or two were hanging around the vicinity of the Odeion, accosting single men, and having some success I saw. I turned my head away. "I'm going home."

I had no heart for going anywhere else, to the few parties that were on offer that night. They would turn into orgies anyway with the mood most of the people seemed to be in. I did not know if Gaius and Drusilla were going to any of them. Although I would have thought they would prefer to be alone together from what I had just seen.

"All right, I'll take you, you can't go alone."

I walked away from him. A couple of men standing together tried to accost me. "All on your own darling? You can come with us." One of them said, they caught hold of me, I fought them off frantically, I hardly realized what I was doing. Marcellus arrived, I screamed, he pulled the man away from me and punched him in the face. His companion tried to knock Marcellus down, he remained upright and shoved him out of the way. I clung to him weeping, I was distraught by now, he put his arms across my shoulders, I was shaking.

"Come on," he said.

Arriving at my door Marcellus followed me in. I ran to my bedroom and fell on the bed, I was weak all over. I lay face down still sobbing, he came into the room and sat on the end of the bed. He tried to take me into his arms, but I pushed him away. "It's all your fault, giving me such a shock, tonight of all nights."

It was a night for romance, and for me it was over. He would go away, and I would lose him, I had been so happy with him, and now the idyll was over. That's all it had been, just an idyll, there was nothing substantial in our relationship. It was not built on solid ground as I had assumed, my life was over I thought.

"Stop this," Marcellus said suddenly. "There's no need to behave in this way."

"Yes there is," I sobbed. "You're going away, there's nothing left for me. What am I supposed to do without you?"

"You'll find something, I'll be back before you know it."

"You won't," I wailed. "Look how long Flavia's parents were away, and they only went to Hispania. You're going to the Orient, it's much further."

"Well I should hope you won't do anything as silly ad Flavia did."

"Of course I won't, the situation isn't the same, you must see that."

"I know," he said, "I was only teasing, I don't think you're like Flavia. Not so stupid, at least I hope not."

I turned around to face him. "I could do better than a slave I should hope."

"Come on," he moved close and reached a hand up my skirt, I tried to push him away, still annoyed with him. He pushed my dress up and put his hand between my legs tantalisingly. I was trying to move away, but my attempts were half hearted by now, his hand was arousing me, he removed it from between my legs and thrust my gown up around my waist. He never believed in wasting time, before I knew what was happening he was inside me. I gave up all pretence and abandoned myself to his lovemaking. Afterwards as we lay locked together I said, "Please don't go away and leave me."

He withdrew and lay down beside me, I rolled over and put my arm across him and gazed at him imploringly. He lay still saying nothing for a while, then he took me in his arms and held me tight. "I'm sorry," he said, "I have no desire to go to Syria, but we are having some trouble with our suppliers there. One of us has to go and see them, or we could be in deep trouble. Our stock flow could cease and we would then have problems with money, and that does not bear thinking about. It may not take long to sort it out, at least so I hope."

"You will be gone a long time," I said. "The journey takes weeks surely. How will you get there?"

"By sea of course as far as it is possible," he answered. "One of our ships leaves from Stabiae in a few days time, I intend to be on it."

"I wish I could come with you," I said, my tears dried up at last.

"You know that isn't possible," he answered. "Making the journey on my own will be much quicker."

"Meaning I'd slow you down," I demanded.

"Frankly yes," he said. "Having a companion, especially a female one, would make the trip last much longer. As I've said I'll be there and back before you know it."

I was silent, my father's business was all local, we had no foreign suppliers, This was something I had never thought about before, having to go overseas on business. I understood that cloth came from lot's of different countries by it's nature. Most silks came from the East, so also did cotton, and wool came from many places, as well as Italy. There was nothing I could do or say to dissuade him, I should not even try. He had a living to make, who wanted to be poor? I certainly did not. Not that I had ever considered the prospect before. I snuggled up to him, "I'm sorry," I whispered. "I realise you have work that must be done. I'll try not to get too impatient as long as you hurry back to me."

He clasped me tighter, "of course I will, can you doubt it?"

After another very satisfying interlude he got up from the bed. "I have to leave now, I'm sorry I can't stay, but I'll see you tomorrow."

But the next day I waited in vain, I spent the day watching and hoping he'd come, but by late evening it was obvious he was not coming that day. I was disappointed and unhappy when he did not appear the next day either. The following day he did come, to my relief, but he was closeted with my father and Gaius for most of the morning. It was time for the noon meal before I was able to see him and speak to him. I asked him why he had not come before this.

"Pressing business," he answered. "I leave in two days."

"So soon?" I asked.

He looked around to see if we were overlooked, then he held me close. "I hope to see you before I leave, if not I'll get a message to you."

But two days later I still had not seen him, when a messenger came to the door. He was a freedman of the Vinicius family, he asked for me. I received him in the tablinium, there was no one else around. He told me that his master Marcellus Vinicius had left the day before. There had been no time for him to visit me himself, but he had sent me a letter and a gift. I could have done without the expensive bracelet, I would have preferred him to have come himself to say goodbye. After the freedman had left I sat alone with the letter and cried until I had no more tears to shed. After this I pulled myself together and walked to my room.

For some weeks after that I stayed at home, I had no heart to go anywhere. I sat with Drusilla bemoaning my fate.

"They always leave me in the end," I said.

She stared at me in amazement. "But you can't think Marcellus has left you surely," she said. "Did he not explain the nature of the reason he had to leave town?"

"Oh yes he explained," I said bitterly. "What difference does that make to me now?" How would you like it if Gaius went away?"

"He doesn't have to," she answered. "But if he did, I should hope I could put up with a few months apart from him."

"Well I can't accept it so calmly," I said. "Suppose he doesn't return?"

"Of course he'll return," Drusilla said. "He has to, can't you see that? He would lose everything if he stayed away permanently. All his business interests are here in Pompeii."

"What about the people he had gone to see?" I asked, aware that what I said was stupid. These people in Syria were only purveyors to his family concern. They needed more than just one cloth dealer for their trade to prosper. There was nothing else for him in Syria to cause him to linger there any longer than was necessary. This Drusilla pointed out to me, "Can't you be patient for a few weeks?"

"It'll be months not weeks," I grumbled.

"Even so, if you are in love with him as you profess to be, you could wait patiently even for a few months."

"All right I'll wait for the six months he said it might take,"

"It will soon pass," Drusilla said. "You should get out a bit, not stay at home all the time. He wouldn't expect or want you to do that."

"I'll try to make an effort to see a few friends," I said.

But socialising depressed me. Everyone was part of a couple. Julia and Drusus were discussing marriage, I felt like an outcast from a charmed circle. If only Flavia was here I thought, we had always found plenty in common. It was only the last year before she disappeared that things had gone sour between us.

The weeks and months passed slowly, my nineteenth birthday went by. I did not give a party, what would be the point? I would probably be the only one without a partner, how depressing that would be. No one expected me to celebrate under the circumstances anyway. Marcellus had been gone only about two months, and it had gone slowly. I had attended the Festival of Augustus with my family, and his parents had joined us again. I smiled and tried to appear happy, it was fun of course, but I kept remembering the previous two years when he had been with us.

The six months passed, and it was the middle of winter. There was no sign of Marcellus, but I put that down to the weather, a ship would have a rough passage in the high winds and seas that whipped around the coasts, and was accompanied by heavy rain that flooded the streets and saturated everything. He would return when the spring came I reasoned, it could not be long now.

But the spring arrived a month later and Marcellus did not. But then I told myself he would have been stuck in port somewhere while the storms raged, and would have only been able to set sail when the weather turned calm. The nearest he could possibly have been to home was probably Alexandria in Egypt. Which would mean another two months before he could possibly reach Stabiae. It would be mid-summer by then at the earliest before I saw him. It was a dismal prospect, I was already somewhat isolated socially by now, not liking to attend parties on my own. So unless it was a special occasion I stayed away. I was becoming a recluse, to my dismay. This was not like me at all, I had always been at the centre of things, outgoing. I disliked my self-imposed seclusion, I discussed it with Drusilla. "I don't know how much longer I can go on in this way," I said. "It's as if I am old before my time, sitting at home every evening. I am so bored, but what else can I do?"

"Get out and enjoy yourself, this isolation is entirely self-imposed. No one is asking you to shut yourself away, certainly not Marcellus. It's getting on for a year now since he left, I don't think he'd grudge you a social life."

"I suppose not," I said. "Where could I go though? I don't want to latch onto you and Gaius all the time."

"You're quite welcome to come out with us any time, why not join us tomorrow night? We're going to the theatre, we'd be pleased to have you with us."

I agreed to go with them the following evening. It was at the larger theatre, and was to be a short tragedy followed by a comedy. A lot of people would go just for the comedy, but they would sit through the tragedy, to get their money's worth presumably.

After the tragedy was over there was a short intermission, and we decided to stroll around the quadriporticus where we would probably meet some of our friends. As we were walking together on the lookout for company, Gaius and Drusilla were hailed by another couple who I did not know. After they had introduced me they began a lively discussion that I lost interest in. I looked around me, I caught sight of a man who looked vaguely familiar from the back. It was likely a mistake I thought, I can't place him.

Suddenly he turned around and saw me, he seemed pleased to see me and made his way over to our group. His dark chestnut hair gleamed in the late sunshine, he was extremely handsome. Where had I known him from? He greeted me with delight.

"It's Claudia isn't it?" he asked.

"That's my name," I replied. "I'm Claudia Livillia."

"Don't you remember me Claudia Livillia?" he asked.

"I'm Marcus Luccullus, we met some years ago at a party at the home of Clodius Publius."

I was stunned, I stared at him, I was pleased to see him.

"Of course I remember you," I answered.

CHAPTER ELEVEN

THE WEDDING

Marcus and I gazed at each other. The interval would soon be over, in a few minutes we would have to return to our respective places. I made up my mind. "Call on me tomorrow morning." Drusilla turned around to look for me. "Come on Claudia, the next play is about to start."

"You remember Marcus don't you Drusilla?" I asked.

She look startled, "Marcus? Yes of course, I recall meeting you in the garden, with Claudia. It was a long time ago it seems."

"About three years," Marcus replied.

"I'll see you tomorrow," I said.

I accompanied Drusilla and Gaius back inside the theatre. But my mind was not on the comedy, in fact I would have been hard pressed to remember anything about it if anyone had asked me.

The following morning I waited in the peristyle. I did not know what I felt now. This was the man I had vowed to wait for no matter how long it took, things had changed in the time he had been away. There was Marcellus for one thing, he had been gone for about a year now, with no word to either me or his parents in that time. How would I feel confronting Marcus alone after all this time, and of more significance, after my relationship with Marcellus. Who I was sure I still loved, in spite of what I considered his neglect.

My reflections were interrupted by the arrival of Marcus. I jumped up, and asked the slave to bring wine as he was shown through to the garden. I hoped it was not too early for him, but I needed courage. I was not sure how to greet him, he took the initiative by coming towards me, and taking both my hands in his, he kissed me on the mouth. I was uncertain how to respond, as my feelings were still confused.

"Is that the best you can do?" he asked. "I thought last night you were pleased to see me again."

"Oh I am," I replied, "but it has been a long time since that night at Clodius' party."

"Is there someone else?" he asked.

I was saved from replying by the return of the slave with the wine. I poured two cups and handed one to Marcus, I raised my glass to him, "Saluti," I said, and took a deep draught. He returned the toast, and sipped the wine, studying me over the rim of his glass. "Well, is there?"

I was not sure how to answer this, it was a more forthright question that I had expected. He was obviously ready to pick up where we had left off. My own feelings were conflicting. Marcus was a very attractive man, he had dark chestnut hair with auburn highlights, which were accentuated by the brightness of the sun. A lean handsome face with deep brown eyes. He wore a light summer tunic in a cream colour.

"There was someone," I said. "but I haven't seen him for a year now." I lowered my head, he came over to me and putting his arms on my shoulders, he lifted my head up to look into my eyes.

"It doesn't matter, I never expected you to remain faithful for the time I have been away. There were no vows to bind us, we made no promises to each other. Of course I assumed there had been someone else in you life. But if it is over now, as you seem to be saying, why can things not be the same between us as they were, however briefly, three years ago?" He gazed down into my eyes, I had no choice but to return his look, I nodded.

"Why not?"

Putting his arms around me he held me close. I stayed still in his embrace for a moment, then I pulled away. I was not going to make it too easy for him, as he had just said we were not bound to each other in any way. I picked up the jug of wine and refilled my glass, offering some more to Marcus. He shook his head, "I have a lunch appointment with a high ranking official. If you are interested I will see you later."

"All right," I said, "You can come here for dinner tonight if you like."

He agreed and we parted. I sat down on the bench in the garden, and pondered what I should do. There was time enough to tell Phito that we would have a guest for dinner. Also my family could wait a while I thought. But then I saw Drusilla approaching from her quarters, she joined me on the seat. "Did he come?"

"Yes, he's just left."

"So what are you going to do?"

"I've asked him to dinner tonight."

"I meant," she said, "how do you feel about him? And what about Marcellus?"

"What difference does it make to Marcellus, he's not here, or likely to be, it seems."

"He will return some time."

"Perhaps, but it could be years before he reappears." I got up from the bench, "I'd better tell Phito we have a guest tonight," With that I left her, I was not up to any interrogations at present. I had not decided what I should do, I would have to think this through in private.

That evening I introduced Marcus to my parents, explaining when and where we had originally met. The dinner went well, they had no objection to Marcus, as indeed why should they. He was very presentable, and made himself agreeable to us all. Just before he left he said to me, "tomorrow night I am having dinner with Clodius, would you like to come with me? Clodius won't mind if I bring someone, and he knows you anyway."

I agreed to accompany him the following evening, and he took his departure.

The next day he called for me, and we made or way to the home of Clodius Publius. When we reached the house, we were shown into the triclinium, Clodius rose to greet us.

"How good of you to come Marcus, and I see you've brought Claudia Livillia with you. I'm pleased to see you Claudia." We shook hands, and settled into dining couches. We were handed cups of spiced wine, and met the few other people who were there. A young woman who was obviously a close friend of Clodius. She was called Lucia, and was very attractive. She wore a pale green gown that floated diaphanously around her, and her dark hair was curled around her face, and coiled up at the back. I too was wearing a rather gauzy dress, in pale blue, which seemed to complement Marcus' tunic of heavy silk, in a darker shade of blue. There was one other young couple there who I did not know. As we were introduced I saw that they were older than I had first thought, perhaps around thirty, as was Clodius. I was the youngest person there, though Marcus was only twenty-four. As the meal was served Clodius engaged Marcus in conversation, he was always interested in military matters, which was obviously the reason he had invited Marcus to dine. They discussed the current situation in Britannia, the present governor was Seutonius Paulinus. As they debated the political state of affairs there at the moment, my attention wandered. I studied the triclinium, I had never been in this room before. A large fresco depicting a stag hunt covered most of the wall opposite me. Other frescoes showed the customary deities in various poses, I turned my attention back to my plate. The main course had now been served, it was garden piglet, stuffed with sausage meat, dates and smoked onions. It was served with a sauce of garum, rue, sweet wine and honey mixed with oil. I helped myself to the vegetables proffered by the chief steward, as it was a small, intimate gathering, Clodius only had a few picked members of his household in attendance this evening. The main course was followed by dessert of cakes and fruit.

Afterwards we sat over a fine wine accompanied by various spices, this was followed by another wine poured from an ornate flask of blue Syrian glass. I excused myself and went in search of a lavatory, then I wandered out to the peristyle door, and stood there enjoying the night air, and the peace of the well tended gardens. Marcus came up behind me, "I thought I might find you here."

"Yes," I answered, "I needed some fresh air, and I did not want any more to drink."

"Yes," he agreed. "They will carry on until they fall asleep or pass out I should think." He moved towards me, putting his arms around me he began to kiss me. The wine had had some effect on me by now, and suddenly I was responding to him. After all he was very handsome, and I had known I was still attracted to him from the first time I had seen him again at the theatre. If there had been no one else on my mind I would willingly have fallen into his arms before now. What had I got to lose I thought, for all I knew Marcellus might never return, although it seemed unlikely he would stay away for ever, he had too much to lose. But it could be a long time to wait for him, and in the meantime why should I not have some fun?

Our passion grew more intense, we fell onto a large couch in the tablinium, almost before I realised what I was doing we were making love. All my inhibitions had gone, and with them my self control. Breathlessly I clung to him, matching his ardour with equal enthusiasm, the first wild desire was soon assuaged. He was as insatiable as he had been the first time, his almost desperate eagerness aroused me, as it had done before. As we began our lovemaking again, I was conscious of a slave entering the room. Ignoring us he went about his business as if we were not there. I do not think Marcus even noticed him, as the intensity of his passion did not cease. Well there was nothing I could do about it, and judging by the man's indifference he had probably seen it all before in this house. He soon left, he only had had to draw the curtains leading to the garden, it barely took him a moment. I returned my attention to the matter in hand as Marcus yelled loudly. He held me tight in his embrace and looked down into my eyes, "Marry me,"

I stared at him in astonishment, "What?"

"Marry me," he repeated, "before I go back to my post."

"I don't know what to say."

"Why don't you just say yes."

I thought about it, "How long have we got before you have to leave again?"

"About two months, it's time enough if you agree. I'll go and see the priest at the temple of Jupiter tomorrow."

I was swept off my feet, why not I thought, it would be fun. I had been miserable for too long. I hugged him. "Yes, let's get married."

The following day I had the prospect of informing my family of my decision, I was not sure how they would take the news. They could have no objection to Marcus as a son-in-law I reasoned. None of us knew his family, but Marcus was a tribune in the army, that alone meant he must be at least eques class. We were merchant class, there was no problem there, we were the new elite, and could if we wished marry even into the senatorial class.

I wandered through the house and found my mother in the kitchen. She looked up in surprise as I entered. "I've got something important to tell you." I said.

She followed me out of the kitchen and into the atrium, "What is it?"

"Perhaps we'd better sit down," I suggested.

Just then Drusilla came through.

"You'd better stay and hear this as well," I told her.

She looked startled, "Is something wrong?"

"I don't think so," I said. "I've decided to marry Marcus Lucullus."

There was an astounded silence. "Are you sure Claudia?" my mother asked. "You hardly know him."

"I know him well enough," I answered. "We have met before you know."

"Yes, but how long for," my mother asked.

"Long enough," I said.

Gaius appeared, coming in through the front door, Drusilla looked at him. "Claudia has decided to marry Marcus."

"Rather sudden isn't it?" he asked. "How well do you think you know him Claudia?"

"He's all right," I said, "I know all I need to know about him."

Gaius smirked. "Yes I expect you do, but there are other things to be taken into account."

"Don't be so crude Gaius," Drusilla admonished him.

He sat down on a chair, we were all still in the atrium, not the most private of places for a family discussion.

"When were you thinking the marriage would take place?" my mother asked.

"As soon as possible, it has to be," I replied. "Marcus has two months of his leave left, he has gone to the temple of Jupiter to see the priest, and arrange the date this morning."

"It doesn't give us much time," said my mother. "I've got the wedding veil of course, that won't be a problem."

I nodded, that would leave the gown still to be made.

"Is Marcus coming here today?" My mother enquired.

"Yes," I replied, "This afternoon, he will tell me how he fared with the priest. It is just a matter of arranging the day, we'll find that out when he arrives today."

"Tell me when he gets here so we can discuss this," she said.

When Marcus turned up after lunch my mother and Drusilla joined us in the tablinium. I wondered what his parent's reaction to the news had been.

"You're to come to our house for dinner tonight, so they can meet you," he said.

"All right," I agreed. We would have to arrange a meeting between our two families before the wedding.

The meeting with Marcus' parents had gone well, and they were due at our house tomorrow evening. We would marry in two weeks time, there would be a great deal of preparation in the meantime. It was agreed that Marcus would live in our house after we were married. There was no time for a separate establishment to be found in the time we had before Marcus had to return to his cohort. Not that I would have wanted one at this stage, I would have been lonely after he left without the company of my family.

The time passed quickly with so much to do, and before I realised it the day of my wedding had arrived. I dressed myself with Meriope's help in the white gown and saffron overdress. The flame orange veil was made of silk. I would go with my family to the temple of Jupiter in the Forum. Marcus would already be there, having witnessed the taking of the auguries before I arrived. It was a messy business, and always done by the bridegroom alone with the priest and augers. When we got to the temple my father took me by the hand and led me towards Marcus. We stood in front of the priest of Jupiter as he recited the marriage rite. Then I approached the altar and presented the cake I had brought with me for sacrifice to the gods.

Afterwards we all repaired to our house for the wedding feast. The food was laid out in the atrium, all our friends and acquaintances, including my father's business contacts were there. There was goose liver pate, truffles and oysters to begin with. Followed by the main course, which consisted of smoked ham from Germania, which we always had in our food stores, accompanied by salads. This was accompanied by a roast wild boar, a hare, and vegetables, large asparagus, leeks and onions, and broccoli. For dessert there were honey-layered cakes, and pastries filled with raisins and nuts. Followed by cheese of all varieties with breads. Wine was passed around, with a special falernian for the toasts, this was circulated freely during the celebrations, and once the formalities were over I joined in without restraint. After all this was supposed to be my special day, so why should I not enjoy myself. I did not want to think about Marcus leaving me, as he would have to do once his leave was up. But at least with him I had the satisfaction of knowing we were committed to each other. That I was his wife, he had at least thought enough of me to marry me, and show the world he cared for me.

Julia came over to me, she was a little drunk I noticed. "Well you've beaten me to it, I thought I was going to be the first to get married in our circle."

"You'll be the next," I said. "I look forward to your wedding, although I shall have to come alone as Marcus will be back in Britannia by then I expect."

Her black hair was piled up on top of her head, with curls artfully escaping, she looked dishevelled. I looked around for Drusus, he was talking to Marcus I saw, I pointed this out to Julia. "Oh yes," she said, "Marcus is a soldier, Drusus would admire that, although he only fights in the arena himself, they probably have a lot in common."

"I expect so," I said, "Shall we join them?"

Together we made our way over to where the two men were standing.

Marcus was still fairly sober, but Drusus had been imbibing rather heavily I noticed. He put his arm round Julia amorously, she clung to him equally tipsy. I wondered how far they were planning to go, they staggered out to the garden. I turned to Marcus, he smiled. "an interesting young man. He told me he fights in the gladiatorial arena, I told him I hoped to see him in action next week, during the Augustan Games."

Of course! It was the festival next week, it was all go at the moment.

"Are you enjoying the party Claudia?" Marcus asked.

"Of course, why wouldn't I?"

He put an arm around my waist. "I'll be quite glad when it's over so I can, hopefully, have you to myself for a change."

It was true, we had not really had a moment alone together since the night at Clodius' house. Just then Clodius himself came over to congratulate us. "I hope to see you again before you leave Marcus. You disappeared the other night." He looked at me, "I can imagine the reason, and I don't blame you."

"That's when I asked Claudia to marry me," Marcus said.

"Well I'm glad I had a hand in it, however remotely," Clodius said.

As the hours went by the party continued, I began to feel tired, and rather intoxicated. Some people it seemed were quite prepared to stay all night. Finally I staggered into my bedroom scarcely knowing where I was, a room had been prepared specially for us, but forgetting that this would no longer be my room, I threw myself onto the bed, and still in my wedding finery I fell into a heavy sleep. I came to suddenly. It was very quiet, it appeared that everyone had gone. I got up from the bed and removed my gown, then I went to the bathroom and washed myself. I then returned to my room and lay down again and went back to sleep.

It was Meriope who found me in the morning. "What are you doing in here? Your husband is looking for you."

I awoke startled, then I began to realise what I had done, I felt shocked at myself. How selfish of me I thought, whatever will Marcus think of me? "What did he say?" I asked.

"Well he was a bit the worse for wear himself by the end of the reception," Meriope answered. "So I doubt if he was unduly worried about where you had got to. But now he is up, and is asking for you."

Just then Marcus appeared in the entrance, "I'd like to be alone with my wife Meriope," he said.

"Yes Dominus," Meriope said, and left us alone together. I was sitting up by now, Marcus wasted no time, he came to the bed. After removing his wrap he took me in his arms and set about consummating the marriage.

"I'm sorry about last night," I murmured.

"Never mind about that," he answered. "We both over-indulged rather, let's make up for lost time now. We haven't been alone together since we decided to marry."

We spent the morning making love in my bed, we would move to the suite prepared for us later that day. About mid-afternoon we emerged from my bedroom, and went to sit in the shaded colonnade around the peristyle. I wore a new gown of sheer silk, in pale green.

"You look like a water nymph in that dress," Marcus remarked.

I smiled contentedly, we had ordered wine, well watered after yesterdays excesses, to be brought to us. I stretched out on the couch and took a large swallow of the wine, I was all of a sudden very thirsty. It was peaceful in the garden in the late afternoon sunshine, it was very hot of course, but I was used to it, and for Marcus it was a welcome change from the climate of Britannia, which he complained was damp, and often cold. The milder weather of Italy was a luxury to him. Our garden was a riot of flowers and merging colours. The fountain sprayed water plentifully into the air, sprinkling the nearby plants and shrubs. It was an idyllic scene I had always thought, and Marcus agreed with me. No one disturbed us in out tranquillity, we were newly weds after all, and our time together was short.

The Festival of Augustus was the following week, Marcus' parents were to join us at the amphitheatre. We arrived early as usual, and the show began. This year there was to be gladiatorial contests between our town and the neighbouring town of Nuceria. The earlier tournaments went off peacefully, or as peacefully as was possible in combats in the arena. Unhappily, towards the end of the day's battles the mood of some of the spectators turned nasty for some reason. We had won quite a few of the contests, and so had Nuceria. But suddenly angry shouts broke out in the crowd. This was followed by fighting amongst the audience, people were beating each other up, Marcus grabbed hold of me. "Let's get out of here quickly." I looked to see if the rest of our party were all right, they also were holding onto each other, none of us wished to be involved in this kind of lawlessness. There would be arrests at least, maybe worse, some of them looked as if they might kill each other.

Afterwards we heard that that is what did happen. There had been murder committed in the streets my father and Gaius told us the next day. And Pompeii was getting most of the blame for the disturbance. We heard that the injured and the dead had been carried up to the Forum. The dead were all from Nuceria, and Pompeii had come off best with only a few injuries sustained.

The Senate at Rome was going to issue a decree we were told, there was much displeasure about what had happened.

We waited apprehensively to hear what the verdict would be. When we finally heard it there was outrage and shock throughout the town. We were told that the Senate had issued a decree forbidding Pompeii to hold gladiatorial contests for ten whole years! We could hardly believe it, what would we do? It would affect our whole lifestyle, the games were part of almost every festival, the main part.

More personally I was wondering how this would affect Drusus and others like him, whose livelihood it was. I was worried about Julia, what if he had to leave Pompeii to find work elsewhere? They were planning their wedding I knew. I mentioned this to Marcus, he shook his head, "There's nothing we can do about it. I'm more concerned about you, I shall be leaving soon to return to Britannia."

I forgot Julia's troubles in my anxiety about losing Marcus.

CHAPTER TWELVE

FAMILY LIFE

The remainder of the festival went off comparatively quietly. There were the theatre performances, and finally the chariot races. We did not hear about the result of the edict until after the festivities were over, so we were able to enjoy the rest of it fairly happily, though subdued. As the Senate's decree was hanging over us, putting a damper on the proceedings.

I was anxious to see Julia as soon as possible, but this was difficult because of Marcus, he barely let me out of his sight, and he was a demanding lover. This was understandable as our time together was so short, but I did feel concerned about Drusus. Perhaps, I surmised, Julia's family might help, after all they were perfectly happy about their marriage, surely they would be desirous of keeping them both in the town.

One day about a week after the festival had finished, I managed to persuade Marcus to let me go and see Julia. "You could come with me, we would still be together," I told him.

"And you have met them at our wedding party."

He agreed to accompany me to Julia's home, and we set off one morning. Julia's family were also wine merchants, although not in such a big way as we were. But they only had a daughter, they had no heir to carry on the business as Gaius would, and indeed already did. He and my father were in partnership. There was also Lucius, who we had not seen or been in touch with for some time. This was because he had decided he wanted to travel after finishing his studies at Rome. We had no way of knowing where he even might be at present.

Arriving at the house we were ushered in by a slave, and shown into a small sitting room. The house was a lot smaller than our own, or indeed of most of our other acquaintances, I had not realised this. I had never been to her house before. It had a small atrium, with, we could see several rooms opening off it. These were closed with curtains, even the main room, which I assumed to be the tablinium only had a curtain covering the entrance instead of a door. But though it was modest in size it was not poor. Julia appeared in the entrance carrying a tray containing wine. "I hope wine is all right for you Claudia," she said, "Or would you prefer something else. It is maybe rather early in the day for some people for drinking wine."

"That'll be fine Julia," I said, "You know my husband don't you?"

"Yes of course," she answered "Ave Marcus." She busied herself pouring the wine into beakers, "It is nice of you to visit me, both of you."

"We're worried about you and Drusus, what is he going to do about the edict?" I asked.

She shook her head, "I don't really want to talk about it at the moment."

"But what are you going to do?" I asked, "Your wedding is next month."

"Maybe," she said

"You mean you're not sure?" I gasped, "what will happen then?"

She was very subdued, "There is no longer any employment for Drusus in Pompeii."

"But couldn't your father employ him, take him into the business or something?" I asked.

"How could he?" she asked. "There is not really a job for him in the vineyard, it is quite small and slaves do most of the work. My father runs it single handed, he can manage easily, why would he want to employ anyone?"

"What are you going to do then? What does Drusus say?"

"He says he will have to look for employment elsewhere, where they still have work for trained gladiators." She started to cry, I went to comfort her.

"What about Herculaneum," Marcus said suddenly, "That is not very far away, could he not find work there?"

"I don't know," Julia sobbed.

"Herculaneum would be the nearest," I said, "Nuceria is definitely out after what happened."

"Otherwise," said Marcus, "Neapolis might be the best. It's a lot bigger too. There may be more openings, surely there is always work for trained fighters. Look why don't I talk to him?"

"Yes," Julia said, "He'd listen to you, but the barracks here will be closing soon, and he will have to go away."

"Could you not bring the wedding forward?" I asked, "So you could get married before he goes. Surely he could live here with you then, at least until he finds another job."

"I don't know about altering the wedding date," Julia said, "But I have already suggested he move in here temporarily when the barracks close."

"What did he say?" I asked.

"He has agreed it is the best idea," said Julia, "After all he has stayed here often enough with me."

"Well that solves the problem then," I said.

We sat talking awhile longer, then we rose to leave, we would return next week to see Drusus we said. He would have moved in by then, and Marcus could give him advice.

The following week we again visited Julia, this time Drusus was there. We sat in the small peristyle garden and drank borage tea. Drusus lounged on a couch beside Julia, he was wearing a green tunic, he looked extremely handsome, his dark blonde hair needed a trim, but its unruliness suited him, enhancing his flashy good looks. Julia glanced at him in adoration, she looked a lot happier than when we had seen her the previous week.

We sipped our tea, then Marcus asked, "What are your future plans now Drusus?"

Drusus gazed around the small garden in satisfaction, "I've not got any plans at present," he said. He stretched out luxuriously on his couch. "This is the life, why should I be in any hurry to leave it?" He reached out and took Julia's hand, she gave him a melting look, "I certainly don't want him to go away, I'd be quite happy for him to stay here indefinitely."

"I dare say," said Marcus, "but Drusus has to find work eventually surely."

I took a mouthful of borage tea, it was strong, but quite pleasant, and kept silent during the discussion. It was clear to me that Julia and Drusus would be content to let him laze around indefinitely. I could see no problem with that if they were both happy, and it seemed that they were. Perhaps we should not interfere if they were contented to live this way. If her parents did not object of course. "What about your wedding?" I asked.

"That's still on," Julia said, "Next month as arranged."

I smiled, "I'll look forward to it."

Marcus frowned, rather disapprovingly I thought. "But you will have to find work eventually Drusus, Julia's family are not going to be able to support you indefinitely are they?"

Julia looked annoyed. "My father hasn't said anything about Drusus not being welcome for as long as he cares to stay." She snapped.

"Well he wouldn't would he?" I said. "But you said yourself there is no work in the vineyard."

I knew Julia's family were not as affluent as most of us in our circle. He could not have been pleased at the prospect of Drusus lolling around permanently with no money of his own. But was it really our business to interfere? But Marcus ploughed on, "Are you planning to continue to fight in the games, or would you prefer to find something else to do?"

"Such as what?" Drusus asked.

"He doesn't want to do anything else do you Drusus?" Julia said.

"Ever thought about joining the army?" Marcus asked.

"No!" Julia exclaimed, "He hasn't, nor do I want him to, it could be dangerous."

"No more than being a gladiator," Marcus replied. "The chance of getting killed is about the same, though there are safe posts in the army, such as being stationed somewhere there is no war going on. As I am myself in Britannia, Claudia needn't worry about being widowed, Camulodunum is secure."

"Could your father not find work for him?" I asked.

"After all you have no brother."

Julia was silent, but I thought if Drusus was going to hang around, he might as well do something.

"Let's leave it till after the wedding," she said.

"Yes," I said, "But I thought that while Marcus is here he could help with advice."

"It's kind of him of course," said Julia. "And as you say my father might be able to help us."

Marcus stood up, "We'd better get home Claudia."

As we made our way through the town he said, "Drusus seems quite content to idle away his time in luxury, that wouldn't matter if he had money, but he seems to be insolvent."

"But surely," I said, "He must have made some money with his fights. I thought they got paid after every display in the arena, as well as a retainer when they are just practicing."

"If that's the case why is he living at what appears to be Julia's father's expense."

I thought about it for a moment. "Perhaps he hasn't been paid yet for the recent games. He might not have saved anything, but spent lavishly when he had money."

"Yes that is certainly possible, I don't know what else to suggest."

It was the hottest time of the day now, though with August over it was much more pleasant, and the open air bars were full of people having their midday meal. The tables spilled out onto the pavements, making it necessary for us to walk in the road which was not so pleasant. It had not rained for some time, and filth had piled up, running down the gutters, and the centre of the street. It was a relief to reach our house, we made our way to our room to prepare ourselves for the noon meal. Marcus raced ahead of me to reach the room first to my surprise, what was his hurry I wondered. When I finally arrived he was behind the curtain where our chamber pot was kept, although he had not troubled to draw the curtain completely across as he urinated into the pot. So that was the reason for his hurry I realised. I changed hastily into another light gown, "Come on, my parents will be expecting us," I told him. We were both hot and sweaty, and he also changed his tunic.

When we joined the family my father and Gaius were there as they quite often were, they all looked up as we entered the hortas, the small summer dining area.

"How did you get on?" my mother asked.

"Well Marcus tried to give Drusus advice," I said.

"So what happened?" she asked.

I looked at Marcus, he said, "I suggested he join the army, after all he's well qualified, and it is a steady job."

"I'll bet he didn't like that," Gaius grinned, "I'll bet he prefers to lounge around at Julia's parents expense."

"Julia didn't want him to," I said

"Their wedding is soon," Drusilla joined in, "why not wait until after that?"

"Yes," I said "But I wanted Marcus to help if he could while he's here."

We discussed the matter all through lunch, not that it was really our problem, but it worried me anyway. I did not want Julia and Drusus to have to part unless they had to, as we unfortunately did.

Afterwards we retired to our quarters, I was still interested in debating the subject, but Marcus had other ideas. Throwing off his clothes he flung himself onto the bed, "Come on, I want to make love to you."

Nothing loath I joined him and the afternoon passed very pleasantly. Our time was getting short now and I was going to miss him dreadfully.

The next few weeks passed much too quickly, and it was my twentieth birthday. A party was out of the question so soon after the wedding party. Not that I wanted one anyway. I preferred a private celebration. We went to the Odeion to see a mime, it was fun, it was risqué and vulgar and we never stopped laughing the whole way through it. It cheered me up and I loved it for that reason, afterwards we went to a high-class taverna for dinner, and made jokes about the play which we laughed at uproariously. Our laughter had an edge to it however, if I had not laughed I would have cried.

The time for Marcus' departure was drawing inexorably nearer, we only had another two weeks left. Still I cheered myself up at least we had that time left, we would have to make the most of it. This we did by mainly remaining in our room, Marcus could not leave me alone, he had always been an insatiable lover, but now there seemed to be an almost desperate edge to his lovemaking. The time passed quickly to our dismay, and sooner than I'd thought the last day arrived. We had a farewell dinner in the tablinium with both our families. I could barely eat anything I was so close to tears, Marcus said goodbye to his parents that night as they left. He was leaving at noon the next day, this would be our last night together.

After bidding goodnight to everyone we went together to our room. He pulled me to him as soon as we got there, we fell onto the bed, I held him tightly, he took me fiercely, I responded sobbing with both grief and passion, this had to be a night to remember. The next morning we again made love, then he got up to finish his packing, finally he put on his army officer's uniform. He looked so handsome in it that my heart nearly broke as I looked at him. "How long will it be?" I asked. There was no need to specify what I meant, I knew he had been away for three years last time. I hoped that it would be sooner than that before I saw him again. He held me in his arms, the metal on his tunic hard against my bare flesh, I wore only a flimsy wrap. He was a real turn on in his uniform I realised, I had never seen him wear it before, I looked into his eyes, "have we got time?" I asked breathlessly.

"Why not, it certainly won't take long," he said meaningfully. It was true, we were both on fire with desire, sensing my state he removed his metal kilt and we fell on the nearest day couch. It was soon over as I had known it would be, and he was again arrayed in full kit.

The final leavetaking was heartbreaking for us both, he held me in the atrium as I sobbed. Finally Drusilla appeared, she stood for a moment waiting to se what was going to happen when he left me, which of course he had to. The door slave came to assist him, and carried his gear to the entrance. With one final hug he turned and hurried out, he had left it as late as he dared. I sank onto a couch limp and distressed, Drusilla seated herself beside me, she enfolded me in her arms. "He'll be back" she said, "The time will pass, at least he's your husband now and nothing can alter that, you are bound to each other. That should be a comfort to you."

"Yes, but I'm going to miss him so," I wept, "It is such a long way away."

We had of course arranged to get messages to each other from time to time, when it was possible. It would not be very often, even though communications were good in the military.

"Come on let's go and sit in the garden," Drusilla said. I agreed and accompanied her outside to the peristyle. We lay in the afternoon sunshine, and I thought of Marcus and how we used to enjoy sitting out here together.

The next few days passed in a haze of misery for me, I was alone in the room we had shared, I missed him terribly. I was also feeling unwell, reaction I supposed, I had had a hectic two months. One day I lay in bed feeling too ill to get up, Meriope came in and looked at me. "When did you last have your menses?" she asked.

"What?" I asked in astonishment, I remembered having had one about a week before my wedding. Now I came to think about it I supposed I had not had one since my marriage. I stared at Meriope aghast, it couldn't be, could it? I rounded on her "why didn't you remind me? You always have in the past, this has never happened before."

"I forgot I'm afraid," Meriope answered, "Or if I thought about it at all I assumed maybe you did not wish for it, as you're married now."

"What do you mean I did not wish for it, why would I not?"

"I don't know, if you're pregnant it could be because you wished to be."

I was horrified, this was no part of my plans, how could I cope with a baby without Marcus beside me, I had no strong maternal feelings. "What am I going to do?" I asked, "I don't need this at all, I've no wish for a child, can you help me?"

She shook her head, "You could be anything from three weeks to six weeks on. If you were single with no hope of marriage I might have tried to do something, but I won't give you the briony tincture now. It would be too strong a dose, far stronger than the one I used to give you to bring on your courses each month. It is dangerous taken as strong as that, and why anyway? What is so wrong with having a baby now? It could help you in your present circumstances."

"In what way?" I demanded, "If it means feeling like this all the time I can't put up with it."

"Yes you can, this will pass in a week or two, you'll feel better, and I'll help you all I can, now and after it's born."

"It's your fault," I moaned, "If you'd made up the potion like you always used to. You never forgot before did you?"

"Of course I never forgot before when I knew you needed it, but I thought this time you would have asked me if you'd wanted it."

I had not had to take the medicine for the past year, not since Marcellus had left. It was no wonder with all the excitement of the wedding preparations we had both forgotten it. But how was I going to cope with a baby? Miserably I sank down in the large bed, this was a blow, how could I have let this happen, it was not as if I was inexperienced, I had known what to do to prevent this. But I had forgotten, as Meriope said she had, and now I had to take the consequences.

"I'll get you a drink of goats milk," she said. "And I'll tell your mother shall I?"

"No, I'll tell her myself, just say that I'm not well and I want to see her."

Meriope nodded. "All right."

My mother came into the room carrying the milk. "Here you are, what's wrong Claudia? Meriope says you're ill, what is it?"

I took the milk and sipped it slowly, carefully, "I'm pregnant."

"What?" she gasped, "Oh darling how nice for you," she hugged me. I stayed still in her embrace. "I don't want to have it."

"Why ever not?" she exclaimed, "It will be nice for you, can we get word to Marcus?"

I shook my head, "I don't imagine so, he boarded a ship at Misenum the day he left here. Besides I don't want him told yet, He'd only worry about me and there's nothing he can do."

"He'd want to be told, surely you can see that. Do you know where the ship docks at all after leaving Misenum?"

I thought about it, "It'll have left Ostia by now, that was it's first port of call. I suppose Masillia in Gaul would be next, but there's no hurry, we can get a message to him when he reaches Britannia. He'll reach Londinium in a week or so."

In fact I did not want him told before he reached Camulodumum after all something could go wrong before that time. Why bother him until I was at least three months pregnant. In the meantime there was Julia's wedding to attend, I cheered slightly, the milk had made me feel better, I would be well enough for it, I had feared I might not be.

The day of the wedding was bright and warm, it was the end of October, the weather was still quite hot. I was feeling better on the whole, although still a bit sick first thing in the morning. My mother and Meriope assured me this was normal, and would pass eventually. I hoped so, I could not stand much more of it. I dressed, with Meriopes' help in one of my new gowns, how long before I would be unable to get into them I wondered. It did not bear thinking about, I resolved to enjoy the occasion even though I missed my husband. I was happy for Julia and Drusus.

After the ceremony at the temple, we all adjourned to Julia's house for the wedding party. It was on a much smaller scale than mine had been, as they did not have the space for a really big reception. The food was laid out in the garden, as the atrium was not big enough. Julia looked lovely in her saffron and orange finery, though she removed the rather cumbersome veil immediately on arriving home. Arrayed solely in her white gown and saffron overdress, she stood with Drusus receiving their guests. I hugged her and congratulated her, "I'm so happy for you."

Drusus embraced me and kissed me, he too looked good in his best toga. Julia's parents stood beside them, they were a handsome couple too I saw. I did not know them really, until I came here with Marcus about a month ago, I had never visited the house before.

Sipping a cup of spiced wine I sauntered towards the small fishpond, where a group of people were gathered. Most of them I knew, as we moved in the same circles, Antonia and Titus were holding hands I saw, they seemed pleased with life. I had hardly had a chance to speak to them at my own reception two months ago, I smiled at them. "Don't they look happy?" I indicated Julia and Drusus. "I suppose you will be next."

They exchanged looks, "Well," said Antonia, "we are making plans for next spring possibly."

"That's good, I'll look forward to that. About April will it be?"

I would easily be seven months pregnant by then, it was a dreary prospect. Whatever would I wear I wondered.

"What a pity your husband isn't here," Antonia commented. "You must miss him a lot."

"Yes I do, he left two weeks ago."

I was not intending to tell anyone about my condition just yet. After all I was only a few weeks on at the most, things could go wrong yet I thought. I was still unhappy with the unexpected gift that Marcus had left me, I took another glass of spiced wine from a passing slave, things might look better if I drank enough. We went over to where the tables were laid out, and collected heaped plates. More wine was passed round, and I joined Antonia and Titus at a small table.

After a while things grew hazy, I also felt more than a little sick. Rising unsteadily to my feet I looked round in panic, I would not throw up in public, not that humiliation please! In a house this size there was probably only one lavatory. People were crowding all around me, I pushed my way towards the house, Antonia followed me. "What is it, aren't you felling well?"

I shook my head, and taking my hand she led me through the atrium, I was starting to retch by now. As we reached the latrine a man was coming out, I pushed past him without ceremony and vomited miserably onto the floor outside, unable to make it to the lavatory. I lay huddled unhappily on the latrine floor, Antonia helped me up. A slave had arrived, and was already mopping up the mess.

"Come on," said Antonia, "sit down here," she found a bench in the small sitting room I had visited when I called here with Marcus. I did not feel all that well disposed towards him at the moment.

"You must have had too much wine," Antonia said, "although I did not think you had any more than the rest of us. You've drunk as much before and been all right, what could have caused it do you think?"

Julia came into the room, she ran towards me, "what's wrong Claudia? I hope it isn't anything you ate here."

Neither of them guessed the truth, they probably assumed I had taken the usual precautions after my marriage. They likely would I thought, Julia would not be so stupid as I'd been, if only Meriope had remembered, I was not sure I believed that she had really just forgotten. She probably fancied the idea of having a baby to take care of again. Meanwhile I was stuck with the result, and would be unable to enjoy myself properly for the next seven or eight months. And even afterwards there would be problems, although I would see that Meriope did most of the work of caring for the child. After all it was just as much her fault as mine I thought. In the meantime what should I tell my friends? In the end I settled for the truth, they would have to know soon anyway, I could be two months pregnant already. And I did not want them thinking I could not hold my wine, "I'm expecting a baby," I hung my head, I felt foolish.

They gasped, "Are you?" Julia asked, "Are you quite sure?"

"I'm sure," I answered.

"Have you seen a doctor?" Antonia joined in.

I nodded, "He thinks I'm nearly eight weeks on."

They went on staring at me, then Julia asked, "Did you plan it? Is it because Marcus is away a lot that you decided you'd like a child, as a reminder of him?"

I shook my head, I was not so high minded or sentimental. Which did not mean I did not love Marcus, but I would not deliberately put myself through pregnancy and childbirth for any man if I could avoid it. "It was an accident," I said. "I didn't plan it, it was a lapse of memory, with the wedding having to be arranged so hurriedly, certain things slipped my mind."

They looked at me uncertainly for a moment. "Aren't you a bit pleased though?" Antonia asked. "I would want a baby some time."

"Well I don't intend to have one at present," Julia said. "And I can sympathise with you Claudia."

"I'd netter go home," I got to my feet, I felt better now but the party was spoiled for me. "Tell them to bring my chair," I told Julia.

Ensconced in the sedan chair, I waved to Julia and Antonia as the two slaves lifted it up, and carried me home.

CHAPTER THIRTEEN

YOUNG LARIUS

After Julia's wedding I stayed at home and did not venture out again for some considerable time. I feared a repeat of the humiliating sickness I had experienced at the reception. I was not feeling too well anyway, and had no desire to go anywhere. I spent my days in my room, or on a couch in the tablinium, the weather was cold too, and I preferred the heated rooms in the house. Drusilla kept me company quite often, and Antonia called to see me now and again. I did not see Julia, and assumed she was too engrossed with Drusus and her marriage. I was still annoyed about my carelessness in allowing myself to become pregnant, as well as with Meriope for forgetting to give me the contraceptive potion.

I wondered how my mother could have gone through this three times, apparently quite willingly. I had no intention of allowing it to happen to me again, once was quite enough I decided. Drusilla told me that she had in fact had a miscarriage soon after her marriage, but had told no one, as it had been too early in her pregnancy for anyone to have known about it. She had not even told Gaius about it she said, he had just thought her to be unwell for a few days.

Now I come to remember it, I did recall her being confined to bed for some days soon after she had married Gaius. I had not thought about it at the time, being too concerned with my own interests. I had been involved in my first love affair at that time, and had been indifferent to anything else that might be happening. She was not in a hurry to try again, in fact that had been a mistake, as mine was. I told her she was lucky it had turned out that way. "I wish that that would happen to me, perhaps it still might, after all I'm barely three months pregnant yet."

"I was only about three weeks on," she said, "I hardly had time to realise it before I lost it. I was careless the first couple of weeks after my wedding, but never since."

I sighed, "It looks as if I'll have to go through with it, but I loathe feeling like this."

"I did not have time to feel ill," Drusilla said, "Before it was over."

"What am I going to do?" I moaned. "I haven't any experience with babies, how can I look after it?"

"Meriope will help you," Drusilla said.

"She'd better, it's mostly her fault anyway."

Drusilla laughed, "That's one way of laying the blame. You're saying she's responsible for your condition?"

"And Marcus of course,"

"Not you at all then, you weren't even there at the time it happened."

Drusilla went on laughing, it was extremely annoying of her, she must have known what I meant. How could I be expected to remember everything with all the wedding preparations to think about.

The days passed slowly, but by Saturnalia I was feeling better. I was by now about four months pregnant, still able to fit into all my clothes, which was a relief, soon I would have to get some loosely fitting dresses I knew. Drusilla agreed to accompany me to the Hall of Eumachia to pick some material out. We went together early in January, it was a chilly day, but muffled in our cloaks we did not feel the cold too much. The Hall was quite crowded, and I hoped I would not be taken ill, I had not been so far from home since Julia's wedding, as I kept away from crowded places. We made our way through the throng towards the new spring fabrics, I chose several in wool for now, and some in thinner cloth for when it got warmer, as it would in two to three months. I looked around to see if I could see anyone I knew, finally I caught sight of Julia, she seemed to be shopping alone, with just a slave in attendance. I waved to her, and she made her way over to us.

"How have you been?" she asked me. "I'm sorry I haven't been to see you since our wedding, but I've been busy."

"How's Drusus?" I asked, "What is he doing or planning to do?"

"Well at the moment he's helping my father in the vineyard," she answered.

"Oh so your father did manage to find a place for him then?"

"Well we're seeing how things work out first, before he makes a final decision. He might still decide to return to the arena."

"Where would he go?" I asked

"I'm not sure yet, probably Neapolis. But I'm hoping that it will work out for him in the vineyard, then he needn't go away."

I nodded, married quarters did not exist at gladiators barracks, so they would have to be separated, "I hope it works out for him," I said, "And you of course."

Julia's slave was now laden with her purchases as was our own, we decided to send them home with our shopping, and go ourselves to a wine bar for a drink. After leaving the Draper's Hall, we found a good class one near the Forum. We sat down and ordered wine. I was drinking wine in moderation at present, that way I found, I did not make myself ill. Julia studied me, "You still look slim, I had thought you might be quite fat by now."

I shook my head, "Not yet, I might still be all right for a week or two if I'm lucky."

"In any case," Drusilla added, "they say you don't show too much with the first one. Not until much later anyway."

"The first!" Julia exclaimed, "Are you planning others then?"

I shuddered, "No I'm not having any more, once is quite enough for me. As you know I did not plan this one."

"But I expect it will be nice once it's born." Julia said.

"I hope so," I said.

"What are you going to do about feeding it?" Julia asked.

"I'll find someone," I said. "We'll find a slave girl who's just given birth, I'm not going to do it."

"I should think it would hurt," Julia remarked, "I wouldn't either."

As we left the bar she said, "I'll come and see you soon."

"Please do," I said, "I rarely go out, I could do with some company." With that we parted to return to our homes.

The time dragged by and I suddenly became cumbersome and awkward. I loathed it. I was also terrified of the birth, partly I wanted it to be over, and partly I dreaded it. The summer came, I lay on a couch in the sun most of the time now. Drusilla sat with me often, we sipped herbal tea and talked. I had moved back to my original bedroom by now, as it was more convenient. The one I had shared with Marcus was away from the main house, at the end of the colonnade, opposite to where Gaius and Drusilla had their quarters.

One night as I was preparing to go to my room I was suddenly doubled up with pain. I screamed and a slave came running.

"Fetch Meriope quickly." I said

She arrived immediately and picked me up off the floor where I had collapsed. "Are you all right?" she asked.

"Of course I'm not all right," I snapped, "Do I look all right?"

The pain seemed to have gone, so I staggered through the atrium toward my bedroom. I lay on the bed, Meriope undressed me, I was not wearing much, it was very hot, and I only wore a loose robe. She covered me with a sheet, "Do you want anything?" she asked, "A drink or anything?"

I shook my head, "No but I feel better now."

"You probably will for a while," she said, "Try and sleep a little, there's plenty of time."

I dozed off, then another excruciating pain woke me. I yelled for Meriope, she came immediately, "I've told your mother, I'm to inform her when the pain comes again."

"It already has," I was doubled over in agony. I hoped this was as bad as it would get, I could not stand much more. A young slave girl came into the room carrying a beaker of milk, Meriope took it from her. "Here drink some of this, you have to keep your strength up."

I did not want it, but I sipped it obediently.

"Go and fetch the domina," Meriope said to the girl, she left the room.

A few moments later my mother came into the room, she came over to me. "How are you feeling Claudia?" She sat down and put her arm around me.

"How long have I been sleeping?" I asked

"About three hours I think," Meriope said.

The pain had stopped again, I felt drowsy.

"Don't sleep too much," my mother said, "It will only prolong the labour if you keep dozing off."

"How long will it last?" I asked in panic.

"It varies from one person to another," she said. "But falling asleep too much stops things moving along, and delays the birth."

"What am I supposed to do then, wait for the pain to return?"

"More or less, yes," my mother answered.

"Will it get worse?" I asked in trepidation.

"I'm afraid it will, but if you're lucky it could be fairly swift."

I closed my eyes, I lay there for some time with only an occasional twinge of pain. Meriope brought me some broth, "This will keep your strength up." She fed me with a spoon, I tuned away after one or two mouthfuls.

Drusilla appeared suddenly, "I'm so sorry I wasn't here earlier, but I've only just heard that you were in labour."

"It doesn't matter," I answered, "There's nothing you can do in any case."

"Are you all right?"

"I've been better," I answered sarcastically.

Just then I experienced the worst pain to date, I bent over, "Help me!" I screamed, "I don't want this." The pain subsided, I lay back again.

"Is it too soon to call the midwife?" Drusilla asked looking at me anxiously.

Meriope came over and put her hand on my stomach, "It isn't time yet, the pains are too far apart."

"I can't take much more," I said, "Not if it's going to get worse."

"I'm afraid it will get worse before it gets better," said my mother.

"What a pity Marcus isn't around," Drusilla remarked.

"I don't want him here," I said. "What could he do anyway? It's better he's not here."

He had of course been informed of my pregnancy and had written to me as often as possible considering the distance between us. He had expressed concern, but was pleased about the baby. My replies had left him in no doubt about my feelings, but he said he understood that in my present circumstances I would feel that way. But once the child was born, he said, I would feel different. I was not at all sure he was right, all I wanted was for the birth to be over, so I could get back to normal again. I had left him in no doubt that there would be no more children. One was enough, why go through this again.

A spasm of pain shot through me, all three women held me down as I thrashed around on the bed. I lay still for a while, then an even worse pain contorted me, by now I was screaming and crying. Meriope left the room and returned with the birthing chair, I stared at it in horror. "What am I supposed to do with that?" I shrieked.

"It is better to give birth in an upright position," my mother assured me.

"I can't, I sobbed, I did not want to leave my bed until it was over.

"Not yet," my mother said. "But in a while we will help you, and support you on it."

I stared at my mother. "How could you go through this three times?"

"It's as well for you that I did," she laughed, "Or neither you or Lucius would be here."

"Even so," I persisted, "How did you do it?"

"It got easier after the first time," she assured me.

I shook my head, "I'm not going through this again. I'm not surprised most of my friends are only children." I shrieked suddenly as another pain shot through me.

Meriope left the room again, when she returned she said, "I've sent the girl for the midwife, it shouldn't be long now."

By now I was writhing in agony, "why don't you send for the doctor," I managed to gasp out.

"I hope that won't be necessary," Meriope said, "If all goes well we won't need him."

My mother bent over me, "Calm down Claudia, it's no worse for you than for anyone else. We all have to go through this sometime."

"Never again," I screeched, the agony grew worse, Drusilla bathed my face with cologne, I could see she was glad it wasn't her. I doubted Gaius would get himself an heir now. He would have me to thank for that I thought, for putting Drusilla off childbirth for good.

My mother and Meriope restrained me as I struggled, "Be still" Meriope said, "This won't help you."

But I was past hearing anything now.

The next thing I knew the midwife had arrived, she was a bustling little woman of about forty I guessed. Removing the sheet she parted my legs and felt about inside me, I moaned, it hurt.

"Relax," she said, "You're much too tense." She turned to my mother and Meriope, "I'm not sure, the head seems to be stuck somehow."

"What does that mean?" I asked apprehensively.

My mother and Meriope stared at the midwife, Drusilla stood wide-eyed. "What does it mean?" she asked.

I stared at them all appalled, "what are you going to do?" I sobbed.

"We'll have to summon the doctor," the midwife said. The pain was appalling now, Meriope brought a cup to me, "Drink this, it's poppy syrup, it will ease the pain, at least for a while."

I sipped it, I would take anything to stop the agony, however temporarily. A slave had been sent to fetch the physician, all we could do was to wait until he arrived. The poppy syrup had made me feel calmer, as well as slightly helped to ease the pain. Nothing I knew would really cure it until the child was born.

The surgeon arrived, I looked at him imploringly, he was my last hope to put a speedy end to my suffering. He came towards the bed and examined me in the same way as the midwife had, I cringed in fear of more pain. His slave had followed him, he turned to him, "Prepare the poppy juice," he said.

While the man mixed the potion the doctor set about laying out a set of instruments. When the mixture was ready he applied it to my vagina with a sponge. This was done to ease the way for the surgical instruments. I felt numb, though the pain was back in force now. The doctor selected from his array of instruments something which he explained was a forceps. This he then proceeded to insert into me, he nodded to the midwife. She and Meriope held me in position, my mother cradled my head, while Drusilla held my hand. The physicians slave held a cup of poppy syrup to my lips. I was by now past caring about anything I was so distressed.

The doctor suddenly gave a tug on his forceps, I screamed and cried, he pulled harder.

The pain was worse than anything I had yet experienced, then I must have fainted for a moment or so. The next thing I knew it appeared to be over, the doctor and the midwife were standing over me, "there's just the afterbirth to expel now," the woman said. "This will help to shift it."

I was handed yet another potion to drink, I lay back exhausted, the doctor peered up me again, He inserted another device and the cord thing slipped out. Then I became aware of a baby crying, I had almost forgotten in my stressed state the object of all this. I turned my head around to see what was happening. Meriope and the midwife were tidying the bed, putting on a clean sheet, while a young girl helped to support me. My mother came in to the room carrying a baby, she was smiling, "Everything's all right now Claudia, you have a lovely little boy." She held him out to me, I stared at him curiously.

"He's perfect," my mother announced, "you're very lucky."

She held the child out to me again, I took him gingerly and examined him. He was wrapped in a fine wool shawl.

"Hold him for a moment then we must get him dressed."

I studied the baby, he had dark curly hair, his eyes were closed. There were auburn tints in his hair I noticed, like Marcus.

My mother and Drusilla were bending over me admiring the child.

"What are you going to call him?" Drusilla asked.

I thought for a moment, "Larius" I said, "Larius Lucullus, it has a nice ring to it I think."

They smiled, "That's a nice name," Drusilla agreed. "Will Marcus approve do you think?"

"Why shouldn't he?" I said, "It's a nice name I like it."

I was suddenly, unexpectedly tired, I handed the child back to my mother. "I have to sleep now." The opium had added to the strain of the last hours, before anyone could say anything else I fell abruptly asleep.

When I awoke I looked around remembering what I had recently suffered. A young slave girl sitting by the door rose from her seat and came over to me.

"Where is Meriope?" I asked.

"I'll fetch her domina," the girl answered.

Meriope arrived.

"Is the baby all right?" I asked.

"He's with Oenone," she answered. "When he wakes up she'll feed him. Let me see your breasts." She examined them for a moment, "I'll bind them up and give you a draught to dry up the milk flow."

She went away and returned with the strip of cloth and a vial of medicine. "You'll need this several times a day for a couple of weeks."

"Can I see my baby?" I asked. "I won't wake him if he's still asleep."

"It's best to wait until he wakes up and has been fed. But I'll bring him to you as soon as he's ready."

"All right," I lay back, "Thank Juno that's over."

I dozed off again, when I awoke my mother and Drusilla were there. My mother held the baby. I held out my arms, she put him into them, "He's certainly healthy," she said, "you're a lucky girl."

I studied him, he had been dressed in a long tunic of fine linen. He was beautiful, I suddenly felt a rush of pure love for this tiny being, it took me by surprise. I had not thought to feel like this, in fact I had had no notion of what to expect.

"Does everything work the way it should?" I asked.

They laughed, "he's fine," Drusilla said. "He's had his first feed and had his napkin changed once already. There's nothing wrong with him at all if that's what's worrying you."

My mother sat on the bed, "Everyone worries at first, but I assure you there's nothing the matter with him at all."

I looked down at him, he seemed to have gone back to sleep, I cuddled him closely, "Larius," I murmured.

I was still very sore after the forceps delivery, the doctor came to see me again the next day, moving around hurt me, I asked him how long this would last.

"It will hurt for a day or so," he answered, "Try to keep still as much as possible then it won't be so painful."

"Will I be all right?" I asked him worried.

"Yes you'll heal perfectly well, this often happens, and no one is the worse for it in the end."

Marcus' father and mother came to see the baby, they brought me gifts for him. They admired the child, and seemed satisfied with the name I had given him. They informed me that they had written to Marcus in Britannia as we had, but that they had not heard from him for some time. We had sent a message to him in Camulodunum, and were still waiting for a reply.

"It seems rather strange not to have heard from him," said Marcus's mother.

I agreed it was rather surprising that he had not replied to any of us.

In fact it was several weeks before a letter came for me from Marcus. He was no longer in Camulodunum he said, the Governor had pulled them all out of the town to join the legions in Deva on the North Wales border. Seutonius was planning an attack on the island of Mona, which Marcus explained was across the Menai Straight. The Druids were augmenting a rebellion in what was by now the last stronghold of Welsh resistance. I was concerned to hear this, it meant that Marcus was now actively engaged in war, or he soon would be. He had always assured me how safe he was in Britannia, where there was no war going on. Until now it seemed!

Larius was now a month old, my friends came round to see him, Antonia brought Titus with her. Maybe to get him interested in the idea of them having a child now that they were married. I had not attended their wedding as I was very cumbersome by then, and tired easily. It was only a month before I gave birth to Larius, they had understood perfectly. I was really sorry to have to miss it of course, but I had had no choice.

"What was the birth like?" Antonia asked.

I shuddered, "Terrible, I would never go through it again. It took ages to recover from the forceps delivery, it tears you you know."

"It doesn't always have to be that way though does it?" she asked.

"Maybe not," I answered, "I wouldn't take the chance again though, but it might be different for you. I don't want to put you off if you want to have a baby."

"But you're glad now that you've got him aren't you?"

"Oh yes," I gazed down at Larius, he was adorable, "I'm glad I've got him, I love him very much, don't get me wrong. I'm just warning you of the hazards."

"It would be worth it to have one like him," Antonia said.

I looked at Titus, I wondered how he felt about it, Marcus and I had never discussed the possibility, it had never occurred to us. All we had thought about was being pledged to each other before he had to leave Pompeii. I held Larius out to Antonia, "Would you like to hold him?"

"Oh yes please," she answered. She took him into her arms and cuddled him, she looked at Titus, he smiled at her. Antonia sat nursing the baby, then she asked, "who feeds him, do you?"

I shook my head, "I have a wet nurse, that was arranged before he was born."

"Who is it, a slave?"

"Yes, her names Oenone, we bought her in the slave market about three months ago. She had recently given birth when we found her."

"What about her baby?" Antonia asked.

"We bought him with her, she feeds them both. We could not have separated them even if we'd wanted to, as her milk would have dried up before Larius was born."

"Yes of course," said Antonia, "But you wouldn't have made her give her child up anyway would you?"

"No," I said. "My mother would never have allowed it in any case."

Julia also came round curious to see Larius. "He's lovely," she said, "I expect you're pleased now he's born aren't you?"

Again I agreed, "But I expect you would want to wait a while," I suggested.

She nodded, "Yes, it would not be a good move for me to get pregnant just yet."

"But things are all right aren't they between you and Drusus?"

"There's no problem between us, but it's best to wait until I'm sure he's settled into the wine business."

"Do you think he might not then? What exactly does he do in the vineyard?"

She shrugged, "He helps with the accounts mostly."

"Is he good at it?"

Julia looked annoyed, "Just because he was a gladiator doesn't mean he's brainless," she answered sharply.

"I didn't mean that," I said, although I had wondered. He had not displayed any mastermind tendencies when I was around, at least.

Although my father and Gaius ran our vineyard between them, they also had freedmen secretaries to help them. Men who could take charge when their masters were not there.

"But you think he might not remain there?"

"I don't know, he still exercises at the baths most days, so I assume he's keeping in trim in case he should ever want to take up fighting again."

"Do you think he will?" I persisted.

She shook her head, "I doubt it, after all he's better off where he is, it's just that he could make more money in the arena."

"What does he say?" I asked. "Anything to make you think he might not be content at present?"

"Not really, after all a gladiators life is very precarious, he could get killed at any time in the arena, and I don't want that, and neither does he."

"No," I said, I told her about Marcus, she stared at me horrified. "You mean he will have to fight in a war?"

"I should think it's very likely," I answered. "But he is a tribune, he would be safer than a foot soldier. Officers rarely get killed in the modern army."

"So you're not worried about him then?"

I shook my head, I was a bit apprehensive about Marcus being engaged in open warfare. Especially as he had assured me he never would be, at least as far as he knew. But things had changed it seemed, these Druids were some kind of priests I had heard. Not liked by Romans as they did not trust them. They cast spells I assumed, and interfered in politics I knew.

The campaign would not start for a few months yet I assumed, and while at Deva Marcus would be safe enough in the military fort there. All I could do was wait until he came home to me, hopefully uninjured. There was nothing else I could do, and in the meantime I had our baby son to attend to, and to take my mind off my worries. I at least had nothing to disturb me there, as he was a healthy baby. I also was much better, as the soreness had gone, and the doctor had removed the stitches and had pronounced me to be healed from the birth.

CHAPTER FOURTEEN

REUNION

A few days later as I sat in the peristyle with Larius now six weeks old, laid on a sheet on the grass at my feet, Gaius came through the tablinium door towards me. He held a scroll in his hands which he handed to me, "You'd better read this Claudia."

I took the scroll and saw that it was a copy of that day's 'Gazette'. "Why what does it say?"

"There's been a battle in Britannia," Gaius replied, "Some place called Wales it seems."

My heart in my mouth I examined the scroll, under the headline 'Seutonius wins victory on Mona," there was an account of the battle. Anxiously I scanned it. The Roman Army it read, had sailed across the Strait and been faced by an army of barbarians. Shouting and screaming curses, wild women dressed in black with their hair dishevelled were waving torches. The women scared them more than the men, who were reinforced by the Druid priests, who were also yelling imprecations at the invaders. But the auguries had been taken by the Roman priests and had proved favourable. And after the first shock the trumpets blared out, and the legionaries jumped out of their coracles and splashed ashore. The cavalry officers mounted their horses and formed up, the soldiers lifted their javelins ready to hurl at the enemy.

The resistance melted as soon as the Roman army showed that they were no longer in awe of the fanatics. A massacre had taken place on the island of Mona I read. I looked at my brother, "Marcus is all right, none of the cavalry were injured. In fact we probably lost very few, if any soldiers. There was no effective opposition it says here, I'm only upset that I didn't realise the war had started."

"But it's over now isn't it?" Gaius asked.

I nodded, "I think so, I suppose they will be leaving Deva soon, and Marcus will return to Camulodunum. Still at least it's finished now and he shouldn't have to fight again." I leaned over and picked Larius up and held him tightly, as I cuddled him I thought about his father, and wondered how long it would be before I saw him again. Before he could see his baby son, but at least I could be sure he was safe now, with presumably no more wars to fight.

Unfortunately my relief was short lived, the next day again Gaius showed me the 'Gazette'. It seemed there was worse trouble to come. I read with deepening horror of outright revolt in the South of Britannia. Camlodunum had been sacked and burned to the ground, and Londinium was in danger of the same fate. Although there was hope that Seutonius might be able to reach there before the rebels, and rescue it from the same fate as Camulodunum. I was only relieved that Marcus was not there, as he was riding with Seutonius and the rest of the cavalry towards Londinium.

This was terrible news, I was frantic with worry, I had no way of knowing what was really happening in Britannia. People escaping the sack of Camulodunum had by this time reached Rome, and the tales they told of the atrocities there were horrendous. I desperately read the 'Gazette' every day now to try to find out what was going on. The news grew worse, unable to protect Londinium with just the cavalry, Seutonius had left it to it's fate, which was the same as that of Camulodunum, it was also sacked and burned, with dreadful tortures inflicted on Roman citizens before death.

I was becoming so frightened I hardly dared to read the News Sheet any more. For some considerable time there was no news of the whereabouts of Seutonius and the Roman army. We heard vaguely that after he left Londinium his movements were to us obscure. I knew Marcus was with him, they were, we heard, meeting up with the infantry travelling down from Wales. They were probably stocking up with food and supplies in preparation for the final battle. I was extremely unhappy knowing that this had to come, but I knew it had to take place as presumably if it did not, the British tribes would have the upper hand, and maybe even succeed in driving us out of Britannia. The Roman government would be most displeased if this should happen, and it was up to the Governor of Britannia to see that it did not.

Julia came to visit me one day, she had heard the news from Britannia as who had not by now. "What are you planning to do?" she asked me, "Will Marcus be all right?"

"There's nothing I can do," I replied, "He'll be all right at the moment, but there will be another battle, there has to be."

"Are you afraid for him?" she asked

"I'm terrified, I wish he'd come home, but of course he could never be spared as things are at present."

The waiting for news became intolerable to me.

The Festival of Augustus was celebrated in the town that year as usual, and we all attended the revels. But as we were not allowed the gladiatorial games, to me at least they fell flat. Half-heartedly I accompanied the rest of my family, leaving Larius at home with Oenone. The heat seemed more oppressive than usual somehow, and my mind was elsewhere, in Britannia mainly. People discussed the situation there with great interest, and with horror for the atrocities inflicted on our countrymen by the barbarian tribes of that land. There were theatre events to attend, but my mind was not on the performances, nor did I wish to attend any parties or private celebrations. It was almost a relief to me when the festivities were over for that year. People were sympathetic to me, knowing my husband was involved in the trouble in Britannia.

In fact the festival had only just ended when the news came through of a final battle against the British, led by a queen called Boadicea. This queen of one of the tribes called Iceni, the report said, had been the instigator of the rebellion. She had gathered up an army of sorts, (it said) and they had made their way to Camulodunum and Londinium. Then instead of following Seutonius, they had turned back and sacked a third town called Verulamium. In the time it took her and her followers to do that, Seutonius had gathered reinforcements and supplies, and (it was said) probably left clues of his whereabouts so that the British would find him. If he had not done this, it could have taken many months until the final confrontation took place. This would have been a bad idea as food would have run short on the Roman side, so they left a trail of their route so that the enemy would follow them. Even though Seutonius was short of troops, having only ten thousand including the auxiliaries, it was better to face down the adversary then, than to wait until later. The foe consisted of fifty thousand fighting men, but they had wagons containing their entire families it appeared, including domestic pets and farmyard animals.

It must have been very disorganised compared to the Roman fighting force, which though outnumbered was in a better position, having taken up their own places with care, with a forest at their back, to wait for the approaching tribes, who spread themselves out on the open ground opposite the Roman troops. Then, according to the account in the Gazette, they charged and loosed their arrows. The Roman army stood still, protecting themselves with their shields, until the advancing Celts had loosed their last arrows. Then they flung their javelins, these I knew from history lessons at school, could wreak havoc on an enemy. The British were also charging uphill, an enormous disadvantage, even I could see that, and I'm no expert on military tactics. I am not sure how long all of this lasted, but at the end of the battle there were eighty thousand British dead, and barely four hundred Roman dead, and very few injured.

The details I would have to wait for until Marcus came home, but at least I now knew that the worst was over. There would be a follow up of course, but any skirmishes would be minor, with the enemy decimated as it now was.

I settled down to wait as patiently as I could for Marcus to get leave. It would not be too soon I knew, as there was still a lot to be done in Britannia. Reports came in from time to time throughout the autumn and winter, a war of attrition continued as the Roman army hunted down the remaining rebels, which was basically anyone who had not actively supported the Romans in any way during the insurrection. The facts were not really made clear to us in the occasional reports in the Gazette. I would have to wait for Marcus to tell me the true details, I did not know how long it would be before I saw him again.

One day the following summer I went shopping in the Forum with Julia, we were choosing materials for new dresses. Having made our selection we entered a wine bar we often frequented when shopping on our own. It was the one near the Forum where we had sat the day Drusilla and I had met Julia when I was buying cloth during my pregnancy.

"So Drusus has decided to remain with your father in the wine trade you say?"

"Yes, I'm so thankful he's no longer going to fight in the arena. I feel really sorry for you at the moment, I suppose you've not heard from Marcus recently?"

"No, he's too busy searching. for British rebels to write to me it seems."

"It must be difficult for him though, but I thought army couriers were so good."

"So they are usually, but in the last letter I had from him he said there wasn't time to write very often as they were marching through thick forests and marshy country. And by the time they rested for the night they were all exhausted, cold and damp. It's a dreadful place for weather, they are on foot most of the time, instead of on horseback as officers usually are."

We left the wine bar and walked through the streets towards our homes. The late afternoon sun glared down on us as we strolled.

"A bath would be nice now," I remarked, "With all the trimmings. Tepidarium, caldarium and fridgidarium."

Julia sighed and nodded, "No time though, Drusus is expecting me, he'll wonder where I am as it is."

Regretfully I agreed, I envied her having her man to go home to, how long I wondered before I would see Marcus again.

As I entered the atrium the cool dimness was welcome after the heat outside. The door to the tablinium was half closed, although we usually left it open at this time of day in the summer. I shrugged and went towards it, I wanted to show my purchases to whoever might be there. Probably my mother or Drusilla or both I assumed. Pushing the door open I stopped in my tracks stunned. I could not believe my eyes. My mother was indeed in there, but reclining on a couch at the centre of the room lay Marcus! He had little Larius cuddled up beside him, so they had found each other then. I burst into tears of shock and joy, my knees gave way, I sank onto a nearby couch. They stared at me.

"Come now Claudia," my mother said, "Is that any way to greet your husband?"

Marcus could not move immediately or Larius would have fallen, he sat up and held out his other arm to me. I flew to him laughing and crying almost hysterically, I kissed him on the mouth.

"Tata," Larius informed me indicating Marcus, "he's my tata."

"That's right darling, your tata's come home to us at last." I looked up, "when did you get here?"

"He arrived about two hours ago," my mother said.

"Not quite as long as that surely," said Marcus. He still wore his full uniform, as soon as he arrived word went round and the child was brought to him. Everyone knew I was out, in fact my mother was the only family member at home when he first appeared. She came over now and took Larius from Marcus, he screamed suddenly, "want tata."

"Hush darling," said his grandma, "your mama and tata want to be alone to greet each other."

"It's all right, " I said, "let him remain in the room."

"Yes," Marcus agreed, "I've got a present for him in my baggage."

"He can have it later," my mother said, "he's over excited as it is. I'll change him, he's wet."

"Don't take him too far away," Marcus said. "I've only just met my son."

"Bring him straight back in here when he's ready mama," I said.

After they left I flung my arms around Marcus, we embraced and kissed. "Our son was impressed that I was a soldier," Marcus said.

"Oh yes, he would be, he's seen soldiers in the street from time to time as well as having toy ones to play with. You being in the army would impress him, although of course he's too young to understand what we've been saying about you being involved in the war in Britannia. Tell me about it," I wound my arms around his neck. "I've been so distressed with everything we've been hearing about what's been going on. I more or less guessed that you were all right as a cavalry officer. Were you in any danger at all?"

Putting his arms around me he pulled me closer and kissed me thoroughly, fiercely, I returned his ardour with interest, we clung to each other. His metal cuirass got in the way, I laughed, "I'm not the enemy you know, you don't have to wear full armour for me."

"Mmmmn, I'm too tired it seems to take my clothes off," he went on kissing and cuddling me. I was excited, I would have liked to make love to him then and there, but just then my mother returned with Larius. "Are you sure you want him in here now?" she asked.

We broke apart, Marcus held out his arms to his son, "Come to tata Lari."

He toddled unsteadily across the floor, I went to pick him up, he yelled again, "tata, want tata."

I handed him over to his father who rose to a sitting position and took the child onto his lap. Larius stopped crying and gazed at his father enraptured, he was totally fascinated with him. Then Marcus said, "Tata's tired Lari, he needs to sleep."

Finally we managed to pacify Larius, and assure him his tata was not going to disappear. Then arms entwined, almost leaning on each other we made our way to our apartment at the end of the colonnade. I helped Marcus to remove his uniform, he had taken off the brilliant red cloak earlier and had left it in the tablinium. He collapsed onto the bed, I joined him, but suddenly he fell fast asleep lying flat on his back. He began to snore loudly, I rose from the bed and withdrawing from the room, I left him to it.

Marcus slept for the rest of that day, when I retired to bed he barely stirred. We arranged a celebration dinner for the following evening, with our family and Marcus' mother and father. It must have seemed strange to them him not going home to their house as soon as he arrived in Pompeii, but for them to have to come to our house to see him. The baby was allowed to attend the very early part of the meal, he was eating with a spoon by now. But Oenone came with him to attend to him while he had his supper. When our main course was brought in she lifted him up and took him to his bed. Marcus was enchanted with his son, he could hardly bear to be parted from him. The attraction was certainly mutual, Larius screaming when he had to be separated from Marcus, although tonight he was luckily almost asleep when Oenone removed him.

Marcus had already told me something about the fighting in Britannia, now he explained the situation to his parents. Seutonius, he said, had now been recalled to Rome, although not in any disgrace, he was going to stand for consul again. And he would surely be elected, as the campaign in Britannia had made him if anything even more popular that he was when he first became Governor there. There had been an enquiry led by an Imperial freedman named Polyclitus, and some discrepancies had been found, mainly a number of ships and their crews appeared to have gone missing. Seutonius would not have a triumph in Rome because of this and a few other problems. But the army supported him, so the Emperor's secretary had to be careful how he proceeded.

The trouble had started because the Procurator, Catus Decianus had resorted to extortion in Seutonius' absence in Wales. He had called in loans of monies that had been given to the Iceni tribe, which they had been assured that they did not have to repay. After the death of the Icenian king Prasurtargus, Catus sent in his troops to collect the money, which he claimed belonged to Rome and the Emperor Nero. Half the king's fortune had in any case been left to Nero, but Catus insisted that Rome should have it all. The soldiers he sent were from his personal guard, as Seutonius had pulled all the others out to fight in Wales. These men were presumably of the same type of person as the Procurator himself, they had flogged the queen and raped her daughters.

All this Marcus told us that evening at dinner, I had heard some of it from him earlier as I have said, but this was the full story. Catus, he said, had fled the country when the revolt began. The fact that he was a coward was harder to forgive than the fact that he was a crook.

"What was this queen like?" I asked.

"Well," Marcus replied, "She rode in a chariot, the small wicker sided ones that the British have. Although most of the others were on foot as our soldiers were."

"Yes, but what did she look like?" I persisted.

Marcus thought for a moment. "A big woman with long reddish hair. We were rather busy at the time, and we were facing a screaming charging horde. Individuals, even queens tend to look much alike when one is riding up and down on the flanks of an army. As an officer has to do in battle, then we charged with our lances."

"Were you in any danger at all?" I asked again.

"Most of the cavalry wasn't really as the enemy became a rabble quite quickly. Of course there's always some danger in a battle, but less for a tribune than for a legionary soldier."

"What happened to the queen afterwards, was she killed in the battle?"

"No she escaped with her daughters who were with her. But after she returned to her home she apparently killed herself by taking poison."

"But that battle really won the war," Marcus' father joined in, "that's what we heard."

"Yes pater, but there was open rebellion even when the war was supposed to be over, and Boadicea had killed herself and presumably her two daughters as well. We could not afford to leave the rest of the Iceni and Trinovante tribes to wage possible guerrilla war on us. It was no fun I can assure you searching for them through woods and marshes in the rain."

Gaius joined in the conversation, "I expect Seutonius was annoyed that all this should happen just when he had won a victory in Wales."

"Oh yes, he wasn't at all happy, he was in a bad mood all the time we rode around trying to gather reinforcements. Having to withdraw from Londinium was aggravation enough as it was. He was furious about the rebellion succeeding when we have such a good intelligence service. Usually we know about any insurrection while it is still in the planning stage, to let this one get out of control was bad enough. Then when we reached Glevum the commander of the fort there flatly refused to join us."

"But why?" we asked practically in unison, "why would he refuse to fight?"

"Who knows," Marcus replied, "We had no idea why he refused. He wouldn't have been Camp Prefect if he had been a physical coward. The actual Legate was not there and Postumus was in his place. He committed suicide when he heard about the battle, but with the second legion we could have held Londinium. It was awful having to withdraw and leave them to their fate, and what a fate!"

"Not now Marcus," said his mother, "we did hear about what happened there."

"And then she made her big mistake." Marcus continued. "It was an error on her part not to have persued us from Londinium. But instead she turned around and sacked Verulamium, a bad mistake. It gave us the chance to get ourselves together, even though we were outnumbered."

After the meal was over he looked exhausted again, "Come on let's go to bed," he said to me.

The following day Julia and Drusus paid us a visit, eager to hear the news about the war from Marcus.

"We've read about it in the Gazette of course," Julia said, "But when we heard that Marcus was home Drusus couldn't wait to hear a first hand account of what's been going on in Britannia all these months."

It was true, there had been trouble there ever since Marcus had returned from his last leave. He had not had a moment's peace, but had had to ride to Deva immediately, to join Seutonius and the legions.

We sat in chairs in the garden around a table and drank watered wine and ate honey cakes. Marcus looked relaxed for once, he had been tense since returning home, he had had a difficult time these last few months. He and Drusus were talking about the war again, Drusus desperate for first hand information. His former colleagues had all left Pompeii after the riot in the amphitheatre, and he was lonely for masculine company of his own age. He and Marcus got on well together, and he admired Marcus although he was not anxious to join the army himself.

"Is Marcus going back to Britannia when his leave is up?" Julia asked me.

I shook my head, "I'm not quite sure what he's got in mind. I'd like him to get a local posting."

"Do you think he will?"

I looked at Marcus now chatting animatedly with Drusus, telling him what he had told us last night at dinner. "To be honest I don't think he knows himself what he wants. But I don't think he'll return to Britannia after all the trouble there, it was pretty horrendous to say the least. Anyway he's been there quite some time, he's due for a change, but whether it will be near here I can't say."

"I'm sure you're glad to have him back aren't you?" Julia asked. "You've been alone so long, it must be good to have him back with you."

I understood her meaning, she was curious to know about our love life. "Actually he's been too tired up to now for any lovemaking, if that's what you're asking about."

"You mean not at all? And he's been home for three days!"

I nodded, "I'm sorry to disappoint you but no, but he seems livelier today."

"Disappoint me!" Julia exclaimed, "Surely you're the one who's disappointed."

Uncomfortable with this line of questioning I turned my attention to the men, hoping to divert Julia from my sex life. They were still discussing the war, Drusus said, "So how many legions did you have in all then?"

"Two when we finally met up, the fourteenth and the twentieth, but that only made up ten thousand troops on the ground as well as the cavalry."

"And how many men did the enemy have?"

"Fifty thousand actually fighting, but they insist on bringing their whole families to war, women, children and animals as well. With unwieldy wagons following behind them. It was a shambles."

After they had left Marcus said "Where's Larius?"

I went to find him, he was playing with the toy chariot that Marcus had brought him, I lifted him up. "Come and see tata darling."

I carried him through to the atrium where Marcus waited, he held out his arms, I handed the child over to him. Drusilla don't you feel tempted to have one like him?"

She did not know what to say I could see, after all she had seen the agony I went through, but did not like to say so.

"What does Gaius say?" Marcus continued, "Doesn't he fancy the idea?"

I wished he'd stop talking along these lines, it was embarrassing for Drusilla, and worried me, although I think he was quite satisfied with the one we had.

"There's time enough," Drusilla said, "Gaius is in no hurry."

It was true there was no hurry for them to have a child, Larius would inherit if they did not anyway, why could Marcus not keep quite? I lifted the baby up from the floor where Marcus had deposited him, and hugged him, "Let's go and find some lunch."

I had hoped to have Marcus to myself that afternoon, but some ex army friends of his called to see him. It was not until we retired to bed that night that I had him alone, and hopefully in the right mood at last. My hopes were realised that night, his passion aroused he attended to me at last. It had been worth the wait, none of his ardour had been diminished I found to my delight, (I was a bit worried, it had been three days). We made love fiercely, neither of us could get enough of the other, it was dawn before we fell into an exhausted sleep.

I was not sure what Marcus' future plans were, he had finished his tour of duty in Britannia. Especially with Seutonius Paulinus no longer the Governor there. I was still hoping that he would get a local post near Pompeii, though I hardly dared to ask him. "Why did Seutonius decide to fight the Druids anyway?" I asked idly.

"They had to be put down, they practiced human sacrifice for Jupiter's sake, what else could we do."

I stared at him in disbelief, "what do you mean?"

He shuddered, "They put their victims inside wicker cages, then set fire to them. It was terrible. We could not allow that sort of barbarity to continue, we had to put a stop to it. They had these oak tree groves where they performed their rites, we burnt them all so they could no longer engage in these monstrous activities."

We were reclining in the peristyle in the hot sun, it was August again and the heat was punishing, but Marcus was enjoying it. It was a treat after hunting insurgent tribesmen in the rain he said.

"What are you planning to do now?" I ventured, "Have you any idea where your next posting will be?"

He was silent for a moment brooding, finally he said, "I'm trying to get an appointment in the local militia, I'm going to see the commanding officer tomorrow. After all I've done my duty to the Empire by now I think."

He had been in Mauretania before Britannia, not an easy posting either. It would be nice if he could be near here, then he could come home every time he had a few days off. I hoped for this, "Have you got an appointment?"

"Yes, I told you, I'm going tomorrow," he sounded irritable.

"I'm sorry I didn't realise, I thought perhaps you were going on the off chance, is there any likihood do you think?"

"We'll have to see won't we?" he said.

The following evening he came home looking pleased, he hugged me, "I've got it, I start as soon as my leave is over."

I was thrilled, "We should celebrate, what shall we do?"

"Whatever, but not tonight I'm tired." He was also relieved, it was a load off his mind obviously. In the meantime he had three months leave, things were definitely improving for us, we would not have to be separated for any length of time again. He would come home here on nights when he was not on duty or on call, we would be together.

CHAPTER FIFTEEN

FATEFUL ENCOUNTER

It was early in January, Marcus had started his new job with the local militia. He was settling in well, and enjoying being near his family after being so long on Frontier Outposts, with no hope of seeing them for several years at a time. He had been on local duty for just over two months, and we saw each other about once a week. We had been invited to a large party at the home of a mutual friend, and we were hoping that Marcus would be able to get time off so we could attend it together. I had no intention of going on my own, but I did want to attend.

Finally, as the time drew nearer Marcus came home and told me he had two days leave. We were delighted, as I at least had never been to that particular house before, and did not know what to expect. As it happened I got more than I bargained for. Marcus and I set off together on the evening of the party, travelling in a litter.

We reached the house which was some way outside the town, almost into Oplontis, our nearest neighbour. Although the house was some way outside the village itself. It was an enormous mansion with two large colonnaded wings, one on each side of a tall central edifice built on lofty pillars. It was very impressive and imposing, especially as it was lit up. Some tables were laid out in the entrance, these were laden with wine of all varieties. Including of course hot mulled wine, which was appropriate to the winter weather. Pausing we helped ourselves to beakers of the hot wine, then we entered the atrium. This was spacious and full of bronze statues in niches surrounding the central space which was crowded with guests.

We looked around for our host, who we really had only a cursory acquaintance with. I assumed we had only been invited to swell the crowd, as it seemed to be the kind of gathering where quantity was the main concern. Not that there was anything wrong with the quality of the entertainment, as obviously no expense had been spared. Gaius and Drusilla came up behind us, they had arrived in another litter carried behind our own, and had just come in. We turned to them, "Where are the people who are giving the party?" I asked them. They shook their heads, "I can't see him at the moment." Gaius said. They also carried cups of mulled wine. "What do you think of this house?" Drusilla asked.

"Rather ostentatious I think," replied Gaius.

There were both colymbadian olives in olive oil with herbs, and the halmadian kind soaking in brine. Sausage meats, dishes of lettuce sliced with leeks, and tunnyfish pieces with sliced eggs. There were also more large bowls of wine standing on the tables.

The atrium led into a large triclinium which was also packed with guests, we moved towards it, still searching for our host. Not knowing him very well made this difficult, he could be anywhere in this enormous house I thought. Temporarily giving up on finding him we stopped by a laden table. There was potted salad made with bread layered with chicken slices, cucumbers, pine nuts and cheese, with a rich dressing poured over it. We helped ourselves to small portions of this which was chilled in snow. It was rather cold fare for the winter weather, and we looked around to see what else was on offer. A lot of people were already reclining on the dinner couches that were, of course spread around, some of these were scattered in the atrium as well. As we stood there a large florid man in a flowing dinner gown came in, seeing us he came over and shook hands with us all. "I'm so sorry I wasn't here to greet you, I had to check that the main course was ready to serve. Really some slaves these days! You can't trust them to do anything without supervision."

We smiled and nodded sympathetically at him, we only knew him slightly as I have previously stated. His name was Diomedes, a rich Greek merchant with obviously a love of extreme ostentation. A hunting scene covered one wall, on the opposite one Bacchus sported with Ariadne, while maenads rampaged around them.

"Ah," said Diomedes "Here come the slaves with the food," he rushed to superintend them, we looked at each other. "I've never met him before," Gaius said, "Have you?"

"No," Marcus replied. "But my parents know him, they should be coming tonight."

I tore my gaze from the rampant paintings, "Is that why we're invited? I was wondering" I had not questioned the invitation too thoroughly, any party was amusing, why examine too closely the reason for being asked, even if one did not know the people too well, or even not at all.

Clodius came towards us, thank the gods, someone we knew at last! He had his pretty dark haired girl friend with him I noticed. She had been at his house on the night that Marcus had proposed to me. Like myself and Drusilla she wore a gown of soft felt, hers was in black, which suited her, she was very beautiful I thought, no wonder Clodius was fond of her as he must be. He tended not to keep the same women friends for very long, this one appeared to have lasted.

"Do you know our host well?" I asked him.

"Yes, quite well," Closius replied, he turned to Marcus and inquired what he was doing now, Marcus told him. "So you're stationed locally then!" he exclaimed, "that must please you Claudia."

"It does," I answered, "I'm glad he's no longer posted abroad."

"Let's eat," said Lucia, Clodius' friend, "I'm hungry."

Together we all approached the tables, we helped ourselves to oysters stewed in wine, followed by lobster baked in coriander sauce, with fish pickle sauce also added. This was accompanied by green beans, leeks and fennel. Large cups of wine were passed around to accompany the main course. There was even a dish of boleti mushrooms (very expensive) nothing but the best here it appeared.

Suddenly a fanfare sounded, we looked up, "Oh no!" Gaius groaned, "Look at that, it's flamingo!"

Marcus looked up, "I don't believe it, how vulgar can he get?"

I stared in astonishment, "I've never seen it in real life before, only in novels."

"One particular novel," said Marcus, "About a vulgar freedman who tries to outdo everyone else."

"Are we actually supposed to eat it?" Drussila gasped.

"I'm not," Gaius replied, "Are you Marcus?"

He shook his head, "Let's disappear into the crowd."

The idea of actually eating such a bird was repellent to me, but some people were literally going to have some of it. The flamingo was served up with it's plumage, so there would be no mistake as to what it was.

"I need another drink," Marcus said, "Come on lets move to the atrium."

Flagons of falernian wine stood on much decorated marble tables. We poured ourselves some into goblets of blue Syrian glass, and watched to see what would happen next. This happened to be dessert, rich sweet cakes peppered with cinnamon and nutmeg, we helped ourselves to dates with almonds rolled in cinnamon inside, as well as the cakes.

A man approached us, it was Cealius who Julia had once had a fling with, I recognised him from the night I had first met Marcus. He was delighted to see Marcus now, he picked up a flagon and poured wine for himself and Marcus. They retired together for a chat to a bench that had just emptied, Marcus looked at me but I shook my head, I had to find a privy.

Afterwards I wandered round the other rooms of the house, most of them were crowded with guests. There were some smaller rooms furnished with couches, it was obvious for what purpose. There were openly lewd lamps in each of them, most of a phallic shape. As I turned to leave and find my way back to the party a man suddenly loomed up in front of me. He wore a handsome toga over a purple tunic, it was Marcellus! I stared at him rigid with shock, I had never thought to encounter him anywhere suddenly like this.

"I suppose you do recognise me?" he asked. "Or had you forgotten all about me, with your grand marriage to the tribune." I was unable to find an answer to this, he went on, "you couldn't wait for me to return from the East, oh no, you couldn't wait to bed the tribune could you?"

I shrank back, "It wasn't like that."

"What was it like then?" he asked.

"You had been gone a long time when I met Marcus again. I was thinking you'd never come home."

"Surely you knew I'd have to return sometime, why did you have to marry the tribune, couldn't you have just had an affair with him?" I could have excused that, I was away for a long time I admit, longer than I had expected to be. But no, it had to be marriage, and I hear you have a child as well." I nodded. "How old is the child now?"

"He's eighteen months old." My knees felt weak, I was in shock, I had not expected this kind of confrontation, especially not at a social gathering. There was no one else in sight, I looked around hoping someone would come and unwittingly rescue me from this unendurable situation. He smiled and barred the entrance to the small room he had managed to manoeuvre me into. I was trapped I realised, there was no escape from this encounter. "My husband will be looking for me," I tried.

He grinned, "Oh I don't think so, the tribune is completely engrossed with his friend."

I gaped at him, "How do you know where he is? Did you plan this?"

He smiled unpleasantly, "Oh I knew you were here, I saw you all come in earlier."

"I didn't see you."

"No I made sure of that, I was afraid you might try to avoid me if you were aware I was here, I wanted to speak to you alone."

"But why?" I was concerned, there was no escape, I turned on him suddenly, "It's as much your fault as mine that things have turned out the way they have. If you hadn't gone away, and stayed away so long, maybe things would've been different. As it is I'm happily married to Marcus Lucullus and we have a son. I don't know what you expect to gain by confronting me like this, I would like to leave now."

He barred my way, "Not until we've had a chat, I didn't think you were the maternal type, but you willingly it seems, had this man's child. Something I notice you would not have been willing to do for me, even if I had wanted it."

I stared at him in astonishment. "I never knew you wanted at child, we weren't married in any case."

"I would have married you, surely you know I'd have married you if you'd become pregnant. But you made quite sure that you did not."

I was stunned, having a baby was never on the agenda during my affair with Marcellus, why was he using this against me now? He was obviously jealous because I had deliberately he thought, got myself pregnant by Marcus. But why should I explain to him that it had been an accident, unplanned by either of us, I would not give him the satisfaction.

Before I realised what was happening he moved towards me. Pulling me into his arms suddenly, he forced my lips apart and kissed me thoroughly, insultingly, I tried to pull away, he gripped me tighter. Shoving me against the wall he pushed my skirt up.

"No!" I screamed, "Not this please!"

He was violently angry I could see, I had never known him behave like this before. He tore off my silk undergarment, "No!" I screamed again.

"There's no one to hear you," he taunted, "I'll have you once more at least."

"Please no," I sobbed.

Turning he flung me onto the divan which was so conveniently placed for assignations between party guests. But this was not like that, I was terrified, I tried to protect myself with a cushion, he tore it from my hands. This was rape, he was already parting my legs, I fought wildly, he laughed, "I'll make you want me."

To my shame feelings of pleasure began to sweep through me. Still I struggled to get away, but the feelings of gratification became stronger, my struggles grew less. Abruptly he stopped, "You did desire me, maybe you're just a whore."

I burst into tears of shame and rage, "How dare you, I never asked you to make love to me, if that's what you call it."

He looked at me in contempt, "No it's not what I call it, I despise you, go back to your husband, I want no more to do with you."

Adjusting his clothes he stormed from the room.

I lay on the couch where he had left me, I was shaking all over, appalled at the way Marcellus had violated me. And by his scorn of me, and the contemptuous way he had looked at me afterwards. I do not know how long I had lain there when I heard sounds outside, other people it seemed were coming to make use of the small side rooms. Someone peered round the curtain at me before finding an empty cubicle. Pulling myself together I struggled to repair the ravages to my clothing. My green felt dress was disarranged but intact, I hid my torn undergarment under a cushion on the couch. Peeping out I saw the coast was clear, sound came from behind drawn curtains in some of the other rooms, no one saw me as I made my way back to the party.

A full-scale orgy was in progress as I entered the atrium, I looked for

Marcus, but could not see him. Where was he, had he got involved with a woman somewhere I wondered. After all everyone else was at it, so why not him, or had he gone looking for me? How could I possibly explain my bedraggled appearance. I took a step further into the room, two men writhed together at my feet, I stepped over them and continued to search the main reception rooms.

There was no sign of Gaius and Drusilla either, had they disappeared somewhere together I wondered. Uncertain what to do I stared around me, some people were still in groups talking together. Our host was surrounded by a large crowd, he had a pretty slave boy on his lap as he sat conversing with his friends. I turned away, I had no desire to be seen by him at present, he could not help me in any case.

A young man grabbed me and pulled me towards him, he was I saw handsome enough, and after what I had just been through with Marcellus any appreciation was welcome. At least he did not despise me as Marcellus had, I turned and embraced him, after all why not? I expected Marcus was doing the same. My self-esteem was in shreds, and I was frustrated after Marcellus had so scornfully cast me aside, if my husband was also being unfaithful to me why should I care what I did, or with whom. My companion put his arm around my waist and began to lead me in the direction of the private cubicles, I pulled back. "Not there, they're all full anyway."

He stared at me a moment, then he grinned knowingly, "Been there already have you? All right this corner will do."

"You have to pass that way to find the privy," I justified myself.

He nodded, "All right I believe you." Not that he cared anyway, he was pressing himself against me, I did not fight him off, nobody was bothered anyway. Not even my husband presumably, I could have been anywhere for all he knew or cared it seemed.

Mushroom caps were being passed around among some of the partygoers, my companion reached over and took some from a passing guest. He handed me one, I took it, why not? He laughed, "Be careful, too many and you'll hallucinate."

"I know that," I nibbled one and looked around, "I'd like some wine," I had not had time to pour myself a drink since I returned to the party, I sorely needed one. My would be lover filled a goblet from a flagon on the table and handed it to me. I drank deeply, he laughed again, "You seem determined to be unconscious it appears,"

I wanted to forget the events of the past hour, at least temporarily, I nibbled another cap mushroom, things went hazy, I clung to my partner and kissed him hotly, he responded with enthusiasm. We sank onto the floor, all other places were taken, and lots of people were embracing on the floor anyway. I helped him remove my dress, most people were naked by now, we joined them. Keeping my mouth on his I wound my legs around him. I was shameless, brazen, I did not care what anyone thought of me now, I was certain my husband was similarly occupied, and I was getting my own back on both him and Marcellus.

After it was over I passed out still clutching my companion. When I awoke Gaius and Drusilla were there, they were engrossed in an argument of their own, and paid no immediate attention to me. I sat up and reached for my gown, Drusilla threw it at me, she was angrier with Gaius than with me.

"Where's Marcus?" I asked, they shook their heads, Drusilla's hair was disarranged as mine was, they both looked the worse for wear I noticed.

"Dress yourself," Gaius commanded me, I struggled into my gown, "Come on we're going home."

I followed them out of the house, slaves were hanging about waiting for their masters, we located our's and ordered them to bring our litters. It was still dark and I felt cold, I could not find my wrap, neither could my brother and his wife, finally we located them in the litters.

"What about Marcus?" I asked, "How will he get home?" Gaius shrugged, "If he's up to what I think he is, let him find his own way home."

I glared at him, "What about you? What have you been doing all evening? Whatever it was it was not with your wife I'll bet."

I noticed that Drusilla's dress was torn, I gazed at it meaningly, they could not criticise me I decided when they had both been up to no good themselves. This was the reason for their dispute it was obvious, although surely in their case they could let bygones be bygones considering they were both guilty of promiscuity with at least one other partner. I was too, but I was not making a scene about it, even though I knew Marcus must be with someone. Just then he appeared, he also looked the worse for wear, I avoided his eyes, I did not want an argument just now, we were both culpable, it would be no use blaming each other. Better just forget about whatever happened, I had no intention of seeing my lover of the previous night again, and I assumed it was the same for the others. I hoped so anyway, I glanced side ways at Marcus, he gazed straight ahead as we lay in the litter.

When we finally reached our home we all four quickly made our way towards our respective quarters. When we reached ours, still not meeting each others gaze we removed our clothes and fell into bed. I was much too tired for a discussion now and so was Marcus, we were soon asleep. When I woke I saw by the waterclock by the bed that it was nearly noon, Marcus still slept. My head swam as I tried to lift it from the pillow, pulling the bedding tighter around me I gave up any attempt to rise. After a while it became imperative that I move, throwing a cloak around me I ventured out into the portico and made my way to the latrine in the main bath area. A bath would be a good idea now I thought, and have the added advantage of not having to face Marcus just yet. Climbing into the bath I ran water from the showerbath over myself. I needed to feel clean again after last nights excesses, including the unpleasantness with Marcellus which had led to my later unrestrained behaviour. I sat in the bath, the water was delightfully hot, as I relaxed I pondered. I did not wish to tell anyone about the scene with Marcellus, not my brother and his wife and especially not Marcus.

As for Marcus, what was the situation between us I wondered, could I confront him and demand to know where he had been and with whom? He would not know of my own immoderate behaviour so perhaps I could brazen it out with him and exact a confession. I could just let it go of course and let things carry on as if nothing had occurred, after all these things happened, we all did them at occasions like last night, and usually carried on as normal afterwards. If I had been single I would have thought no more about it, so why make trouble in our marriage because we had both got carried away at a party, it would likely happen again, though not too often I hoped.

Climbing out of the bath I dried myself and wrapped my cloak around myself again. It was a chilly walk back to our room, Marcus was awake when I got back, we stared at each other, we could hardly go on not looking at each other indefinitely. I began looking for a warm gown to put on, Marcus sat on the bed, I turned to him, "Let's go and find something to eat, it's lunch time."

He nodded and putting on a tunic he followed me out of the room.

A meal was laid out in the winter dining room, a small family room to the right of the atrium. Gaius and Drusilla were in there reclining at the table eating a pine nut omelette, we asked for the same, and a slave served us, we drank fruit juice. I glanced at the other two to see if they had made it up yet between them. They gave no sign, in fact they were not looking at each other, but they both looked curiously at us. I tried a smile, Marcus kept his eyes on his food, nobody asked if anyone had enjoyed themselves the previous evening.

"Cold isn't it?" I asked

"What do you expect it is January," Drusilla snapped.

"There's no need to be so bad tempered," I said, "Can't we forget what happened or didn't happen last night?"

All three of them glared at me, I took a bite of my omelette and decided to keep my head down for the moment. Everybody was hung over, and I was probably not the only one who had had to hurry to the lavatory this morning.

Gaius rose from the table, "I've got a business meeting with father and Marcellus."

I was stunned, "you mean he's coming here?"

"And why shouldn't he?" Gauis demanded, "we're still friends, just because you -." He stopped suddenly, Marcus looked up. "I spoke to him last night," Gaius continued, I gaped at him, when I wondered, was it before or after our encounter? Surely Marcellus had not said anything about it to Gaius, I shrank back.

"Olympos!" Gaius exclaimed, "What is the matter with you? Marcellus and I have business interests in common, what did you expect?" He left the room, the rest of us remained,

Drusilla rose, "I'm going to rest, I'm still tired."

Marcus and I were left alone, "what was all that about?" he asked.

I shook my head, "Nothing, just Gaius in one of his moods."

"Who is this man Marcellus anyway?" he asked. "You looked shaken because he was coming here today."

"Just a business friend of the family," I got up, "I think I'll go back to bed too."

When Marcus returned to our room I was sitting at my cosmetics tables staring into a silver mirror.

"I thought you were going to bed, you said you were tired."

"I am," I moved to the bed and lay down on top of the covers still fully dressed. Marcus lay down on the opposite side, "Maybe I'll go back to work today instead of waiting for tomorrow, it'll be an early start from here anyway."

I looked at him in trepidation, "Why? You said you had two days off."

"I have, but if I went back today I could save myself the rush."

We lay in silence, I was upset by this, what had gone wrong between us, he could not know of my behaviour last night, he had been too occupied with his own. He did not join us until we were in the litters, he was not there when Gaius and Drusilla had found me, so what could he know? I turned towards him, "what's wrong, why are you behaving like this towards me?"

"Behaving like what?"

"So coldly, what happened last night?"

"Nothing" he snapped, "What should have happened?"

"Well you weren't around, I wondered where you'd gone."

"You were a long time returning yourself, you said you were only going for a piss."

I had not put it quite like that but I let it pass, "I got waylaid."

"Who by?"

"No one you'd know, we got talking," I lied. "You were busy talking to Caelius when I left."

He did not answer, I turned away from him, "I'm going to sleep for a while."

Marcus did not leave that night to my relief, but we still preferred to join the family rather than be alone together for the rest of that day. But when we retired for the night he turned towards me in bed, and took me in his arms. I returned his embrace, this was better, we made love enthusiastically, I was relaxed for the first time that day. Afterwards we held each other, he ran his hand down me "you've got a beautiful body, try not to be so free with it in future."

I laughed shakily, "And the same goes for you."

"I love you, you know that, what happened last night meant nothing."

I cuddled up to him, "the same with me."

The following afternoon I found Drusilla in the small side sitting room, it was warm in there. I was not sure if my father and Gaius had any meetings planned, so I avoided the tablinium. My sister-in-law looked at me sourly, "you're looking very pleased with yourself. Marcus left this morning I assume."

I nodded and smiled happily, "Everything's all right between us now. He was very loving last night."

"Does he know about what happened? Come to that what did he get up to?"

"It doesn't matter, we confessed everything to each other. None of it meant anything to either of us. I just wanted to get even with him that's all, I knew he must be with another woman. How are things between you and Gaius?"

"They've been worse, but I don't think we've forgiven each other yet?"

"I don't see why my brother should blame you, he's guilty himself."

"I know that, but it doesn't necessarily make it easier between us."

I sighed, why did everything have to be so complicated, it was not as if anybody was in love with anybody else. I pointed this out to Drusilla, she agreed. "He'll come round," I comforted her, "He has to really, surely that's obvious."

As the days passed the tension gradually eased, Gaius and Drusilla seemed more relaxed together. I would see Marcus again in a couple of day, I was looking forward to it, I was contented with life.

Unfortunately this did not last long. One afternoon I was passing through the atrium when there was a knock at the door. A business friend of my father's I guessed, the door slave opened the door, a minute later Marcellus entered the house. I was petrified after what had happened at the party, where was everybody? I stood my ground, "I presume you've come to see my father or Gaius."

He stood looking at me for a moment, he did not seem a bit abashed about what had happened between us, and his attack on me. "I have an appointment with Gaius yes, you surely didn't think I'd come to see you," he sneered. Just then Gaius arrived, he looked disconcerted to see us together, the atmosphere was leaden, I made my escape. This was something I had not foreseen, that there would still be business meetings in our house between my family and Marcellus Vinicius. Of course I should have known, but he had been away so long I had forgotten how close our two families were.

I was happy to see my husband when he came home for two nights leave, I felt safe and protected, although he had no idea he was supposed to be defending me from anyone or anything. We had a blissful day together, with Larius who was with us a lot of the time. Marcus and he had barely seen each other the last time Marcus was home. What with preparing for and attending the party, and the miserable feeling between us the following day, the child had been almost forgotten. We made up for it this time though, taking him out with us, well wrapped up against the cold.

The day after Marcus left I encountered Marcellus again, to my dismay. He was just leaving the house, there was no sign of my father or Gaius, or anyone else, we confronted each other. After all there was nothing he could do, it was my home and all I would have to do was call out if I needed help, he would know that.

"We can't go on like this can we?" he asked.

"No," I agreed. "We'd better have it out between us."

I led him towards a bench in a corner of the atrium, people would have got the wrong idea if we had gone into the private sitting room. In any case Drusilla was probably in there, but we had to talk to clear the air if, as was likely he was to continue coming to the house. I did not know where to begin, or how, come to that, I looked at him hesitantly. "You never wrote to me as you promised."

"Yes I did, I wrote regularly, but I believe you when you say you never had the letters, my parents didn't get theirs either. I explained in the letters the reason I was delayed, there were complications with the suppliers, it took longer than I expected. But I was coming to see you as soon as I returned to Pompeii, but of course I heard the news of your marriage, so naturally I didn't visit you."

"I'm sorry," I said, "But I really had given up hope you ever seeing you again."

"Surely you knew I'd have to return, I wouldn't just leave everything and remain in the East, whatever for? My family and all my business interests are in this town, you must've known I'd come home eventually. Why didn't you wait?"

"All right I assumed you'd come home ultimately, but I didn't know how long it would be. I could have waited for years, you could even have met someone else."

"Instead of which it was you who met someone else, but why the hurry to get married? You could've just have had an affair as I've said."

"And I expect you had affairs while you were away, I don't suppose you were celibate all the time."

"Whatever I did I didn't marry anyone, I intended to return to you, but you couldn't wait, you had to marry the tribune, and now you have a child."

I rose to my feet, "There's nothing more to be said, there's nothing to be gained by arguing."

He also rose, "All right, I'll go now, but I still have reasons to visit this house, so we may as well be pleasant to each other when we meet."

I nodded, "Yes, I don't want to quarrel, I'm sorry about how things turned out." I looked at him, he was as handsome as ever I thought.

He put his hand on my shoulder, "I'll see you."

His touch was electric, to my dismay I felt a shudder of desire for him, he still had an effect on me. I did not want this, my life was contented and pleasant, I had everything I could want, this complication I did not need. I moved away, he grinned knowingly, "Well I'll say goodbye." He left, I stood in the atrium appalled at my reaction to him, I had a husband and child, this could ruin everything if allowed to get out of control. I must control my urges towards Marcellus, it was over between us. Drusilla appeared, she had been in the small sitting room, "Is anything wrong? Who were you talking to?"

I shook my head, "No one," I ran towards my apartment.

CHAPTER SIXTEEN

EARTHQUAKE

January continued cold and chill, but as February began the weather turned warmer. One day early in the month the sun shone brilliantly out of a cloudless sky, though there was a feeling reminiscent of an impending thunderstorm, unusual at this time of the year. Then we heard a rumbling sound which we at first mistook for thunder. Minutes later the ground shook, there was the sound of falling masonry, we all ran out of the house to see what was going on. When we reached the gate of our dwelling we saw that buildings had collapsed, as we stared around us the ground heaved again and more buildings fell. We were horrified, an earthquake of fairly large proportions had occurred.

People began to rush through the streets, we tried to ask passers-by what was happening, but nobody would stop to talk to us. There was myself, my mother, Drusilla and some slaves huddled together by the gate. Where were my father and Gaius I wondered, were they caught in some damaged building? They had not gone up to the farm today, so they would be in the town.

The quakes seemed to have died down by now, I stepped further into the street and gazed around me. The nearby houses and shops did not seem as badly damaged as I had thought at first, but some devastation was apparent. Meriope pulled me back, just then my father and brother came hurrying into view.

"What's happening?" I asked.

Larius was crying in Oenone's arms.

"The Forum is nearly destroyed," my father got out, "All the main temples have collapsed."

"The rebuilt temple of Venus is a total wreck," Gaius told us, "and the others look ready to follow it."

"Is anybody badly hurt?" my mother asked.

"We're not sure yet," my father answered her, "but there are bound to be some casualties. We did not stay to check, but came quickly back here to see if you were all all right."

"It seems like it," I said, "our house appears to be undamaged, but we ran outside as soon as we heard the noise, so if there is any harm done we probably would not know yet."

"Come on, let's go inside," my father said. "The upheaval has stopped now, but of course there could still be danger of falling masonry."

Shaken and appalled we all re-entered our home, "I hope Marcus is safe," I said.

"He should be," Gaius said, "The military barracks are some way outside the town."

"But he'll be worried won't he?" Drusilla said, "He'll want to know if we're all right here."

After a time during which we managed to eat a light lunch, Gaius and my father went out to see what news they could find out. When they returned they looked grave, a lot of people whose homes had been destroyed were apparently wandering hopelessly round the streets, unable in some cases to help themselves. A lot of them seemed to have lot their wits completely, and would have to be cared for somehow. The destruction of the town, and of their homes had sent them mad. A large flock of sheep belonging to one rich farmer had completely disappeared. Swallowed up by a fissure that had opened up in the ground beneath them, this would be a serious financial loss to someone. A large reservoir had given way causing flooding in some areas, which only added to the general confusion and destruction.

Later, in the evening Marcus came home, he was relieved to find us unharmed with only minor damage to the house. We could soon put that to rights, a few pillars had collapsed, causing our quarters, and Gaius and Drusilla's quarters to be uninhabitable for the moment.

Marcus and I moved into my old bedroom, while Gaius and Drusilla used the room Gaius had slept in before his marriage.

Marcus had gone to see if his parents were safe. While I waited for him to return I helped Meriope and some of the slaves to move our clothes and personal possessions out of the wrecked room. It would not take long to get that part of the house repaired, but it was unsafe at the moment for us to remain in the room. The larger bed was moved into my original bedroom, which left us rather short of space. But at least we would be secure there, I waited anxiously for Marcus to return, I hoped he would find his parent's home unharmed, and them safe. When he came home after supper, (he had stayed and had a meal with his parents) he told us there was no serious damage to their house either.

Fortunately our water supply was still in working order, as the reservoir that had collapsed was not the one that we got our supply from. It had served several important public buildings, including at least one bathhouse, the pipes were broken and would have to be repaired urgently.

By now the move to our temporary room was complete, and we retired to bed. We fell into each other's arms as soon as we reached our room, the strain of the events of the day taking their toll of me. Sobbing, partly with relief that we were unharmed, I clung to Marcus unable to let him go.

"Come on," he soothed me, "Calm down, everything's going to be all right."

"But what about our town," I whimpered "Nothing will be the same again."

"Yes it will," he cheered me, "they will soon reconstruct it, you'll see."

I pressed myself against him, lust flared up in me, "Make love to me," I whispered.

He lowered me onto the bed, I tried to remove my clothes without letting go of him. Our lovemaking was intense, I did not want to stop, neither did he.

The next day Drusilla told me that it had been the same with them. It was the shock, and the relief that we were safe, and that the danger was now past. It was I suppose a celebration of life, after what had been terror of death. Marcus had gone back to his job, the military would be needed in the clear up operations. Some buildings would have to be shored up quickly to prevent further collapse, there was still danger of falling brickwork which could result in loss of life.

There had been casualties unfortunately, I dreaded to hear if anyone I knew had been injured or worse. I went to find my son, he was playing happily with Oenone's son Hector, I snatched him up, and hugged him to me. He objected to this form of treatment vehemently, Hector stared at us. Reluctantly I put Larius down, I kissed him, which he also objected to, then I left them. I had to find out about Julia and her family, ordering a slave to accompany me, I set out for their house. To my relief it appeared to be unharmed, I was admitted, Julia greeted me by throwing her arms around me. "I'm so glad you're safe."

"You too," I answered, "Wasn't it terrible?"

She nodded in agreement, "I've never been so scared in my life, I thought the world was coming to an end."

"Your house appears undamaged," I remarked.

"Yes we've been lucky, what about you?"

"Some minor damage, mainly to the colonnades, which means our room is uninhabitable, so's my brothers."

"So what are you doing?"

"Using my old bedroom."

"Of course," she said "but we're still using the room I had before we were married anyway. Your house is so much bigger than our's."

We sat sipping hot honey laced with cinnamon, it was delicious, and warming against the winter cold.

Gradually, slowly, things began to settle down again, the normal routines of people's lives were resumed. There had been some damage to the buildings on the slopes of Vesuvius. And the country areas had come off badly, a lot of the mansions in the countryside around the coast of the Bay of Neapolis had had to be abandoned by their owners. Presumably they would rebuild eventually, and things would be as they were before the earthquake.

Most of the buildings in the Forum were being shored up, the temples of Jupiter and Apollo were covered in scaffolding, but the temple of Venus was a write off. Some saw this as unfortunate, as Venus was the patron goddess of Pompeii, and this was seen as an ill omen for the town by some people. But it was not long before some people were scribbling invocations and exhortations to her on the walls again. Begging for her intervention in their love lives, or maybe giving thanks to her if things were going well in that part of their lives.

Builders and masons were in great demand, as were plumbers. It was lucky that the town was so resilient and economically sound, as were also the surrounding towns. Herculaneum had been almost totally destroyed, as Pompeii almost had. Nuceria had suffered a lot of devastation, but not so bad as Pompeii and other nearer towns. The quake had also reached as far as Neapolis, Neapolis had suffered some havoc in an earlier earthquake that had hit that town one day a couple of years ago. The Emperor Nero was performing in the theatre there at the time. That had soon put a stop to that, much to most people's relief, who had been forced to attend, or suffer reprisals. They had had to endure his singing endlessly, which was not most people's idea of pleasure. The minor earthquake had almost been a blessing in disguise to some.

It took quite a lot longer than we had expected to get the destruction to our home repaired, as the workmen were needed on more important jobs, rebuilding the civic buildings in the Forum. So that the life and commerce of the town could resume as quickly as possible. Marcus and I took Larius up to the family farm on the slopes of Vesuvius, as things were not too busy there at the moment I thought. The farm and slave quarters had been destroyed, and were being hastily restored by the farm slaves. This did not leave much time for them to do their usual work. It was strange to see my father and Gaius doing the manual work themselves. Although at this time of year there was not much else to be done. Everything had been stored for the winter now, but storehouses had to be rebuilt. Amphorae of wine and olive oil were in the open at the moment, and my father and brother were hastily erecting sheds of wood, assisted by the slaves. The journey in the cart had been rough over the uneven ground.

"Is it a good idea to bring the child up here just now?" Gaius asked me, "Or even to come here yourselves? Things aren't at their best up here at present."

"I thought it would make a pleasant outing, and I thought you weren't busy at the moment."

"Well you can see that we are busy," he replied, "what are you intending to do up here?"

"I thought we'd have a picnic, perhaps you and father would like to join us."

I unpacked bread, cheese, Lucanian sausage, pork liver sausage, German ham and slices of cold chicken. To drink I had brought a flask of cold wine for us and milk for Larius. To finish there were sweet honey cakes.

I spread a cloth on the ground, there was nowhere else suitable, nothing we could use as a table as everything was ruined. The scene was bleak, being winter the weather was cold as well. We all huddled in our cloaks as we settled ourselves around the food laid out on the ground. My father and Gaius were quite glad to have this feast, they would have had only rough bread and cheese otherwise, shared with the slaves.

After we had eaten we were shown the work in progress, and where the earthquake had taken its toll. Olive trees and vines had been uprooted, fortunately some still stood.

"We must get everything repaired before the spring planting," said my father.

Some slaves were already planting new trees, but they would not be ready in time for this years crop, Gaius was already resuming work on the sheds, we would be all right as we had a store of wine and olive oil, enough to tide us over this year, so our family should not lose money. Some people might not be so lucky.

I looked around for Larius, he had wandered towards the place where the slaves were working, I set off in pursuit. He would not get far, it was hard enough for the rest of us to walk over this terrain. The mountain had suffered great upheavals, jagged rocks of lava had been thrown up by the quake. Larius had fallen over and started screaming loudly, I hurried as best I could over the rough ground to pick him up.

"You'd better go home I think," my father said, "It is really not safe up here, especially for a child."

I agreed, and lifting Larius I cuddled him and calmed him down as best I could, while Marcus prepared the cart for our homeward journey.

Arriving home I handed the child to Oenone, he needed attending to, I was tired, and entering the tablinium I threw myself onto a couch. Marcus followed me into the room, and equally tired lay down on another couch. I gazed at the painted walls, at the stucco work which blended with the murals and the floor. I was glad that the house was still mostly intact in spite of our own apartments that had still not been repaired. But the main thing was that this principal living area was unharmed, apart from a few ornaments being broken, we were very lucky compared to some people, extremely fortunate really.

"I hope your father will be able to rebuild his farm quite soon," Marcus said.

I stretched out on my couch, "Oh I think they will, they should have the new trees and vines planted in time for next years sowing. And we have plenty of stock stored up, that will see us through this year well enough."

"Will the earthquake affect the market at all do you think?"

"There's always going to be a demand for wine and olive oil whatever happens," I replied. "How could there not be, people will always need these things."

"Yes of course," Marcus answered, "I suppose one can't lose if one is in one or both of those trades."

It grew dark early still, the door slave came in to light the lamps as we lay there. Light glimmered, giving the room a greenish glow. The underwater scenes on the walls shimmered in the light, neraids and dolphins sported together. While the variegated marble on the floor showed under the rugs which covered it at this time of year, for extra warmth. The floor and walls were heated by the hypocaust of course, as was most of the house in the winter. A heater also stood in the corner of the room, a wood burning stove with a door that could be opened if desired to give a flicker of flame to add to the warmth both visually and physically. I went across to open the door now, and held out my hands to the heat. Drusilla entered the room, I turned to her, "You should have come with us today, I'm surprised that you did not."

She joined me at the stove, warming her hands, "Gaius wouldn't have wanted me to go up there, I'm surprised he didn't object to you being there.

"He did a bit," I answered, "but he soon calmed down when I unpacked the food."

"Oh well," she flung herself down on a couch, "perhaps I'll go another day."

"Well you'd better take some food with you," I said, "Or you might not be welcome, you know what Gaius is like."

"Even your father told us it was not safe up there," Marcus added, "He told us to go, virtually."

"Yes," I said, "he was thinking of Larius."

Meriope came in with a dish of roasted chestnuts, "I thought you might like these now."

We pounced on them, "Bring us some herbal tea Meriope please," I requested her. She returned with a jug of camomile tea, I poured it for all three of us, we relaxed.

"I expect father-in-law and Gaius will return soon." Drusilla said, "It's getting dark."

"A pity we finished the chestnuts and the tea," I remarked, "But there's bound to be some more."

A few minutes later we heard my father and Gaius enter the atrium, Drusilla went to greet them, they all came into the room.

"We've finished the roasted chestnuts," I grinned.

"Let's get some more," said Gaius, and went to summon a slave.

"I'm glad you got home safely," my father remarked, "It's not the safest of places to take a baby at present. But still no harm done, but keep away in future until things have settled down up there."

I nodded. "All right."

The fresh chestnuts arrived with another jug of herb tea, we settled down companiably. Life was still comfortable and pleasant I decided. Considering what we had been through, some people were less fortunate of course I reflected, with their homes totally demolished. But rebuilding was taking place fairly rapidly I knew, and most of our friends had got off reasonably lightly, as we had.

CHAPTER SEVENTEEN

AFTERMATH

One day as I was sitting in the small family sitting room playing with Larius, a slave came to tell me that there was a young woman outside in the atrium asking to see me. It was now nearly two months since the earthquake, and things were beginning to get back to normal. Some buildings would remain in scaffolding for many months, perhaps longer in some cases. I looked up from my absorption in my young son, "Who is it? Did she give a name?"

"No Domina," the slave answered, "She said you would know her."

It could not be Julia she would not be so mysterious, and why anyway? I picked Larius up from the floor and sat him in my lap, "All right, you'd better show her in."

I did not immediately recognise the young woman who entered and stood uncertainly just inside the entrance. We gazed at each other for a moment, neither of us willing, it seemed to break the silence. Larius fidgeted on my lap, I held him tighter, the girl stared at him. "Claudia don't you know me?"

I stared at her, "I'm sorry, you seem familiar, but I don't quite recognise you."

"I'm Flavia, have I really changed so much?"

I jumped to my feet, almost dropping my child in my shock. "Flavia! Where have you been all this time? And yes you do look different." In fact she looked haggard, and from being a pretty girl, she seemed to have become quite plain. Her once glossy dark hair was lank, and carelessly pinned up into a bun at the back, she wore no make up and her face was pale, she did not look well.

I could not hug her as I was still holding the child, I indicated a chair, "You'd better sit down. Have you any idea of the worry you caused disappearing like that? Yes I'm pleased to see you, and surprised after all this time, I suppose you heard about the earthquake."

"Yes, and hurried home as fast as I could to make sure my family and you were all right."

"How are your parents?" I asked. "Is their house still intact, are they all right?"

She shook her head, "I haven't been to see them yet, I wanted to see you first, they may not have forgiven me."

I sat down again, holding Larius on my knee, "I'm sure they'll be pleased to see you, and relieved that you're back safe."

I summoned a slave by ringing a small silver bell, I ordered some warmed wine, she looked as though she could do with it, also some honey cakes. She gulped the hot sweet wine, and fell on the cakes as if she was starving. I still could not believe the change in her, she looked as if she had has a hard time since leaving the town.

"Where were you when you heard about the earthquake?"

"Sicilia, I've been there since I left Pompeii. I wanted to come home but I had no money, and was anyway afraid to return."

"How did you manage to get back here now?"

"I begged a lift in a carriers cart for as far as it went, then I succeeded in getting a passage on a ship across the Strait of Messina. I told them the reason I had to get home, and they took pity on me and let me on. Then I managed to cadge lifts as far as Nuceria, I walked from there."

I stared at her in horror, "you walked all the way from Nuceria to Pompeii?" No wonder she looked so exhausted, and had lost her looks. She looked at me, "I can see you're very well, you're married I presume, you've got a lovely baby, you married Marcellus I suppose?"

I shook my head, "He went away, I'm married to Marcus."

"So Marcus came back did he, how long have you been married?"

"Just over two years, Marcus was away a lot at first in Britannia. He was involved in the war there recently, but he's with the local military now."

I did not like to ask her what had happened to her, or where her lover was. I ordered more wine and some pastries, she seemed famished. "When did you last eat?"

"About two days ago in Nuceria."

"Would you like some barley soup?"

"I'd love some if it would be no trouble."

I summoned the slave again and ordered the soup. While we waited I tried to find out more details about what she had been doing the last three years or so. After the nourishing tisane arrived she began to talk about her life since leaving her home so suddenly.

At first, she said, things had been good, they were happy, and they had had money. They made for Sicilia, travelling in comfort, it had taken about two weeks. Arriving there they had found lodgings and looked around for somewhere more permanent to live. Finding a small flat they had settled down together, she was content with life, although a bit worried about her parents, but there was nothing she could do about it.

They continued to live together happily for nearly two years. At first they had lacked for nothing, Philocrates had been given his freedom by his master Sabinus which meant he still had all his savings, as he had not had to use them to buy his manumission. Also he had considerable prize money from the races he had won. His master had let him keep nearly half of whatever he won. So they lived richly and extravagantly, and had a circle of friends and acquaintances in Sicilia. But after about eighteen months the money had started to run out, they had started to quarrel. Things quickly got worse between them, and one morning Flavia had awoken to find that Philocrates had left her. He had taken most of the money that was still remaining, and had left her the bare minimum, barely enough for food and rent. She had had to move to cheaper lodgings, then again to something even cheaper. She was finally living in one small room in a run down apartment block with no cooking or bathroom facilities. She had sold her jewellery and most of her clothes that they had bought when things were going well. She had come home with only what she stood up in, which I could see was worn and shabby.

Larius struggled suddenly in my arms, I put him down on the floor, where he promptly made a puddle.

"I'd better get Oenone." I rang the bell and sent for the nursery maid.

"Hello curly," Flavia said bending down to Larius, "he really is beautiful."

"He takes after Marcus."

"Does he? I wondered, I can't really remember what Marcus looks like."

"No well, it's been a long time."

Oenone entered and lifted Larius up, another slave mopped the floor.

"I notice you didn't put him on the rug," Flavia remarked.

I grinned, "No, I knew why he was fidgeting."

"You did put him down rather hurriedly," she laughed.

It was the first time since she had entered the house that I had seen her smile, it was an improvement at least, if my son had caused it I was glad I had had him with me when she arrived.

"Would you like to have some lunch with me?" I asked her.

"I'd love to," she replied, "can I tidy up a bit?"

I took her to my room, "We're using this room, as our own was badly damaged in the earthquake."

"This is the room you used to have isn't it?"

"Yes, Gaius and Drusilla are sleeping in his old room."

"How are they?"

"They're very well."

We returned to the small sitting room, Flavia was in no condition to meet any of my family. I ordered lunch to be served to us in there.

While we were eating fish in cheese sauce with boiled peas, Drusilla entered the room. "What's wrong Claudia?" she began, then she stopped and stared in astonishment at my companion. "Introduce me to your friend won't you?"

"Don't you know her? It's Flavia, she's come home."

Drusilla gaped at her, "I'm sorry, but you look so different, what's happened to you?"

"It's a long story Drusilla," I said, "You'd better go and finish your lunch first."

"I'll bring it in here then you can tell me all about it while we eat." When she returned, carrying her bowl of fish, we told her what Flavia had just told me.

We decided that Drusilla and I would accompany Flavia to her parent's house, as she was so nervous of them. I would have thought that they would be only too happy to see her, and have her at home again after all this time. I offered her one of my dresses so she could at least look smarter when she met them. "We used to be about the same size, although you're thinner than me now, but I haven't put on any weight lately so one of mine should fit you."

We returned to my room where we both changed, as I was not dressed for going out. One of my gowns fitted Flavia well enough, and she looked improved in appearance, although there was nothing to be done about her hair at the moment.

The three of us set off towards Flavia's house, she hung onto me tightly all the way there. To our dismay their house seemed to have suffered considerable damage in the earthquake, we stared at it in horror. Leaving my side Flavia rushed to the entrance, to our relief a slave opened the door. She turned and beckoned us in, and we all entered the atrium, inside it did not appear so bad as it had seemed from the outside, as far as we could see.

"Where's my mother?" Flavia asked the slave. I followed him down a passage where I found Flavia's mother Priscilla in a side room, she rose to her feet. "Claudia! It's nice to see you, it's been a long time."

"I know, I'm sorry I've not been to see you since Flavia disappeared."

"I heard you married."

"Yes Domina, I think you'd better come and see your daughter."

"What do you mean?"

"Flavia's here, in the atrium, she came to see me first as she was afraid she would not be welcome here."

"I must see her," she hurried from the room, I followed her down the passage, entering the atrium where Flavia stood with Drusilla. Her mother went towards her and took her in her arms, "Oh my darling, I thought I'd never see you again," she wept.

Flavia also began to cry, Drusilla and I stood watching them, I said "Do you want us to leave?"

"No, stay and have some herbal tea with us," Priscilla said. Arms entwined, Flavia and her mother led the way into the tablinium, we all sat down.

"Tell me everything that's happened to you Flavia," her mother said.

When she had again related the events she had earlier told us her mother looked appalled. "Why didn't you come home when he left you?"

"I was afraid, and I had no money, but when I heard abut the earthquake I was desperate to find out if you were all all right, so I took my chances and made for Pompeii."

After we had drunk the tea Drusilla and I took our leave, happy to see the reunion between Flavia and her family.

"Well that's good news at least," Drusilla remarked. "I suppose if it hadn't been for the earthquake she would never have come home."

"Oh she might have returned eventually," I said, "still it seems like some good has come out of all the horror."

I usually tried to avoid Marcellus when he came to see other members of the family. But I knew I had to tell him the good news about Flavia returning, and being reunited with her family. Marcus had only the vaguest recollection about Flavia, as he had only met her the once, which was also the first time he had met me. But Marcellus had been very involved with Flavia's entanglement with Philocrates, coming with me to see her family, and trying to break up the relationship. And when she ran away with him Marcellus had been very concerned about it, and had done his best to try and trace them. I owed it to him to let him know she was safely home again I reasoned. And I wanted him to hear the story from me, and not from Gaius, or anyone else.

I found out what time he was expected one afternoon, and waited for him in the atrium. He seemed surprised to find me apparently waiting for him when he arrived, I rose from my seat and approached him. "I've got something to tell you."

He looked astonished, "What is it?"

"Flavia's come home," I told him, "She came to see me first, and then Drusilla and I escorted her home."

"Well that is good news, but why is it so urgent to tell me about it?"

"Because you helped so much at the time of her disappearance, and were concerned about her. I just wanted to tell you."

"I expect you'll be glad to have each other's company again, I'll see you." He went towards the tablinium where Gaius was waiting for him.

Strangely disappointed, though what I had expected I could not think,

I retired to my room. It was now April and the weather was already getting pleasantly warm. It would be better to keep out of Marcellus's way in future I decided, as he might think I was encouraging him. But about two weeks later we encountered one another again entirely by chance in the garden. I had no idea he was out there when I wandered out one morning. He had come hoping to see either my father or my brother, and on being told that they were expected home shortly he had decided to wait for them. As there was no one about he had sauntered out of the tablinium door into the peristyle. He looked startled to see me come through, I also stopped in confusion, "I had no idea there was anyone here."

"Maybe," he said, "it is surprising the reasons you seem to find for encountering me."

"I can assure you it was unintentional," I said indignantly. "Why should I look for reasons to meet you?"

"You tell me," he answered, "I didn't come here today with the intention of finding you, but as we're here we may as well be sociable with each other."

We sat down on a bench, I felt awkward, he seemed as assured as always, I did not know what to say. We stared at the fishpond, the gardens were beautiful, the setting perfect for an assignation I thought. I pushed the thought away, what was the matter with me, I was married to another man, I should not be thinking in terms of assignations with Marcellus, or anybody else.

"Haven't you got anything to say?" he asked.

"It's turning really warm," I tried.

He suddenly reached out and put an arm around me, "Come on, you can do better than that."

What to do, I panicked, his arm was tightening round me.

Wrenching myself away I leapt from the bench just as my father and brother came into the garden. They both stared at me in astonishment, Marcellus rose to greet them, "I came out here to wait for you, Claudia has been keeping me company, haven't you Claudia?"

I was flustered, if they had seen Marcellus' arm around me I was in trouble probably. "I'll leave you to it," I muttered. I would have to watch my step or people would begin to suspect that something was going on between Marcellus and myself. The worst part was that I still found him impossibly attractive, I should not have let him put his arm around me even casually. I resolved to keep out of his way in future, I was doing myself no good by inventing excuses to see him, if that is what I was doing. I did not want to admit this even to myself, today had been sheer chance, I could really not blame myself for it. I had had no idea that Marcellus was in the garden.

Flavia came to see me again, she looked much improved. She wore a new dress of some rich blue material, and her hair had been dressed by a skilled hairdresser. Although it would need a lot more doing to it to restore it to it's former glossiness and shine. It still looked dull, I looked at her, "you need to wash your hair in a cosmetic rinse to bring back the lustrous glow it always used to have."

"There's time for that," she answered, "at the moment I am gradually getting myself a wardrobe, which takes time."

"Your dress is lovely," I said, "I'll come shopping with you if you'd like me to."

She smiled, "I'd like that, but there is a lot of damage in the Forum."

"Yes but they managed to get the Hall of Eumachia restored, I hear it's even better than it was before."

"That's true, come with me then tomorrow morning."

"I will, I'll call for you if you like, so we can walk there together."

"All right."

The following day I called for Flavia as arranged, and we set out for the main shopping area in the Forum.

We enjoyed ourselves enormously, it was like old times. The new summer fashions were in and we both chose materials for dresses. I had not at first intended to buy anything for myself, but I could not resist buying a couple of new gowns.

As we were leaving the Hall we met Marcellus on his way inside, he stopped (it would have been rude not to). "Ave Claudia," he said, he looked curiously at Flavia, as if not certain who she was.

"Aren't you going to say hello to Flavia?"

"Of course, I'm sorry, Ave Flavia."

"Most people don't recognise me," Flavia said, "people say I've changed a lot."

"Oh I think I would have known you eventually." Marcellus replied, "But it has been a long time."

"Don't let us keep you," I said, "I expect you're very busy."

"Well I do have business here," he said "so vale Claudia and Flavia."

"He's still very handsome" Flavia remarked. "he doesn't alter at all, I'm surprised you didn't hook him while you had the chance, he's wonderful looking."

"Yes, well I'm happily married to Marcus now. Let's go and have a cup of wine."

We went to the wine bar I usually frequented with Julia.

"Have you seen any of our friends since you've been back?"

She shook her head, "Is there anything I should know about any of them?"

I nodded, "Julia's married, so's Antonia, Antonia married Titus, you remember them don't you?"

"Yes," Flavia agreed "I remember them, who did Julia marry?"

"A gladiator named Drusus."

"A gladiator! Did he fight in Pompeii?"

"Yes until the trouble with Nuceria, we've been banned from gladiator shows ever since."

"Yes I heard about that, so what does Julia's husband do now?"

"He works for Julia's father in the vineyard."

"Doing what?"

"Keeping accounts mainly apparently."

"Is he good at it?"

"She says he is."

We finished our wine and went out into the street again. A lot of people were crowding round some signwriters who were painting something on a nearby wall.

"Let's see what the excitement is about," I suggested.

We went nearer, it was impossible to see through the audience that had gathered. "What's going on?" I asked.

The people beside me were also having difficulty seeing what the sign was. Some people nearer to the front turned around, only too glad to impart their knowledge. It was hard to hear what they were saying as they all spoke at once. Finally a man rather nearer to us said "it says that because of what we've been through with the earthquake, The Senate has decided to allow us to have the games again."

"That's wonderful news," I said, "Does it mean that we can have gladiator fights and everything."

"Oh yes!" several people shouted at once.

"But we'll have to get the amphitheatre repaired first," someone said. Flavia and I looked at each other "That's exciting news," I said, "I wonder how soon they can repair the amphitheatre. You'd better join us for the first show."

"Lovely idea," she answered.

When I reached home my family were already gathered for lunch, I joined them. "Have you heard the news?"

"Yes we've heard if you mean about the games," Gaius said. "There are signs about it all over town, there are workmen already starting work on the amphitheatre, it won't take long to shore it up, it's not too badly damaged."

We discussed the subject of future games excitedly for the remainder of the meal. "I've asked Flavia to join us for the opening show."

"Yes, I expect some other people will be joining us too," Gaius said. He looked at me meaningly, "Maybe it's time that Marcus was introduced to Marcellus."

I had not considered this possibility in my thrill at hearing the news of the gladiator shows resuming. This was difficult, I could hardly forbid them to invite Marcellus and his family, they were still all friends as well as business associates. It would cause embarrassment to me, and suppose Marcellus said something? Relations between us were still extremely fragile, and I could not see any way to prevent a confrontation.

"But we'll be a large party won't we?" Drusilla said, "It shouldn't cause trouble if we all behave like civilised people."

I nodded, I hoped so, it would spoil things though, for me anyway.

If only life did not have to be so complicated, I could see no way out of this dilemma. But maybe Marcellus would feel the same way, and would not choose to join us, I hoped that this was what would happen. Meanwhile there was still time before the date for the games would be fixed, a lot could happen in the meantime I thought optimistically.

CHAPTER EIGHTEEN

IMPERIAL VISIT

The Emperor was coming to visit our town to see for himself the damage inflicted by the earthquake. Everybody was very excited, and arrangements were being made to entertain him and his entourage. Work on the amphitheatre was being stepped up so that the Imperial Games could be staged. The first gladiator show would be in Nero's honour. Enthusiasm for the forthcoming event had reached fever pitch, as everyone was hoping to get into the amphitheatre on the momentous day. We were of course quite certain of getting a stand on that day, there was no doubt about that, the question was whom we should invite to join us in our box.

I waited in trepidation to hear whether Marcellus would be joining us on that occasion. I could not wait to see the Emperor Nero and his wife Poppea, who came from Pompeii herself originally. Her family were known to own five properties in the town, and to be extremely rich.

As the day approached for the arrival of the Imperial visitors, which would be followed by the Games on the following day, I learned that Marcellus and his parents would indeed be joining us at the arena. Flavia was also joining us, as I had asked her previously, we would be a fairly large party, consisting of the family of course, with the Vinicius family, Marcus and Flavia. I could only hope that Marcus and Marcellus would manage to get on well enough with each other, and that Marcellus would not make it obvious that he and I had had a passionate relationship in the past.

I went with my mother, Drusilla and Flavia to watch the Emperor arrive in state, Marcus would likely be riding behind him with the rest of the military garrison. It was lucky that he had managed to get the following day off to sit with us at the Games, as an escort would be needed to attend the Imperial party on this occasion. My father and Gaius had business to attend to and so could not join us to see the procession. The anticipation had been mounting in the town leading up to the arrival of the Emperor. GOOD LUCK TO THE DECISIONS OF NERO someone had written on a wall.

The streets were crowded, we were fortunate to find a good position to get a good view of the Imperial party. The town was in holiday mood, the worst of the ravages had been hastily repaired, but there was enough damage evident for the Emperor to be able to see the extent of what the place had suffered.

The day was very hot, we had found some seats outside a café, and we were drinking cold honeyed wine, and eating rich cakes peppered with cinnamon, pastries stuffed with nuts and raisins, and dates stuffed with almonds. The café was packed tightly with people, we had been lucky to get a table, the excitement of the crowd was intense, this was the first time anyone could remember a state visit by an Emperor.

As we sat there waiting we heard the first sounds of the procession come to us faintly on the still air. We would get a good view from where we were sitting we knew, a trumpet sounded, followed by others. The first of the soldiers leading the procession appeared, this was it then! The Imperial party would be here soon, I could hardly contain my excitement. I had never seen an Emperor before, few of us had, although there were several Imperial villas in the Bay of Neapolis. The commander of the Praetorian Guard came next, in full military dress, as were the rest of the troop, these were the elite troops who guarded the Emperor in person. The commander was a tough looking man, his name was Burrus, they all looked pretty tough I thought. They marched in full military panoply, helmets and armour gleaming in the sun. The café we were sitting in was on the main route where most people were gathered, which meant that we would get to see the full ceremony.

The Emperor was riding in a splendid carriage we saw, as it drew near to where the crowd was congregated a great cheer went up. As the carriage came towards us Nero leant out and waved to us all, the cheering grew louder, beside him the Empress Poppea smiled graciously. She was almost a local girl as I have said, although she had not been in Pompeii for a long time. After the Imperial entourage had passed I saw Marcus riding behind with other members of the local militia. I felt so proud of him at that moment, he looked magnificent I thought, as they all did of course. I turned to Flavia, "That's Marcus, that's my husband, doesn't he look wonderful?"

"Yes," she breathed, "you've struck lucky it appears, again."

I hoped she was not going to be difficult again, we had quarrelled over what she called my good luck with handsome men before. Why did she have to spoil things always, she had not always been like this, but then of course she had had a bad experience lately with Philocrates, still she did not have to be so awkward on this occasion, when everybody else was in a joyous mood.

"Aren't you enjoying yourself Flavia?" I said, "It's probably only a matter of time before you meet someone."

"With my luck!" she exclaimed.

"Stop arguing you two," said my mother.

"Come on let's have some more wine," said Drusilla lifting the flagon from the table and pouring wine into our beakers. The procession seemed to have passed and was continuing along the street beyond us, the trumpet blasts still sounding in the distance.

The following day we arrived at the arena early as we usually did, and took our places in the stands. I had Marcus on one side of me and Flavia on the other, next to her sat Drusilla, then Gaius of course, with Marcellus beside him at the end of the row. Behind us sat our parents with Marcellus' father and mother. The stand for the Imperial party still remained empty until all the other stands were full. Then two trumpeters appeared and blew a fanfare, the helmeted commander of the Praetorian Guard came next, surrounded by his men in their shining armour. They formed a guard of honour through which the Emperor and Empress strode to their seats. Another fanfare sounded and Nero stood up and declared the Games open, the crowd cheered. I studied Nero, he was a rather fat young man I noticed now that I could see him clearly, he wore a toga of Imperial purple boarded with gold.

The show was not as spectacular as it would have been under normal circumstances to entertain an Emperor, because the town was still in the throes of recovery from the devastating earthquake. Two pairs of gladiators came on and fought to the death, but the Emperor spared the lives of the defeated ones. The rest was the usual thing, though Nero watched carefully, using a crystal, to see better presumably, he was known not to be as keen on gladiator fights as most people were. Preferring theatrical displays of singing and recitation and drama to the Games.

During the interval the six of us walked among the stalls outside the amphitheatre. Marcus and I, Drusilla and Gaius and to my surprise Marcellus escorted Flavia.

We drank beer as being more thirst quenching than wine, although I do not care for it really. I watched Marcellus seat Flavia on a bench and sit down beside her, his head bent over her's, I stared at them resentfully, surprised at how jealous I felt. I had convinced myself that my passion for him was over, and that I was content in my marriage to Marcus. Gaius grinned at me, diverted, I wondered if the whole thing was designed to wind me up, knowing Gaius and his games. I turned away from him, and the two on the bench, and led Marcus to a stall selling momentos of the occasion. I absorbed myself in the merchandise for sale, and finally chose alabaster statuettes of Nero and Poppea, where I was going to put them I had no idea, it was something to do to buy them. Perhaps when our apartment was repaired I would find a niche for them I thought.

Gaius and Drusilla meanwhile had collected our lunch, sausages and bread and pastries filled with cheese and nuts, carrying a jug of beer Marcus joined us, and we made our way back to our seats. Flavia sat next to me and Drusilla again, much to my relief, I would have to cease this jealousy of anyone Marcellus paid attention to, for my own peace of mind if nothing else. We watched the remainder of the Games, which ended with a gladiator fighting a lion, this was popular with the crowd, although maybe not too popular with our Emperor. He appeared bored with this turn, and held a conversation with his wife and friends while it was on.

The next day was the chariot races, much more the Emperor's cup of wine I knew. He had raced as a charioteer himself, this was frowned on we all knew, especially among the upper class. We settled ourselves again in our box at the amphitheatre to watch the races. To my dismay I saw that Flavia had got herself seated beside Marcellus, I glared at them both, but there was nothing I could do about it. Marcus fortunately still did not know that Marcellus and I had had a love affair, he looked at me curiously, "What's wrong Claudia?"

"Nothing, there's nothing wrong at all, why should there be?"

"I thought perhaps you had quarrelled with you friend Flavia," he said, "you seemed upset with her."

"No," I answered, "I'm not upset with her, I was just looking at her, why should I not?"

"No reason, you just looked angry I thought."

Flavia was too engrossed in talking to Marcellus to notice anything that was going on, so the exchange between Marcus and myself passed unnoticed by her. Drusilla sat on Marcellus' other side, with Gaius on her other side, I wished she would engage Marcellus in conversation so he would pay less attention to Flavia. But she seemed absorbed with Gaius at the moment, I turned to Flavia, "What do you think of Poppea's dress?" I asked.

To my relief she turned to me, and we began discussing the fashions in the Imperial box. I would have to stop envying any woman that Marcellus paid attention to I knew, it would do me no good. I was in fact appalled at my reaction to this, it appeared as if my feelings for him had not changed at all. I sneaked a look at him, he was talking to Gaius and Drusilla now, I tried to draw Marcus into the conversation between myself and Flavia.

Suddenly there was a hush, the Emperor had risen and was making a short speech before declaring that the chariot racing could begin. I tried to pay attention to what he was saying, and forget my own concerns for the moment. He was announcing aid for the town to help rebuild after the earthquake, there were cheers and applause for this speech.

The racing began, it was a good turnout as certain citizens had provided the chariots and their drivers, and they had not stinted on this. I turned to Flavia, "There's Caius Sabinus in that stand near the Emperor's, you'd better be careful he doesn't see you."

She looked apprehensive, "perhaps he's forgotten all about me by now, it has been a long time."

I realised this, I did not think he was still likely to be resentful about losing Philocrates, but I was annoyed with Flavia at the moment and wanted to shake her up a bit. Perhaps she would not be so pleased with herself about Marcellus paying so much attention to her. I also knew that Marcellus was a match for Sabinus any time, and could, and probably would protect Flavia from him if it came to a confrontation between them. I did not care to contemplate this too closely, as she would make capital out of it if it came to that. She obviously fancied Marcellus, and thought with me out of the running, she likely stood a good chance with him.

I sat brooding on this, paying no attention to what was going on in front of me in the arena, until Marcus remarked "The Greens are doing well, the Emperor will be pleased. He's bound to have a bet on them to win, he supports them, as most of the Imperials do."

"What?" I asked, startled at having my thoughts interrupted so suddenly.

"I just said the Green's appear to be winning," Marcus answered, "aren't you paying attention? What's the matter with you?"

"Nothing," I said, "Of course I can see that the Greens are winning." I hurriedly turned my attention to the race in hand. It was just finishing with the Green team in the lead by a head, I applauded enthusiastically and smiled at Marcus, "That's brilliant."

The interval occurred then, and we went for a stroll, and to look around the stalls. We bought a small chariot and driver complete with horses for Larius, he would love that. Then we found the others, Flavia held onto Marcellus' arm, I seethed inwardly but fixed a smile on my face.

"We've got lunch, and some wine this time," Flavia said. Thank Juno for that anyway, at least I did not have to drink beer again. It was cool and refreshing, I felt better, after all Marcellus was only being polite to Flavia anyway, what else could he do?"

The racing began again, the Greens seemed to be leading again, I wondered if Sabinus had fixed this to please the Emperor. It would be in his interest to keep Nero happy during the visit to Pompeii. I was actually quite glad when the chariot racing came to an end, and Marcellus and his parents came home with us after we had dropped

Flavia off at her home. Again she clung to Marcellus all the way, much to my exasperation with them both.

When we reached home though there was a surprise in store for us, which quite put Flavia and Marcellus' behaviour from my mind. As we entered the atrium we saw luggage which two slaves were attending to. My brother Lucius came out of the tablinium to greet us, I flew into his arms, "Lucius! I did not know you were coming home, I'm so glad to see you."

"Claudia! It's lovely to see you, I've been trying to get home ever since I heard about the earthquake. I wondered where everybody was, then I heard that the Emperor was in town, and that you were all at the Games."

"What a pity you could not get here in time, and missed the Emperor's visit," I said.

"I've seen Nero before, that isn't important," he replied.

The rest of the family were now all around him, I withdrew slightly, the Vinicius family were almost forgotten until Gaius said, "You remember Marius and Marcellus and Marcellus's mother don't you Lucius? They came to dinner one night when you were home last time."

They shook hands "It's nice to meet you again," Marius said. Marcus of course did not know Lucius, and was introduced to him.

"So Claudia's married," my brother remarked, "I have so much to catch up on it seems. What do you do Marcus?"

"He's a tribune in the army," I answered proudly, "He rode in the procession with the Emperor when he entered the town."

"You're with the local militia then?" Lucius asked, "Is that how you met Claudia?"

"No," I said, "it's a long story, and as you say you've got a lot to catch up on."

We all entered the tablinium, ordering the slaves to bring refreshments, Lucius had only been home a short while, and had not had anything to eat, though wine had been brought to him. Food had been prepared for our return from the Games in any case, a dish of meat and fish prepared in a seasoned cheese sauce flavoured with herbs and wine was served. We ate informally in the tablinium, I shared a couch with Marcus, Lucius shared with mother, she was so pleased to see him she would not let him leave her side anyway. We drank Setinian, a good wine we kept for special occasions.

Lucius had been in Antioch when he heard about the earthquake he told us, he got a ship as far as Rhodes, then the weather held them up. It was February at the time, the same month that we had had the earthquake. It had taken him till now, nearly June to reach home. I reached for the Setinian and poured myself another cup, filling Marcus' cup as well.

"I wondered if you'd come home when you heard about the earthquake."

"I would have been here sooner if I could."

"We realise that," my mother said, "we don't blame you for not getting here earlier."

"Have you decided what you want to do yet Lucius?" my father asked him.

"Give him a chance," said my mother, "he's only just arrived home!"

"Of course there's no hurry," father answered, "I was only asking."

"Actually I might join you and Gaius in the family firm eventually, I've travelled enough for now."

"That's good news isn't it Gaius?" father remarked.

Gaius nodded, "We could do with extra help of course, especially now since the earthquake. If you're sure about settling down, you'd have to start at the bottom of course, learning the trade."

"I realise that," Lucius answered, "As I've never taken much interest in wine making before, unlike you."

Gaius nodded again, "Marius and Marcellus are in the cloth trade by the way, but we have investments in common and see a lot of each other."

Lucius nodded politely at Marcellus and his father, "Glad to know you."

It grew dark as we lingered far into the night, the Vinicius family took their leave as we went on talking. Lucius told us about his travels in the East, he had got as far as Parthia, a long way off. "I intended to reach Cappadocia eventually, before I heard the news from Pompeii, and felt I had to come home to see if you were all safe."

"We got off fairly lightly, the only damage to the house were the quarters occupied by Gaius and Drusilla, and Claudia and Marcus. When the repairs will be done we still don't know," mother told him.

Marcus yawned suddenly, I nudged him, irritated by this, after all Lucius was my brother, and I had not see him for several years, Marcus need not be so rude. "I'm sorry" he whispered, "But I do have to get to work tomorrow."

The others had not noticed this exchange fortunately, "All right," I rose "Marcus has to work tomorrow, guarding the Emperor presumably."

"Of course," Lucius rose too, "I'm rather tired myself."

When we reached our room Marcus said, "I'm sorry, I did not mean to be rude, I'm pleased to meet your other brother."

"It's all right," I answered, "It's late anyway."

The next day Nero was touring the town, seeing the destruction for himself, Marcus was indeed in attendance on the Imperial party. Lucius and I went to watch the proceedings to see what we could see. Crowds thronged the streets hoping for a glimpse of the Imperials. We had brought little Larius with us, he had been introduced to his uncle Lucius earlier in the morning. I lifted him up to see the proceedings, he was getting heavier I noticed, he would be two years old in another week. Lucius took him from me and carried him through the crowded streets, the throng pressed forward, filling the cobbled streets and pavements.

All traffic had been barred while Nero made his inspection of the more damaged buildings in the town. We could not see much of the Emperor's party from where we were standing, and we debated whether we should push our way through the hordes of people, or wait on the chance that the Imperial party might move closer to where we stood. We were now near the Forum, and it was almost impossible to force our way any further towards where Nero was examining the main temples.

"I hear the temple of Venus is a complete write off," Lucius said.

"Yes" I answered, "it was only recently completed too."

"Seems a shame," Lucius said.

"Yes, not having a temple to Venus is quite upsetting to some people."

"Well she is our Patron Goddess after all."

"Yes, that's why it upsets them."

Most of the market stalls had been banned for the day, as they would have caused an obstruction, although a few stalls selling food and drink had been permitted. We bought sweet cakes fried in olive oil with honey poured over them, and sprinkled with nutmeg for our selves. And for Larius cakes soaked in milk, also fried in olive oil. This kept him occupied for a few minutes.

"Ate you all right carrying him?" I asked my brother.

"Oenone can hold him if you like."

"No I'm enjoying getting to know my nephew," Lucius said.

"He's getting a bit fidgety," I said.

"It's all right he's fine," Lucius said.

Oenone was following behind us, she carried a basket containing necessities for Larius over her arm. But she could still take a turn with the child quite easily. We moved forward towards the Imperial party, shoving our way through the crowds, someone elbowed me in the ribs, I turned round furious, it was Julia. She had Drusus in tow, I had not seen her lately, not since Flavia had returned.

"Julia!" I exclaimed "How nice to see you, do you know my brother Lucius?"

"Not very well," she answered, "But we have met before."

They could not shake hands because Lucius was holding Larius.

"This is Drusus," I said, "Julia's husband."

They nodded at each other.

"We're trying to get closer to the Emperor," Julia said.

"Yes," I said, "so're we, let's see if we can push our way through this mob together. I'll take Larius, Lucius, then you'll be free to force a way through."

We came up against a barrier when we finally reached the Forum, a cordon was fencing off the Imperials from the people, this was as far as we went it seemed. Larius squirmed in my arms, he was wet but I could not do anything about that at the moment. I could now clearly see the portly form of the Emperor with his wife at his side, and a gaggle of town decurions and aediles surrounding them. Nero again wore a purple toga with gold stripes, I stared at the Empress Poppea, "Isn't she lovely?" I said to Julia.

She agreed, it was impossible to find a place to sit down as every seat in every café was taken. The Praetorian Guard stood around, with some of the local militia, I looked for Marcus, he did not appear to be there, he must be on duty somewhere else I thought.

The Imperial party moved on towards the theatres, to inspect the fairly minor damage they had suffered. I turned to Julia and Lucius, "Let's get away from here, there's really no more to see now."

They agreed and we turned away, and made our way out of the Forum.

Finally we found a large café/bar with a table still available, thankfully we all sat down. I handed the child to Oenone, "Take him and change him, then bring him back here, there's a reasonably spacious lavatory at the back."

We sat relaxing after our hectic morning, a waiter appeared at last. We ordered cool white wine, when it arrived we all drank deep, and gave our order for lunch.

We ordered fish stew with cheese sauce added, and for Larius, who had now rejoined us and was sitting on his uncle's lap, a small portion of fish stew, and milk sweetened with honey to drink. I turned to Julia, "Have you seen Flavia?"

She looked surprised. "No, is she returned then? I had not heard."

"No, well she's keeping a fairly low profile at the moment I think. She came to see me before she went anywhere else, even her own home."

"Did she, what happened? Is her lover returned with her?"

I shook my head, "No, that's well and truly over, he left her destitute in Sicilia. She managed to beg her way home when she heard about the earthquake."

"How is she now?"

"She's feeling a lot better now, she came to the Games with us yesterday."

"We didn't see you at the Games, we were there."

"I daresay," I said, "It was impossible to see everyone anyway."

Lucius who had been feeding Larius looked up suddenly, "Flavia! Your friend, what happened to her did you say?"

What to say? Flavia had fancied herself in love with Lucius, and although he did not appear to reciprocate her feelings, might in the future. I did not want to say anything to discourage him if she should still feel the same way. I realised that Philocrates had been on the rebound for her after Lucius left Pompeii without showing her any encouragement. But what if Lucius should change his mind now he was home for good more or less. I did not want to put him off her if there was any hope for Flavia with him. Of course she thought herself infatuated with Marcellus at present, it had seemed yesterday, I should like to discourage that, and what better way than to re-introduce her to my brother.

I did not want to examine too closely my reasons for putting Flavia off Marcellus, I did not want to admit even to myself that I was jealous. I knew I had no hope of Marcellus myself now I was married to Marcus, but I still felt resentful of anyone else whom he might show an interest in. Julia looked at me "What are you brooding about Claudia? You look quite grim all of a sudden, has someone annoyed you?"

"No," I answered "no one's annoyed me particularly, I was just thinking."

"I wouldn't like to be the person you were thinking about."

"I'm all right, if everyone's finished eating we'd better go."

"Oh let's have some more wine," Lucius said, "There's no hurry is there Claudia?"

"No I suppose not."

We ordered more of the cool wine and sat talking, Lucius telling Julia and Drusus about his travels. Larius fell asleep on his lap, I reached over, "I'll take him now."

"If you insist," Lucius handed him over, I cradled him in my arms.

The café emptied and filled up again as we sat there, finally we left and made our way home. We were tired by now, we left Julia and Drusus and made our way to our house. I had sent Oenone home before we had our lunch, and I handed the child over to her when we reached home, and went to tidy myself for the evening meal.

Marcus would be home shortly, I changed my dress just before he came into the room swinging his helmet in his hand. "Ave Claudia." He said, he put his arms around me, I shifted away from his embrace.

"You'd better get changed, there isn't much time before dinner."

His hold on me tightened "Come on, I'm not that late."

I moved away from his hold, "I'm going to join the others, after all I haven't seen my brother Lucius for years. I want to spend some time with him."

I did not mention that we had been together all day, I was not in the mood for lovemaking with Marcus at the moment. I left the bedroom quickly before he could get hold of me again.

CHAPTER NINETEEN

FAMILY STRIFE

It was lovely having Lucius home again, and it appeared he was staying for good this time. During those first few weeks of his return he was having a rest after his travels before starting work in the family firm. He and I spent a lot of time together, going about the town, sometimes taking Larius with us, sometimes going alone. I was happy in this situation, and I did not want it to come to an end. As of course it would have to when Lucius began work.

One day as we walked around the market stalls in the Forum, a man I had never seen before greeted Lucius. I stood studying the merchandise on a nearby stall while they talked. Eventually Lucius turned to me and introduced me to his friend, "We're going to a wine bar Claudia, you'll join us of course."

I had no choice but to agree, although I had no objection to this arrangement in any case. The July sun beat down on us as we seated ourselves around a table outside a bar. Lucius' friend who was called Popilius Varus turned to me, "I'm giving a party next week, I've invited Lucius, would you like to come as well?"

I looked at my brother, "if you're going I'd be happy to accept. I have a husband by the way."

"Then bring him along by all means, I'll be pleased to meet him. It's been simply years since I've seen Lucius, I was so pleased to meet him today."

The wine arrived, Popilius had ordered Setinian, we drank deep of

the superior wine. We nibbled anchovies fried in wine sauce, and a dish
of pine nuts.

Later as we made our way home Lucius said, "I am not sure what kind
of party it will be. But in the past when we were younger his parents
used to give good parties. But the house belongs to him now, so things
will be bound to have changed, it should be fun."

Unfortunately Marcus was unable to come to the party as he would
be on duty that night. "But you go with Lucius" he said.

On the night of the party I dressed carefully in a diaphanous gown of
bright scarlet. The weather was hot, and the dress was both cool and
glamorous. I doused myself in a new perfume I had recently acquired
called 'Poppea', after the Empress. It was very popular at the moment
among young women in Pompeii. Maybe we hoped some of the
Empress' glamour would cling to us if we wore the perfume. I had gone
in for the whole range of cosmetics as well as the scent. I was quite sorry
that Marcus would not be there to see me that night. When I was ready
I joined Lucius in the atrium, and we set out for Popilius's house
together.

The house was large, though not so big as Clodius' enormous mansion,
but pretty spacious all the same. Only a few people had already
congregated for the evening at yet. Popilius Varus greeted us in the
atrium, I apologised for Marcus being unable to attend that night.

"Never mind," Popilius said, "we'll find you a partner for the
evening, there's bound to be someone unattached."

I looked at Lucius, I had assumed he and I would stay together. He
shrugged as I gazed at him, "I think Popilius has someone he wants me
to meet. However I can still stay near you if you prefer."

I shook my head "I'll be all right," I did not want to be a drag on
Lucius if he had other plans, I could amuse myself if I had to. A slave
offered us a tray containing spiced wine, we both took a cup, I looked
around. The atrium was large, but no tables were laid out there, we were
obviously going to eat elsewhere. The floor was of variegated marble, the
impluvium in the centre was filled with small fish which was unusual to
say the least. In fact I found it so odd I stared at it hard, I nudged Lucius
and indicated the pool. "Yes trust Popilius to be different," he said.

"I've never seen that before," I said.

Other people began to arrive now, dishes of nuts and olives were handed round, Popilius had disappeared. I sipped my wine and nibbled olives, a slave offered more wine, I took another cup.

"This wine is quite strong," Lucius said to me, "be careful, there'll be other wines at dinner."

Popilius reappeared with a very attractive girl in tow, he brought her towards us, "This is Fanina," he introduced us. She was I had to admit a remarkably pretty girl, I looked at Lucius, he seemed impressed. Fanina had masses of light brown hair piled high on top of her head, and large brown eyes. We exchanged civilities for a few minutes, then Lucius put an arm around the girl, "Would you like some more wine?" he asked her.

"Yes I would," she answered.

"Let's go and find some," Lucius said, "will you be all right Claudia?"

"I'll be fine," I said "enjoy yourself."

I wandered into the main reception room which I assumed to be the tablinium. Egyptian scenes underfoot I noted, the wall paintings also had an Egyptian theme, and several ornaments and statues also echoed the style. I wondered if Popilius was a devotee of Isis, lots of people were. The temple of Isis was one of the largest in Pompeii, and had a large cult following. Could Popilius be a member?

I stared around me and saw a familiar face, with a shock I recognised Faustinius. I turned away hurriedly, I did not want to speak to him, I did not trust him. I wondered if he had had any hand in Flavia's liaison with Philocrates, as he had had quite an influence on her at the time. Also his treatment of me at the Rites of Bacchus was an unpleasant memory too. I left the tablinium wondering where supper would be served, I soon found out as Popilius and his major-domo came to usher us into an enormous, (or so it seemed to me) triclinium.

There were comparatively few guests assembled I noted, for a house of this size it was a fairly select gathering. Lucius and Fanina were at a table on the opposite side of the room to where I was seated. The couch beside me remained empty, presumably someone would be set to be my dinner companion. The light was dim, opposite me to my dismay Faustinius reclined with an extremely attractive woman. He did not appear to recognise me, he was already caressing the woman beside him. I had heard that the mystery villa had been quite badly damaged in the earthquake, and the inhabitants had abandoned it, and left Pompeii. It was being converted into separate apartments by freedmen of the original family, they were going to run the farm, and live in the house with their families, it was said.

Honeyed wine was being poured into our cups, hor-d-oevres of lettuce and leek salad, dormice covered with honey and sprinkled with poppy seeds, tunneyfish and sliced eggs, and grilled sausages, were served. We helped ourselves from serving dishes held out by slaves. The couch beside me seemed destined to remain empty, until suddenly in the dim light a figure appeared and took it's place on the couch. I was absorbed in the food and did not immediately look up. Then I turned my attention to my dinner partner, it was Marcellus! I stared at him aghast, I had not expected this. He smiled at me, "Ave Claudia, how nice to see you."

I was suddenly furious, was all this arranged so that Marcellus and I could be together, "Did you plan this?"

He shook his head, "No, believe me I'm as surprised as you are, I had no idea you were going to be here tonight. But as we're here we may as well make the best of it and not quarrel. I'm sorry I'm late by the way."

I believed him because until I arrived this evening Popilius would have assumed I would be accompanied by my husband, even so I still felt suspicious. Music was being played on an assortment of instruments, but mainly it was flute music. But as the main course was served other musicians started to play, Lyre, panpipes and sistrum joined the flutes.

The main course was roasted venison marinated in a spicy sauce. The slaves passed among us with dishes of vegetables, carrots in a peppered sauce, parsnips in coriander and chive sauce, and greens stewed with pepper and thyme. A thick strong red wine was passed around with this part of the meal. For the moment I concentrated on my food, I would not let Marcellus upset me at this juncture, I was enjoying the meal.

I took a draught of the wine and saw Faustinius, he also held a wine cup in one hand. With the other he stroked his partner who was also drinking the wine. Putting her cup down she turned her attention to her plate, I looked away from them and also attacked the food on my plate. I gazed surreptitiously at Marcellus, he was also enjoying his dinner, he seemed unconcerned about whether or not I was enjoying mine. I lifted the flagon off the table and poured myself another drink, I drank deep. Marcellus glanced at me, "Be careful of this wine, it's quite potent."

I put the cup down and reached again for the flagon.

"Of course if you wish to drink yourself insensible don't let me stop you," Marcellus said.

The dessert arrived, I was quite full by now and took a small dish of custard sprinkled with nutmeg. A sweet wine accompanied the dessert course, served in tiny cups. I looked around, Faustinius had his hand up his companion's skirt I noticed, he certainly did not remember me, for which I was thankful. I watched them bemused, they were kissing now, I wondered how far they intended to go in public before they sought privacy. Marcellus laughed softly, "Stop staring so blatantly at other people, or is that how you amuse yourself now?"

I turned on him, "How dare you suggest such a thing, you seem to have no shame at all."

"Oh and you do I suppose, which is why you are staring so hard at that couple opposite. Do you know them by any chance?"

"No," I lied, "I don't know them, I was just fascinated."

"That's obvious, you couldn't take your eyes off them."

He reached over and put a hand on my thigh, I moved away indignantly.

"If you think I'm going to make a show of myself in this gathering you must be crazy."

"Rather find somewhere a bit more private would you?"

I glared at him, "I expect you're sorry that Flavia isn't here aren't you? You'd rather be sitting next to her wouldn't you? You must be really disappointed to find only me as your dinner partner."

"Flavia!" he exclaimed, "your friend? Perhaps she would be more fun than you are at the moment. But what makes you think I would want her here now?"

"You paid enough attention to her at the Games, you obviously fancy her, why deny it when it was obvious to everyone at the arena."

"I don't suppose everybody at the arena was paying that much attention, but it evidently bothered you."

"I didn't say it bothered me."

"I'd say you made it eminently clear that it upset you."

"Why would I be upset by anything you do?"

"You tell me."

"You do have a strong hankering for Flavia don't you? Have you seen her since that day?"

"No, as a matter of fact I haven't, until now I've barely given your friend a thought."

"I don't believe you."

From the corner of my eye I saw Faustinius and his companion leave the room, arms entwined.

"There go your friends, they're not wasting time arguing at least."

"They're not my friends, I told you I don't know them."

"So you did, you're full of surprises Claudia, I never know what disreputable types you're going to be acquainted with next."

"What do you mean disreputable?"

"The man Faustinius is, or was an important member of the Bacchic cult. Presumably that is why you know him. Still he seems to have the right idea, let's stop arguing." He reached across the cushion that formed a partition between us on the couch and put an arm around me, I struggled to pull away.

"Look at me Claudia."

I tuned towards him and melted, all my antagonism ebbed away, he was beautiful. It was the only way to describe him, in every way he was beautiful. Passion gripped me, our lips met, we kissed, the kiss grew fierce. I lost all restraint, I had always known that this was inevitable, from the time I met him again. I flung my arms around him. The flute music grew more insistent and voluptuous, arousing us both. His hand crept up my skirt, mine crept under his tunic, I moaned, so did he. I tried to reach inside his undergarment, the size of his erection made this difficult, he was already caressing me intimately. He broke away from me suddenly, "Come on let's find somewhere more private before we both lose control of ourselves." Taking my hand he led me to a small side room which was furnished with bed large enough for two people to lie close together. A small table with a lamp on it, and a chamber pot in a corner was the only other furnishing, curtains hung round the walls, I noticed all of this vaguely as I removed my dress. Naked we fell onto the bed, I glued my mouth to his, his response was immediate. Our tongues writhed together, followed by our bodies. He glowed with health, his bronzed body gleaming in the dim light. I caught my breath and twined my legs around him in a paroxysm of lust. He returned my ardour enthusiastically.

"You're gorgeous," I whispered, "how can I resist you?"

"You're not are you?" he laughed, triumphantly I thought.

I laughed softly with him, then I groaned ecstatically as he led me to a shattering climax.

We remained intertwined, he raised his head and looked into my face, "I'm going to make love to you all night."

I sighed with content, "I hope so."

We shifted slightly on the bed to get more comfortable as we lay there in each other's arms. I resolutely shut all thought of the future from my mind. All I wanted to think about was the present, lying here in Marcellus' embrace. I ran my hands over him, his skin felt smooth and silky, it always surprised me that men's bodies felt like this. I hoped mine felt as sleek to his touch. Our passion began to mount again, he pulled me over on top of him, I writhed against him in an agony of lust. He was ready again, I impaled myself upon him crying out in ecstasy as I felt myself start to come. He pushed himself up me, then turned me over onto my back, shouting out exultantly as he reached fulfilment. We stayed glued together for a long while after we had finished. Then in spite of what we had vowed about making love all night, we realised we would have to leave, and return to our own homes. Rising from the bed we pulled our clothes on, then, looking cautiously around we exited from the small room.

"I'd better escort you home," Marcellus said. He pulled me to him and kissed me lovingly.

"No," I said, "it's better not, someone would be sure to see us, there would be gossip."

"Who cares? It would be true anyway wouldn't it?"

I began to feel nervous, I was not ready for a confrontation with my family, let alone Marcus! "It's best not to, we've brought a slave with us, he can escort me home."

His arm was still around me when we entered the atrium, I froze, shocked. Lucius stood there talking to our host, he was obviously waiting for me. I disengaged myself from Marcellus' grasp and confronted my brother. "Marcellus was just escorting me to find you," I improvised hastily, "I did not know if you would still be here."

"So I see," he stared at me, "Ave Marcellus, I think I'd better take my sister home now."

"I'm sorry I kept you waiting," I said, "we got talking."

"If you say so," my brother answered.

"I thought perhaps you were otherwise engaged, you disappeared with that girl Fanina. I didn't see you again, where is she by the way?"

"Fanina has gone home, as you should, and me as well, come on let's go," he said, rather brusquely I thought.

We thanked Popilius for the evening, and took our departure. In the litter I avoided Lucius' gaze, he regarded me sardonically, "You look somewhat dishevelled, what have you been up to Claudia?"

"Nothing," I answered, "why should I have been up to anything?"

"Well apart from your rather guilty look, you seem like a cat that got the cream."

I blushed furiously, "I don't know what you mean."

"Oh I think you do, but it's all right I won't tell your husband what you've been up to."

"What is there to tell?"

"You know perfectly well what there is to tell, anyone can see what you've been up to. But no one need see you when we get home, lucky for you Marcus isn't home tonight, as you very well know."

When we reached home I shuffled guiltily past the door slave, fortunately there was no one else around. With a muttered good night to my brother I hurried to my bedroom, the next morning would be time enough to worry about what had occurred that night. I got into bed and was soon asleep.

When I awoke the following morning the full impact of what I had done the previous evening struck me full force! What would happen now? I could of course keep quiet about it, Lucius I knew would not tell anyone, that was not the problem. It would be stupid and unnecessary to say anything to Marcus. No the main problem would be Marcellus. He obviously still felt the same way about me, as I had to admit I did about him. But the full implication about what he would now expect of me was just dawning on me. He would I thought apprehensively probably expect me to divorce Marcus, and presumably marry him. After what had occurred between us he would surely expect no less. I shivered with fear, there would be complete upheaval in my family. And what about my son? I would surely lose him as Marcus could, and probably would, claim custody. As I was the one who had been unfaithful, he would easily get it.

Meriope entered the room at this stage in my deliberations. "Aren't you going to get up Claudia? I realise you were late home last night, but your brother is already at breakfast, and he didn't get home any earlier, as I know you came home together."

"I'm tired," I mumbled, "leave me alone."

"Come on, I'll bring you some hot water and lemon juice, and you can join your brother in the hortas."

Reluctantly I got out of bed and put on a wrap, Meriope returned with the drink, I sipped it, it revived me a little. I went to join Lucius, he was breakfasting in the small garden as Meriope had said. He looked at me as I took a chair opposite him.

"How are you feeling this morning Claudia?"

I shuddered, "fragile."

"Yes, I should just think you are, the less said about what happened last night the better for everyone."

I sighed, "That might be easier said than done."

"Why? Who would want to discuss it?"

I sighed again, "Marcellus"

"Why would he wish to talk about it? Surely it's as much in his interest as yours to keep quiet about it. You're a married woman after all."

I did not answer him, but helped myself to bread and honey, and poured myself a beaker of milk.

"You really think Marcellus would make trouble for you?" Lucius asked.

"I don't know," I answered, "I think he might have taken it seriously."

"But why should he? He knows you have a husband, or does he expect to carry on an affair with you? I thought it was just a one night stand."

I shook my head, "I don't know."

"Has he been your lover at all before last evening?"

I nodded.

"When? For how long? Since you've been married to Marcus?"

"No, not since I married, but we were lovers before, but he went away and I met Marcus again."

"This is beginning to sound more complicated than I thought. I assumed you had got carried away last night at the party, with the wine and the atmosphere. What are you going to do? What about Larius? You do have a child to consider."

"I know, I don't know what I'm going to do if this goes any further."

"Then make sure it doesn't go any further, where's your sense of responsibility? After all it's mainly up to you you know, you'd be better not seeing this man again, even if he is a family friend."

"How can I do that? What if he comes to see me?"

"Make sure Marcus is with you whenever he tries to see you. Or at least a member of the family. Did you say anything to him to make him think you would either carry on a liaison with him, or divorce your husband?"

I shook my head, upset with this cross-questioning of me by my brother. "I thought you might be on my side."

"Not if it means conniving with you so you can continue to carry on with this man. I barely know him, but I'm beginning to wonder if he's an altogether desirable character."

"I've had enough of this," I sobbed, I left the table and rushed into the house. I reached the small sitting room and collapsed onto a couch crying uncontrollably. What sort of mess had I landed myself in, and what did I really want? To end my marriage to Marcus and marry Marcellus? I had believed I loved him last night, but did I want all the trouble and strife that being with him permanently would entail? Did I want to risk losing my child as I would if I left Marcus? There would be too much anguish involved if I left my husband.

I did not believe I had the strength to go through that. No I wanted both I realised, to have my cake and eat it too. I could not bear the idea of Marcellus with any other woman, but what could I offer him? At best a hole and corner affair, meeting in secret, hiding from everyone. And even if I could put up with that, what about him? He deserved better, a woman who could be totally committed to him. And possibly a child of his own as he had hinted once, I could give him neither in my present circumstances. And did I want to lose my own child, I could not bear that. Also there was Marcus to consider, he also deserved better that I would be giving him if I carried on an affair with Marcellus while remaining married to him.

Drusilla entered the room and stopped in surprise. "Whatever is the matter with you Claudia, what's happened."

"Nothing," I said, "it's nothing at all."

"It doesn't seem like nothing to get you in this state. Something must be very wrong."

"I quarrelled with Lucius at breakfast."

"So what happened? What did you quarrel about?"

"Something that happened at the party last night."

"The party! We weren't invited, what went wrong? Did Lucius get involved with some woman and leave you to come home on your own."

I wished it had been something as simple as that, "Why would that bother me so much?" I asked. I got up, "I don't want to talk about it." I left the room and returned to my bedroom.

My mother entered the room soon after I did. "You'll be pleased to hear that the workmen are coming today to start the repairs to your apartment."

"What?" I asked startled, it was the last thing on my mind.

"I just told you that they are beginning the repairs to yours and Gaius' apartments. Are you in a hurry or can they do the others first?"

I pulled myself together, "Whatever, I'm not bothered, let them do Gaius and Drusilla's first. There's no particular hurry anyway."

My mother looked at me curiously, "Is something the matter Claudia? You don't look too good. Did you drink too much last night?"

"Yes I did drink rather a lot." I said, seizing on that excuse. "I feel hung over, I think I'm going to lie down for a while."

"Yes that's a good idea," she said, "You should be more careful at these parties. You'll end up making yourself ill."

"I'll be all right after I've had a rest."

"All right, so you don't mind if the men renovate Gaius' room first then?"

I shook my head, "I don't mind." It was the last thing on my mind I thought after she had gone, what difference did it make which room I slept in I reflected. The way things were going at the moment my marriage would be over in a short while. I lay down on the bed, I would do nothing for the present I decided.

By lunchtime I attempted to get some clothes on, a casual house gown, and joined the family in the hortas. I could not face a big meal even by lunchtime standards. I asked for a cucumber omelette, the others were having a fish dish, I nibbled my omelette. Lucius looked at me quizzically, I avoided his eyes. After we had finished my father and Gaius stood up, "We have to leave you now, we're expecteing Marius and Marcellus in a moment."

I stared down at my plate, I could feel Lucius' eyes on me. I would stay in my room all afternoon, or at least until after they had left.

Much later I wandered into the garden, the roses were exquisite at the moment, I walked to the fishpond. The fountain splashed into it. I stood watching it. A footfall sounded behind me, I turned around startled, to my horror it was Marcellus. "I've been waiting for you," he said, "Been resting have you?"

I nodded, appalled by his intrusion, "What do you want?" I asked stupidly.

"You," he answered, "surely that's obvious." He put his arms around me and kissed me passionately. For an eternity I responded, his ability to turn me on was still apparent, I kissed him back ecstatically, I could not resist him. Then I pushed him away abruptly, "We shouldn't be doing this."

"Whyever not? It's the most natural thing in the world to do after last night isn't it?"

"Someone might see us, I can't risk that."

"But your family will have to know eventually won't they? You'll have to tell your husband you want a divorce."

I sank onto a bench, sitting in the middle so that there was no room for him to sit beside me. He put an arm across my shoulders, "You are going to divorce him aren't you? We love each other don't we?"

"I can't think about all this right now," I whimpered, "There's a lot at stake."

"Last night you did not seem to have any doubts, you implied it was me you loved. Have you changed your mind in the light of day? Judging by the way you kissed me just now I would say you still feel the same way about me."

I turned around and faced him, "I have a child Marcellus, I can't leave him."

"Of course not, you'll bring him with you, if my present house isn't big enough I'll buy another."

"It's got nothing to do with the house, do you think Marcus would allow me to take his son away from him?"

"But if you tell him that you love me he'll realise that you want a divorce, he'd expect you to have the child, you're his mother."

"And Marcus is his father, there's no getting away from that, he'll not give him up without a struggle. I don't think I can go through that."

"So what are you saying? That you're going to stay married to Marcus because he won't let you have your son if you don't?"

I nodded, "Something like that, what else can I do? Also it would cause great upheaval in the family, and what would Marcus' parents think of me?"

"And that's more important than being with me?"

I shook my head, "I can't think straight today, I've got a headache."

"Which you didn't complain of last night."

"I didn't have a headache last night."

"That was obvious! And now you do because you can't face the consequences. Well in that case I'll leave you to it, and find someone else." He stood upright, I could not bear him to leave me like this, I rose to my feet, "We can see each other sometimes can't we?"

"You mean carry on an intrigue behind your husbands back?"

"What else can we do? I don't want to lose you, I meant what I said last night."

He stood looking at me, "I would say you don't know what you do want. But I don't think that that would be strictly true, you want to have things both ways don't you? You want to stay married to Marcus, and have an affair with me, the best of both worlds. What do you expect me to do, creep into your room under cover of business dealings with your father and brother? How long would we get away with it?"

"No," I said, "I could come to your house, no one need know, I could say I was going shopping or meeting a girl friend, or anything?"

"And how would you manage that? Slaves talk as you very well know. You couldn't get away unescorted it would appear very strange."

I thought a minute, "I could come at night after I've supposedly gone to bed, no one need see me. Marcus is only at home one or sometimes two nights a week. No one need know I was going out. I wouldn't bring a slave with me, of course I know they talk."

"You'd walk the streets at night unescorted, by yourself? Don't you understand how dangerous that could be, a woman alone, wandering through the town in the dark?"

"I wouldn't be alone would I? Surely you would meet me outside this house, you could hide until I came out, and escort me to your house."

"You've got it all worked out haven't you? How long do you see this situation lasting? Until you tire of it and me?"

"I'd never get tired of you, I'd want to go on being with you."

"While I remain ostensibly unattached, indefinitely?"

"Why would that bother you? You've never shown any desire to get married since I've know you."

"In the future I might, I was and am prepared to marry you."

I sat down on the bench again, this time leaving a space for him to join me. He remained standing, "I'd better go, I'm not supposed to still be here, I slipped away after the meeting finished. My father will be wondering what's happened to me if I don't join him. I told him I'd meet him at a wine bar. I let him leave first while I stayed to have a word with Gaius. I cut that short to come to find you."

"All right," I said, "but call on me again soon and we can make plans to be together."

"But only when it suits you to meet me, what am I supposed to do the rest of the time?"

"I've told you I'll see you several times a week, as often as you like when Marcus isn't home."

"And there we have it, I'm to be your bit on the side, I don't think so my love, I'll see you." He strode out of the garden, through the house to the street entrance. Someone would have been sure to have seen him, but that did not matter, What did I care? He had left me without any hope of future meetings. I slumped on the garden seat staring at the fish in the pool. When would I ever see him again I wondered, how could I survive without him, without feeling his arms around me, without the sweet lovemaking of last night?

Drusilla and Gaius wandered out to the peristyle, they saw me and came towards me. "Not still moping are you Claudia!" Drusilla exclaimed. "Surely you've made it up with Lucius by now, he seemed all right with you at lunch."

"Why did you and Lucius quarrel?" Gaius asked, "what about?"

"Nothing," I answered, "there's nothing wrong between Lucius and me. We argued coming home last night that's all. It wasn't important." I rose to my feet, "I'd better go in."

"Why are you always running away whenever we meet lately?" Drusilla asked.

"I'm not running away, I've had enough sun for today, that's all."

Gaius stared at me curiously, "I just saw Marcellus leave the house, I had thought him gone some time ago. I was surprised he was still here."

"Oh," I said, "what is that supposed to do with me?"

"You tell me," Gaius replied.

Drusilla looked at me stunned, "you and Marcellus? I thought that that was well and truly over since you married Marcus. You can't be carrying on a liaison with Marcellus can you? You've got a baby to consider, you have a duty to him, to behave yourself like a responsible person. You're a mother, you can't just please yourself."

I rounded on her close to tears (of guilt as much as anything). "Who says I'm having an affair with anyone. What right do you have to castigate me about who I see or don't see?"

"Look here Claudia," Gaius said, "we're not trying to upset you, but don't get involved in something you won't be able to handle. You've got a husband now, you've a duty to him, I'm not moralising here, but you can't behave as if you were still single and unattached."

"Apart from anything else," Drusilla said, "Marcus could divorce you, and you'd be sure to lose Larius, he wouldn't give up his son."

I brazened it out, "I'm not carrying on a liaison," (well I wasn't yet anyway) so just get off my back both of you."

I stormed through the garden into the house, I could no longer face them. What was I going to do? Marcellus had as good as refused me, and my family were harassing me as well. I knew they were right of course, I knew I could lose my child if I was not very careful. I went to find him now, he was asleep, Oenone dozed beside him, her own son Hector held close. I bent over Larius, how could I even contemplate losing him or leaving him. What was I going to do now?

CHAPTER TWENTY

HAPPY EVER AFTER?

Some months had gone by since the party at Popillius' house. I had tried to forget the scene with Marcellus, I had not seen him again after he left me alone in the garden. I had accompanied Marcus to several functions, none of which Marcellus had attended. For which I felt both relief and disappointment. It would of course have caused embarrassment to me if he had been at any of the same events, but I could not help feeling a strange regret that I did not see him. I even wondered if he was avoiding me, I could not blame him if he was I supposed. His rejection of my suggestion for meetings between us had upset me. Although I knew it would not have been practical, and that my family, or worse Marcus, could have found out, then where would I have been? Also I did still have feelings for Marcus, and I did not really want to hurt him or rock the boat of our marriage. So why did I still crave for Marcellus? I would, I resolved, forget him and get on with my life.

It was at this time that I saw Flavia again. We had not met since the Imperial Games. For some reason our paths had not crossed since then. I had been too wrapped up in my own problems to think about helping her in any way. I should be trying to get her back into circulation again I knew. She was not invited anywhere at present, and needed assistance. I wondered if she was still likely to be interested in my brother Lucius.

He was, I knew, seeing the girl Fanina, whom he had met at Popillius' party, but I did not think it was specially serious between them. But one never knew with Lucius. I met Flavia in the Forum one morning when I was shopping in the market. She was examining a turbot on a fish stall.

"Ave Flavia," I came up behind her, "I've not see you for a long while."

"Claudia!" she exclaimed, "Where have you been hiding yourself all this time?"

"Oh I haven't been hiding, I've been around."

"I've not seen you."

I remembered my annoyance with her at the Games, and the reason for it, "No, well I've been quite busy."

Making up her mind she indicated a fish and paid for it, her attendant slave picked up the package. "My mother is entertaining some of her friends this evening, she sent me shopping for her."

"Well send your slave home with the fish, and join me in a cup of wine."

"All right." She spoke to the man and he left with the parcel.

Seated in the usual wine bar I said, "So what are you doing with yourself these days?"

"Nothing much, in fact life has been quite dull since I came home."

"Still you're glad to be back in Pompeii aren't you?" I asked.

"Oh yes, it's better than being stuck in Sicilia with no money. But I wish I could get myself into society again."

The wine arrived and I poured it into cups. "Did you know Lucius was home?"

She stared at me in surprise, "No I didn't know, as I've said I don't get out much. How is he?"

"He's fine," I said, "He's been travelling in the East. You should get him to tell you about it sometime."

She brightened, "I'd love that, would he see me do you think?"

"I don't see why not, why don't you come to dinner one night and meet him?"

Are you inviting me?"

"Of course I'm inviting you, what about tomorrow evening? I'll try and make sure Lucius is there."

"Yes please I'd love to come."

We finished our wine and got up to leave. Of course I knew I could not guarantee that my brother would be interested in Flavia. But he would be polite and talk to her, and at least it would be an evening out for her.

The following evening Flavia arrived. Lucius was in to my relief, as I could not really vouch for him being in that night. I had invited Flavia on the off chance that he would be, and it had paid off. The next thing was to try and get him interested in my friend. I did not know how implicated he was with Fanina. Flavia looked lovely I was pleased to notice, she had obviously taken trouble with her appearance. She wore a white gown draped becomingly across the front, with a stola of pale blue. Not too daring, but enough to be provocative.

"I like your dress," I said

"Do you really? I only bought it this morning."

"You bought it specially then?"

"Well yes, I did not have anything suitable, as I don't go out much."

I hoped my brother would like it, she really did look attractive.

I sat with her in the atrium until my family joined us. We then gathered in the triclinium, with my parents, Gaius and Drusilla, and Lucius.

"Marcus not home yet?" Lucius asked, "He's expected tonight isn't he?"

"Yes," I said, "but we needn't wait for him, he'll likely be late."

I had put Flavia next to Lucius with myself on her other side, leaving the space on my other side for Marcus. The hors-d-oeuvre was served, a simple dish of mussels in a wine sauce.

The main course was being served when my husband arrived, having quickly changed into a simple tunic of light blue. He greeted Flavia, he was probably surprised to see her there as I had not seen him the previous night to tell him she was coming. He settled himself on the couch beside me and set himself out to be pleasant to my friend. To my delight I noticed Lucius was engaging Flavia in conversation, telling her about his travels I surmised. I tried to listen but Marcus was telling me about some problem he had encountered that day. I barely heeded him, I had arranged this evening in the hope of getting Flavia and Lucius together. I was much more concerned with what they were saying to each other than in Marcus's troubles with the army.

The dessert arrived, mainly fruit with a sweet dessert wine. I reached for a fig and surreptitiously watched Lucius and Flavia. They were I saw with pleasure getting on very well together. If only I could be sure he really liked her and was not just being agreeable to her. Marcus stared at me curiously, "What's wrong Claudia? You've not paid attention to a thing I've been saying all evening."

I turned to him, "What?" I asked vaguely.

"Oh never mind," he snapped, "forget it." He turned his attention to the dessert and chose a peach. I nibbled my fig, still listening to Lucius and Flavia. If only I could be sure he would fall for her, she would find it easier to socialize if she had a beau of her own to escort her I thought.

Marcus poured himself another cup of wine and looked around for someone else to talk to, having decided that I was hopeless as a conversation partner this evening. I barely noticed him, or anyone else except my brother and my friend. At the end of the evening I waited to see if Lucius would offer to escort Flavia home. But to my disappointment he did not suggest it, but left her to go home with just her house slave for protection.

After she had left I followed my brother into the tablinium, "Well?" I asked, "How did you get on with Flavia?"

"I got on with her well enough, why should I not?"

"She looked lovely tonight didn't she?" I wondered if I should tell him that she had bought her dress especially for the evening. Perhaps I had better not I thought, best not to admit how eager she had been to impress him.

"Yes," he said, "she's a very pretty girl, I'm surprised not to see her around more. Doesn't she go out socially very much? Why I wonder."

I picked up a scroll someone had left on a reading couch and pretended to be absorbed in it, what could I answer? I did not want to tell Lucius about Flavia's liaison with Philocrates, and her resulting social ostracism. It might put him off her. Eventually I supposed it would have to come out if they were to see a lot of each other. But I did not want to say anything that might put him off at the outset. An affair with an ex-slave was considered a disgrace. Even in Pompeii which I knew had a racy reputation, even compared to Rome where morals were also quite lax. One could get away with quite a lot these days, as indeed I, and most of my friend and acquaintances did. In earlier times things had been stricter of course, but under our present Imperial system people believed in enjoying themselves, and indulging in anything that gave them pleasure. I was certainly happy that I lived in these times. As a woman I would have been kept on a far tighter rein that I was now, during the time of the Republic say. Although I expect people found a way round it if they wanted to even then.

I examined the scroll, Lucius looked at me, "You seem very interested in that book Claudia, what is it about?"

"I don't know," I said, "I just picked it up casually." I looked at it closer, it appeared to be farming poetry, by Virgil or some such. I wondered who was reading it. My father probably, or Gaius even. Lucius took it from me, "Oh the Georgics by Virgil, this gives useful tips on various aspects of farming. I meant to have a look at it anyway." He settled himself on a reading couch with the scroll. I wished I had not picked it up now. I reclined on another couch, "Why don't we arrange an outing together the four of us? Marcus and I, and you and Flavia. We could see a play, or a mime, or maybe go to a concert."

He looked up from the book "All right, why not? Let's arrange it"

I was delighted, "I'll see Flavia tomorrow and discuss it with her."

The sooner I could initiate another date with Flavia and my brother the better I schemed. It would have to be when Marcus was free, I went to find him. He was in the atrium with Gaius and Drusilla, I joined them. I linked my arm through Marcus', "Let's go for a stroll in the garden" I said.

He looked at me in surprise, "Decided to talk to me at last have you? You seemed too preoccupied at dinner."

"I know, I'm sorry, let's go, I want to talk to you."

"Well that makes a change," he said sarcastically.

"Come on," I tugged at his arm.

The spring night was warm, so we were able to stroll outside without having to fetch wraps, "When are you home again in the evening?" I asked.

"After the way you ignored me tonight I'm surprised you're interested."

"I wasn't ignoring you."

"You gave a pretty good imitation then."

I snuggled up to him slipping my hand into his, "I was thinking it would be nice to have an evening at a play or a concert the next time you come home." I looked at him, "I've been speaking to Lucius and he agrees. We could invite Flavia to join us and make up a foursome. What do you think?"

"I don't mind if you want to, it would be pleasant to have an evening out together. If Lucius and Flavia would like to join us fine."

I hugged him, now I only had to ask, or rather tell Flavia. She obviously still liked my brother. Marcus held me in his arms and kissed me, I responded. "Come on," he said, "let's go to bed, you've started something now."

Happily I allowed him to lead me to our apartment.

The following morning I called at Flavia's house, she was pleased to see me and to discuss last night.

"I'm glad you enjoyed it," I said.

"It was wonderful," she enthused, "Lucius was so kind to me."

"You looked lovely," I said, "Of course he was nice to you. Would you like to come with us to the theatre next week?"

"With you and Lucius you mean?"

"Yes, and Marcus, it has to be Marcus' next free evening."

"When will that be?"

"In a weeks time."

"Fine, will you arrange it?"

"Yes, Lucius and I will organise it, and I'll let you know the plan."

"I'll look forward to it."

We arranged to attend a concert at the Odeion. We called for Flavia at her house. She wore the white dress again to my delight. It really did suit her, enhancing her dark prettiness. We arrived at the theatre just before the concert began. I sat between Marcus and Lucius, with Flavia on Lucius' other side. The music commenced, I felt pleased with my plan working out so well. I stared around the theatre at the audience to see if I could see anyone I knew. With a shock I recognised Marcellus. He was sitting with a woman, I went rigid with horror, I had not expected this. Just then he looked across and saw us, he waved. Looking unconcerned I waved back, Lucius raised his hand in token acknowledgement. He did not like Marcellus much after what had occurred at the party last summer.

After the concert was over and the audience exited the theatre I watched for Marcellus. I wondered if it would be possible to have a word with him in private without his lady friend. It would be difficult with Marcus watching, to say nothing of what Lucius would think. I did not want to spoil Flavia's evening but I whispered to her, "Did you see Marcellus?"

"Yes," she answered "I did, I wonder who the woman was that he was with, she looked at least thirty. I wonder if she's married."

I had not thought of that, I felt infuriated that he could possibly be having an affair with a married woman when he had refused to carry on a liaison with me when I offered. What was so special about her. What had she got that I had not. I glowered.

"Cheer up Claudia," Lucius said, "Didn't you enjoy the music?"

I pulled myself together, "yes of course I did."

Marcellus had disappeared, when could I get another chance to talk to him. I was sure I could still get him for my lover. After all I was much younger that the woman he was with. Marcellus was now thirty-eight years old I knew. But the age gap had always been rather a turn on, for both of us I assumed. It seemed it was all right to carry on with a married woman as long as it was not me I brooded. Marcus looked at me, "Stop scowling Claudia, we're going for some supper."

I fixed a smile on my face and accompanied them to a restaurant.

The following morning I found myself breakfasting alone with Lucius, he examined me, "Something upset you last night, was it Marcellus being there with a lady friend?"

"Of course not," I lied, "Why should it have been?"

He stared at me, "I thought perhaps you were distressed that he should be there with someone else. Poor Marcus is completely innocent of your hankering for another man. Don't you think he deserves better from you? He's a decent man, yet you still crave someone else. Don't you think it's time you grew up a bit and behaved like an adult woman instead of a spoilt child?"

"How dare you say that to me." I was furious because I felt secretly guilty of what he was accusing me of. I knew I had sulked last night because I was not able to speak to Marcellus.

"Why, it's time isn't it? Forget about him and think about your husband, he adores you. You cannot be seriously thinking about starting an intrigue with somebody else."

I spread honey on a piece of bread, trying to keep my hands from shaking. Lucius had hit the nail on the head. I was uncomfortable with the situation but I would not show it. I glared at my brother and continued to eat my breakfast. "Anyway," I said, "How did you get on with Flavia?"

"Very well," he said, "as you might have noticed if you'd been interested. But your thoughts were obviously elsewhere!"

I felt annoyed at this, but I knew it was true. I would have been perfectly happy if I had not seen Marcellus obviously content in the company of another woman. Especially if she was married as well, as I suspected. We finished our meal in silence. I did not want an argument with Lucius. Especially now when I was supposed to be trying to get him paired off with my friend.

Later in the morning Flavia called round. We sat drinking herbal tea in the small sitting room.

"Is Lucius here this morning?" she asked.

"No he's gone to work," I said, "I saw him this morning, We had breakfast together." I did not say we had argued, it was not her business anyway. "You got on well with him last night didn't you?"

"Yes, but he has not suggested escorting me anywhere else."

"Give him time," I said, "I expect he will." I was determined he would if I could fix it somehow. I was determined to concentrate on the matter and not get sidetracked by my own concerns. "I'll try and think of something." I poured more tea from the jug, and we settled down to chat. I agreed to go shopping with Flavia to help her choose another gown for when she next saw Lucius. I suggested she stay for lunch, and we go out to the shops afterwards. It would be a chance for her to see my brother again.

We ate lunch in the small triclinium, the family dining room. My father and Gaius were not eating lunch with us today, But Lucius had come home for his lunch.

"Where's father and Gaius?" I asked him.

"They had a business lunch, I wasn't invited. But I've only just started in the firm, so am not important enough to get invited to today's lunch party."

I looked at Drusilla, she appeared unconcerned, she had known about the luncheon, and had not expected Gaius home. So Lucius was the only male member of the family joining us. He reclined between me and Drusilla. I would like to have changed places with Flavia but it was not feasible without causing an upheaval. We ate a light meal of eggs poached in a wine sauce. I told them that Flavia and I had decided to go shopping that afternoon, which was the reason she had joined us for lunch, "Perhaps she could join us for dinner tonight?" I suggested. This was duly approved by everyone, and Flavia and I set out for our shopping expedition to the market.

Entering the Hall of Eumachia I stopped short, Flavia nearly bumped into me. "What's wrong Claudia?" she asked.

"Isn't that the woman who was with Marcellus last night?" I asked her. "Over there looking at those shimmering silks."

Flavia looked in the direction I had indicated. "Yes I think it is the same one. What about it anyway? You can't hope to know everyone he sees can you?"

"No of course not, it's just a strange coincidence seeing her again so soon."

"Not so strange considering everybody comes here to buy clothes. Come on, let's look around."

She made for the same silks the woman was examining. I pulled her back. "They're too exotic for what you want at the moment. You want something you can wear tonight, and it's only a family dinner not a big party."

"Yes of course you're right, What do you suggest?"

"These muslins are nice, it is warm enough to wear them now."

They would be daring enough to be provocative, but not too outrageous for tonight. While Flavia was examining the dresses I glanced surreptitiously at the woman choosing silks. She had fair hair twined round her head, curling in front. She was I had to admit rather beautiful. As she lifted a garment of the shimmering silk I noticed she wore a betrothal ring. My heart skipped a beat, could it be Marcellus'? But no I told myself, if she was married it could not be his, it was probably her husbands. I breathed again, Flavia turned to me, "What do you think of this?"

I turned my attention to the muslins and together we chose a gown for Flavia to wear for supper tonight. It was a pale green, I thought it a good idea to stick to pastels at the moment. The more audacious colours could come later. I wanted her to look demure, even innocent. And she seemed to be getting away with it where Lucius was concerned at the moment. I hoped that if the business with Philocrates had to come out at a future date, then my brother would be well and truly besotted, therefore likely to accept it.

It was at dinner that night that Gaius made his shock announcement. We were on the dessert course fortunately by that time. As we tucked into stewed cold quinces he said to our mother, "We ought to invite Marcellus and his parents and his betrothed to dinner one evening soon."

"What!" I asked appalled.

Gaius turned to me, he grinned, "Had you not heard? He's betrothed to the lady Silia, has been for several weeks, I thought you'd have heard by now. It's common knowledge in the town."

I put my dish aside, my appetite had quite gone, "Who is she? I've never heard of her."

"That must be who we saw him with last night," Flavia interjected. "We saw her again this afternoon," she added.

"But surely," I exclaimed, "She's quite old, at least thirty I'd have thought."

"Hardly old," Drusilla said. "She's about thirty, maybe thirty one, but Marcellus is thirty eight. It's time he settled down."

"Why isn't she married already?" I asked, my voice shook, I tried to sound calm.

"She's divorced," Drusilla answered, "As is Marcellus, they should be well suited."

I was shaking with shock, Lucius looked at me ironically, but kept quiet.

How I got through the rest of the evening I do not know, I could not wait to leave the table. As soon as we rose I fled out of the room, Lucius followed me and took my arm, which must have disappointed Flavia I realised later. I had forgotten about her and my plan to pair her and Lucius off.

"Calm down," he said now, "It's a good thing Marcus isn't here tonight. He would have thought your behaviour most odd."

I turned to him, "I must see Marcellus, I have to speak to him."

"About what? His getting married? It's probably the best thing that could happen in the circumstances. In any case if they come to dinner you can speak to him then."

"I have to see him alone," I said

"I don't think that's a very good idea. In fact I think you should leave it alone and get on with your own life and marriage. And behave like a responsible person."

I shrugged him off and fled to my room, forgetting about Flavia. She followed me in there, I was collapsed on the bed.

"What is it Claudia? Is it about Marcellus getting engaged? Surely you're not upset about that are you, it's been over between you since you married Marcus hasn't it?"

I did not answer her though I sat up on the bed, I was numb with shock. What awful news, I could not bear to think about it.

"Answer me Claudia, It is over between you and Marcellus isn't it? You're not still seeing him are you?"

I did not want to tell her about the scene in the garden when he had rejected my offer. It was too humiliating. I had told nobody about that. Not even Lucius knew. But he was the only one who knew what had happened at his friends' party last summer. Flavia was saying something, I paid no attention to her, I would have to try and see Marcellus alone somewhere I thought. I had no idea what I would say to him. But I would try and persuade him to break off his betrothal to the woman Silia.

The next day unexpectedly I had my chance. I ran into him in the atrium as he was coming out of a meeting with my father and Gaius. I waylaid him, "I have to speak to you."

He nodded "All right, what do you want to talk about?"

"Is it true you're betrothed?"

"Yes, it's true, I'm marrying Silia Galla."

"But why? You still love me, you said so last summer."

"You expect me to hang around until you notice me? No Claudia, it's been over between us for a long time. Since before last summer, it really ended when you married Marcus Lucullus, why not admit it?"

I flung my arms around him, "I still love you, Don't marry Silia, we'll work something out between us."

He removed my hands from around his neck. "Stop this Claudia, you're doing yourself no good. I need a wife and I need and heir, you can't give me that, Silia can."

"How do you know she can? She's past thirty isn't she?" I asked spitefully.

"Silia's pregnant already, we will marry next month."

This was another blow. "Do you love her?"

"Yes I love her, I would not be so calculating as to get a woman pregnant if I felt nothing for her. I'm not that cold blooded. You don't give me much credit do you?"

"But you can't love her, you loved me."

"I did love you, and if you had been prepared to divorce your husband and marry me and give me a child, I would have happily agreed. But we have not seen each other for a long time and things change, have changed in fact. I'm in love with Silia now, she's a lovely girl, sweet and loving, it will be a good marriage this time for both of us."

"Marcellus what we had between us in the past was good. Must we finish everything?"

He nodded, "It was good between us in the past but it's over now. We must put it behind us and look to the future. We had our fun, then you married."

"I thought I'd never see you again at the time I agreed to marry Marcus."

"But you did marry him, and presumably you're contented with him. After all you refused to divorce him last year when I asked you to, so you must be satisfied with you situation."

"I told you–" I began.

"Yes," he said, "About losing your son, you were quite right, I was wrong to press you on this matter." He turned to leave. "I'll see you when we come to dinner next week."

I tried to stop him from leaving by putting my arms round him again.

He evaded me, "Don't Claudia, have some pride, don't throw yourself at me."

He left. I had lost him I knew. How could I bear it with no hope of being close to him again. As for the dinner party I would have to make some excuse to avoid it. I could not bear to look at Silia, the bitch! How dare she snare him, take him away from me. I was not really being logical, we had not even seen each other for nearly a year. But at least he had been available. Now he would belong to someone else and I had no chance to be with him ever again.

Drusilla appeared in the atrium. "Is something wrong Claudia? You look upset, What's happened?"

I sat in a chair "I've lost Marcellus, how can I live without ever seeing him again?"

"What do you mean you've lost him? He's not been near you for months has he? Or is there something I don't know? Surely that's all over isn't it? And what about Marcus, are you cheating on him with Marcellus?"

I shook my head, "Marcellus wouldn't have me."

"What do you mean he wouldn't have you? Did you suggest divorcing Marcus and marrying him? When was this, last summer?"

I nodded "Yes, only I didn't offer to get a divorce, just to see each other sometimes."

"You mean have an affair behind your husbands back. Is that what you suggested to him? No wonder he turned you down, he has some decency at least, which is more than you have if that's what you offered him."

"What else could I do? I couldn't risk losing Larius."

"So you thought you'd have the best of both worlds, how could you be so selfish? The depths you can sink to amaze me. Of course he turned you down, any right thinking person would."

I glared at her, "How dare you criticise me like this, you're not that perfect yourself are you?"

"I've never been unfaithful to Gaius whatever I might have done before I married him. As you very well know, so don't censure me, but your own behaviour leaves a lot to be desired. You should either stay true to Marcus or divorce him, not deceive him with other men."

"It wasn't other men, just Marcellus, and I was only unfaithful once."

"Only because Marcellus wouldn't agree to your plan to carry on an intrigue with him behind your husbands back."

I got up from the chair, "I can't face the dinner party next week, I can't watch Marcellus with another woman."

"Yes you can, don't be such a coward. You'll have Marcus, It's being arranged to coincide with his evening at home."

"But how will I bear it? I still love Marcellus," I wept, "Why did he have to meet this woman?"

"If it hadn't been her it would have been someone else. He was planning to settle down, he needs and heir, he has no brother or even a sister. Someone has to inherit the business, he can't leave it much longer, surely you can see that."

My mother entered the atrium at that point. "There you both are. I wanted to ask you Claudia, do you wish to invite Flavia to the dinner next week?"

I shook my head dispiritedly, "Not really." I had lost interest in matchmaking between Flavia and Lucius at the moment. All I could think of was my own misery. Whatever Drusilla said I could not get over Marcellus' betrothal. I turned to my mother, "Must I attend?"

"It would look odd if you didn't. Marcus will be there, Of course you have to come."

I sat down again and put my head in my hands.

"What's wrong Claudia?" my mother asked.

"I don't want to meet Silia, I shan't like her I know."

"Whyever not? After all it was over between you and Marcellus a long time ago. Surely you're not still hankering after him are you? You've got a wonderful husband, you can't upset him by behaving stupidly over this visit. He'll wonder what's wrong with you. Are you going to tell him you can't get over another man?"

I shook my head, "Of course not, I'll make some other excuse, I'd say I was unwell."

"You'll do no such thing," my mother answered. "You'll behave like a grown up woman. I'm surprised at you. Besides you'll have to meet Marcellus and his fiancée socially sometime."

It was true of course, I could not hope to go indefinitely without ever encountering Silia.

On the evening of the dinner I was forced to confront both Marcellus and his betrothed. His parents were also there. I tried to put a good face on it and greeted them all with dignity. I stared covertly at Silia Galla. She wore a gown of oyster coloured silk cut quite low at the front, and sleeveless. I expected she knew how to excite Marcellus. I seethed. I picked at a dish of snails sautéed in a fennel sauce. My appetite was non-existent. I gazed at Marcellus, he wore a scarlet tunic, he looked devastating. Any stomach I might still have had for the food vanished. I pushed my dish away and nibbled an olive. Marcus stared at me. "What's the matter Claudia? You've hardly touched your snails, I didn't know you disliked them."

"I don't dislike them, I'm just not very hungry tonight."

I stared at Marcellus again, he caught my eye, he smiled at me. I looked away quickly. I remembered the first evening I had met him, at a dinner just like this one in this room. I remembered how we had gazed at each other across the tables, and fallen in love. I fought back tears, I should not have come tonight, I should have stayed away no matter what my mother and Drusilla said, this was a mistake. Silia turned to Marcellus and touched his arm, she said something to him under cover of the general conversation. He smiled at her and nodded. The main course arrived, I did not see the slave who offered me the serving dish, just as it had been on that other night.

"Wake up Claudia," Marcus said. I remembered Lucius saying something similar to me on that other occasion. Scarcely knowing what I was doing I selected something from the dish and picked at it. Marcellus was eating heartily as usual. Surely he must recall that first meeting between us, but he seemed perfectly happy. I stared at him mesmerised, I could not take my eyes off him. Lucius said something to me, I did not hear him. Marcus was looking at me, I would have to pull myself together or he would notice something. The meal continued, we drank a toast to Marcellus and Silia, I barely sipped the wine. Marcus looked at me oddly, I barely noticed, I was trying not to look at the happy couple. It appeared Marcellus had been telling the truth about loving Silia now, that it was over between him and me.

Finally the long evening came to an end, and I escaped to our apartment which had been repaired some months ago. I lay on the bed and sobbed. Marcus appeared in the doorway, he regarded me in silence. I sat up and wiped my eyes, "I'm sorry, I'm not feeling very well."

"Would the reason you're not well be the engagement of Marcellus and Silia?"

"Whyever should it be?" I asked.

He continued to stand in the doorway, "What is, or was, between you and this man Marcellus?"

"Nothing," I blustered, "What should there be between us?"

"That's what I'd like to know," he answered icily. "You couldn't eat your dinner, and I noticed you all but refused to drink the toast to the happy couple. And from what I could see they were happy together, whether you liked it or not. And for some reason you didn't like it at all. So I ask you again, what is or was between you and this man?"

"It was before we were married." I decided on the truth as far as possible."

"Then why were you so upset tonight if it's all in the past? From his point of view I would say it is in the past. He was definitely in love with his fiancée, that was clear. But what about you?"

I was stricken about what Marcus had said about Marcellus not being in love with me any more. I knew it was true. I had seen tonight how he and Silia had looked at each other. I decided to brazen it out with my husband. "I'm married to you aren't I?"

"Exactly, but have you been unfaithful to me with this man since our marriage?"

"No," I lied, Well it had only been once.

"But you've wanted to be haven't you? Was it he who refused to have an affair with you after you were married?"

"No!" I exclaimed indignantly, "I turned him down when I met him again."

"Then why are you in this state now? It seems to me you still have a craving for this man whatever he may feel. Is it because he's getting married and you realise you've really lost him, when before the door was still open if you so desired it to be?"

There would be the wedding to get through next I suddenly thought. How could I bear that. I had never thought he would remarry. It had never occurred to me. I had just assumed he would always be available. I had known he would have married me if I had divorced Marcus, but that he might marry someone else was something I had never envisaged.

Marcus studied me, "Are you sure that nothing has happened between you since you married me? To me you seem to be acting as if this betrothal has come as a complete shock to you. And I would say by the look on your face you still care very much about him."

"He's marrying another woman for Juno's sake, there can't be anything between him and me. I'm your wife, I love you."

"That doesn't always follow," he said sarcastically, "I had thought we did have something special, but now I have grave doubts. In fact I wonder if you ever loved me."

"Of course I loved you, I still do. The thing with Marcellus was in the past, before you returned from Britannia and we agreed to marry."

"Why did you consent to marry me at that time? Was it on the rebound from your affair with Marcellus?"

"No!" I said vehemently, "Juno and Minerva! I married you because I loved you." He had rather swept me off my feet at the time I remembered. But I had loved him.

He sat down on a couch, "If I was sure that it was in the past, I would leave it and say no more about it. But if you are going to carry on as you did tonight whenever we have to meet him, it makes me look a fool, and you too. I presume we will have to attend the wedding, and if you can't put on a better show than you did tonight, I for one will not attend it with you."

I was silent. I had no intention of going to the wedding if I could get out of it. But if I said that to Marcus now his suspicions would appear to be confirmed.

Marcus rose from the couch. "I'm going back to the barracks now, I won't spend tonight with you. By the time I return I hope you'll have come to your senses and accepted the situation with your former lover. Otherwise things don't look good for our marriage."

"No don't go," I pleaded, "Stay with me here tonight, don't leave me."

He shook his head and strode out of the room. I collapsed again, I was alone just when I most needed comfort. What was I going to do? If I was not very careful I would lose Marcus as well as Marcellus, I would not see him for another week now. What had I done? I would find myself divorced if I was not more discreet, though it was a bit late for that now.

Drusilla entered the apartment, "I just saw Marcus leaving so I knew you'd be alone. What's happened, why did he leave tonight?"

"He found out about Marcellus."

"What about Marcellus? What is there to find out?"

"Nothing now, but he got so suspicious I ended up having to tell him that I had an affair with Marcellus before we were married."

"But surely he'd forgive you that. You weren't promised to him when your liaison with Marcellus was going on."

"He knows that, but he's suspicious that it's been going on more recently."

"But it hasn't, or has it? You were telling me the truth weren't you when you said nothing had happened recently with Marcellus?"

"Yes, but Marcus refused to believe me."

"What made him suspect anything anyway?"

"He noticed I could not eat my dinner tonight, and I couldn't bring myself to really drink the toast."

"You're a fool to be so obvious, look where it's got you."

"What can I do, he's gone?"

"Nothing tonight, but you'd better pull yourself together by the time he comes home again."

"If he comes home again."

"Did he say he might not?"

I shook my head, "No, but he warned me about the future of our marriage."

"You're an absolute fool Claudia, you've lost Marcellus, so you'll have no one if this one leaves you."

"I don't want to lose him, I do love him."

"Then forget about Marcellus and set about convincing Marcus that you really do love him."

"If only he hadn't left."

There was nothing to be done about that though as I knew. Drusilla stayed with me for a while, then she left to join Gaius. It seemed everyone had someone except me now. I had been greedy wanting both Marcus and Marcellus and had maybe lost them both.

The invitation to the wedding came the next day. They could not afford to waste much time with Silia pregnant. I tried to hide my unhappiness, and my worry about Marcus. I would have to work hard at my marriage, even if it meant going to Marcellus and Silia's wedding with my family and husband, and putting a brave face on it. Behaving properly, and carrying on as if it was not a problem for me to attend. I did not want to end up divorced, and maybe losing Larius. I did not want to end up with nothing.

When Marcus returned the following week I was waiting to greet him, anxious that he might not come home. My relief when he entered the atrium was so strong that it surprised me. I rose from the couch I was reclining on in the tablinium, and ran to welcome him. I threw my arms around him and kissed him. His arms came round me and he returned my kisses. I clung to him lovingly. He removed my arms from around his neck and turned to acknowledge the rest of my family who were also in the tablinium.

"Where's Larius?" he asked me.

"With Oenone, she'll be putting him to bed soon."

"I want to see him, I barely had time last week."

I bit my lip to stop the retort that if he had not dashed away so quickly he could easily have had time with his son. "All right we'll go together to see him." I slipped my arm through his and led him to Larius' rooms.

The child was eating his supper when we entered. He got up from the table when he saw Marcus. "Tata!" he ran to his father. Marcus lifted him up and sitting on a chair set him on his lap. Larius was excited, he probably would not sleep tonight I thought ruefully. But I did not object as I did not want to antagonise Marcus at this juncture. We stayed about half an hour in the sitting room/playroom, then contrary to my worries Larius began to doze on his father's lap. I signalled to Oenone to take him, then I led Marcus from the room.

It was nearly time for dinner, I went with Marcus to our room and waited while he changed. The meal passed off well enough, with Marcus joining in the conversation happily, and it seemed without a care in the world. Then we separated to go our separate ways. Marcus yawned, "I'm tired I think I'll go to bed."

"All right, let's go to our apartment." I said.

Having no alternative he followed me to our room. Entering he threw himself onto a day couch and looked at me. "Well Claudia what have you decided to do?"

I was shaken. "About what?"

"About our marriage."

"I want to stay married to you, why should I not?"

He stared at me his eyes hard, "I'm not going to be second best because you can't have the man you really want."

"You're the man I want," I went over and got up on the couch beside him. He made no gesture of affection towards me but remained unyielding. I tried to put my arms round him.

"No Claudia, this has to be settled now."

"There's nothing to settle, I'm your wife, I love you, there is no one else."

"Not now, your former lover is about to marry someone else, someone he obviously cares about. The point is can you accept this situation? Or are there to be more exhibitions like last week's when you see him? At the wedding for instance."

"No!" I said vehemently, "I'll go to the wedding with you and my family, there'll be no exhibition." I had been badly frightened by the rift between us, It had showed me how much I cared for Marcus. I was now terrified of losing him. Something I had not considered as a possibility before. He had just always been there when I expected him to be. Life without him was too alarming to contemplate. Especially if he took our child away from me as well. I snuggled up to him on the couch troubled by his coldness. He still made no move towards me. I laid my head on his shoulder and ran my hand up his thigh. He did not respond. "Let's go to bed," I suggested.

"Not until this is settled between us, I have to know, were you still in love with Marcellus when you married me?"

I shook my head, "I wasn't thinking of anyone else at the time of our wedding. I was so pleased to see you again at that time."

"And since you married me? Have you told me the truth about that?"

"I haven't had a lover since we were married, I told you that."

"Yes, but can I believe you? I won't be made a fool of."

"I haven't made a fool of you."

I reached under his tunic, he groaned, I felt triumph, "Come to bed," I whispered.

"Let go of me and I might," he whispered back.

I felt jubilant. I had won him back I thought. I would not think of Marcellus any more, he meant nothing to me now. I would dance happily at his wedding feast with Marcus at my side. I removed my gown and got into bed, and lay there waiting for Marcus to join me.

THE END

Printed in the United Kingdom
by Lightning Source UK Ltd.
98611UKS00001B/263-272